序 言

　　「中高級英檢複試」是在每年六月和十二月舉辦，測驗內容分為兩部分，即「寫作能力測驗」和「口說能力測驗」。本書共有十回，每一回都是一個完整的測驗，題型完全仿照全民英檢「中高級英檢複試測驗」。

　　「寫作能力測驗」包含「中譯英」和「引導寫作」兩個題型。「中譯英」沒有什麼訣竅，就是考英文實力，要特別注意的是，翻完之後，要中英對照檢查一下，是否有把重要的名詞或連接詞翻譯出來，以免被扣分。至於「引導寫作」部分，用字遣詞除了注意正確性之外，也要考慮到詞彙的難易度，寫中高級測驗的作文，當然不能像寫中級測驗一樣，如果從頭到尾都用簡單的字，恐怕較難拿到亮麗的分數。

　　「口說能力測驗」對所有人來說，恐怕都是最難的部分。要通過「中高級口說能力測驗」，其實並不難，只要你能儘量保持沉著，不必刻意用艱深的字彙回答，重點是流利與言之有物，還有不要因為緊張而停頓太久，記住，時間就是分數。本書中的回答範例，完全以「一口氣英語」的方式，三句一組，九句一段，容易背，不容易忘記。

　　本書另附 MP3，每回測驗有五個音軌。第一個音軌完全仿照考試情況，播放試題並留時間給考生作答，考生可以藉此作模擬練習。後面四個音軌是回答範例，由專業的美籍播音員錄製，讀者可跟著練習，模仿他們的語調及發音，說起英文來，就會像道地的美國人。

　　為了提供給讀者最正確的資料，書中所有試題都經專業美籍老師 Laura E. Stewart 審慎校對過，但仍恐有疏漏之處，誠盼各界先進不吝批評指教。

劉 毅

座位號碼：＿＿＿＿＿＿＿＿＿＿＿　　　試題別：＿＿＿＿＿＿＿

第一部份請由本頁第1行開始作答，請勿隔行書寫。第二部份請翻至第2頁作答。

5

10

15

20

25

55

60

65

70

ITTC® 財團法人 語言訓練測驗中心

寫作口說能力測驗 ①

寫作能力測驗

Part I: Chinese-English Translation (40%)

Translate the following Chinese passage into an English passage, and write your answer on the Writing Test Answer Sheet.

現在，你不一定要是個全職的學生，才能得到你的學士或碩士學位了。你可以藉由網際網路，就讀線上的大學。在你方便的時候上課，無論是在辦公室、在家，甚至在路上。任何事情，從註冊、選課、買書，到課堂討論、和資料研究，都在線上進行。整體而言，完成課程大約需要兩年。如果你的必修科目較多，或許還要更久的時間。

Part II: Guided Writing (60%)

Write an essay of **150-180 words** in an appropriate style on the following topic. Write your answer on the Writing Test Answer Sheet.

Studies show that people in Taiwan are making slow progress in English learning. Compared to other Asian nations, Taiwanese students receive lower scores on the TOEFL and TOEIC test. Please write A LETTER to the Minister of Education to suggest what you think the government should do to improve this situation.

口說能力測驗

Please read the self-introduction sentence.

My seat number is （複試座位號碼）, and my registration number is （初試准考證號碼）.

Part I: Answering Questions

You will hear 8 questions. Each question will be spoken once. Please answer the question immediately after you hear it.

For questions 1 to 4, you will have 15 seconds to answer each question.

For questions 5 to 8, you will have 30 seconds to answer each question.

Part II: Picture Description

Look at the picture, think about the questions below for 30 seconds, and then record your answers for 1 ½ minutes.

1. What is this place?

2. What kind of occasion do you think it is?

3. What are the people in the picture doing?

4. Have you ever joined in an activity like this before?

5. If you still have time, please describe the picture in as much detail as you can.

Part III: Discussion

Think about your answer(s) to the question(s) below for 1 $\frac{1}{2}$ minutes, and then record your answer(s) for 1 $\frac{1}{2}$ minutes.
You may use your test paper to make notes and organize your ideas.

What kind of boy or girl will catch your attention? Name some physical features or personal traits that attract you to a boy or girl. Please explain.

Please read the self-introduction sentence again.

My seat number is （複試座位號碼）, and my registration number is （初試准考證號碼）.

寫作口説能力測驗 ① 詳解

寫作能力測驗詳解

PART 1 中譯英 (40%)

　　現在，你不一定要是個全職的學生，才能得到你的學士或碩士學位了。你可以藉由網際網路，就讀線上的大學。在你方便的時候上課，無論是在辦公室、在家，甚至在路上。任何事情，從註冊、選課、買書，到課堂討論、和資料研究，都在線上進行。整體而言，完成課程大約需要兩年。如果你的必修科目較多，或許還要更久的時間。

　　At present, you don't have to be a full-time student to earn your bachelor's or master's degree. You can enroll in an online university via the Internet. Attend classes at your convenience, in the office, at home, or even on the road. Everything from registration, course selection and book buying to class discussions and information research is conducted online. On the whole, it takes about two years to finish the program. If you take more required courses, you may spend a longer time.

【註】 *at present* 現在；目前
　　　full-time〔'fʊl'taɪm〕*adj.* 全職的
　　　earn〔ɝn〕*v.* 獲得　　bachelor〔'bætʃələ〕*n.* 學士

master〔'mæstə〕n. 碩士　　degree〔dɪ'gri〕n. 學位

enroll〔ɪn'rol〕v. 註冊；入學 < in >

online〔'ɑn,laɪn〕adj. 線上的　adv. 在線上

via〔'vaɪə〕prep. 經由　　Internet〔'ɪntə,nɛt〕n. 網際網路

attend〔ə'tɛnd〕v. 上（課）

at one's convenience 在自己方便時

registration〔,rɛdʒɪ'streʃən〕n. 註冊

course selection 選課

information〔,ɪnfə'meʃən〕n. 資料

research〔'risɝtʃ〕n. 研究

conduct〔kən'dʌkt〕v. 進行；做

on the whole 整體而言　　program〔'progræm〕n. 課程

take〔tek〕v. 修（課）

required〔rɪ'kwaɪrd〕adj. 必修的

PART 2　引導寫作 (60%)

Studies show that people in Taiwan are making slow progress in English learning. Compared to other Asian nations, Taiwanese students receive lower scores on the TOEFL and TOEIC test. Please write A LETTER to the Minister of Education to suggest what you think the government should do to improve this situation.

研究顯示，台灣人英文學習進步得很慢。與其他亞洲國家相比，台灣學生的托福和多益測驗成績較低。請寫一封信給教育部長，提出你認為政府該怎麼改善這個情況。

【作文範例】

A Letter to the Minister of Education

October 2, 2009

Dear Minister Lee,

Are you aware that in the latest survey of TOEFL and TOEIC scores in 16 and 10 Asian nations, Taiwan ranked No. 14 and No.7? *Have you ever wondered why* our students, so dedicated to studying English, should perform so poorly? Something is wrong with our education system. Taiwan is notoriously exam oriented. We really need to introduce some fresh thinking into English teaching here.

We are a country that greatly depends on international trade. *Besides*, we have been trying hard to develop and boost our tourism. *Thus*, we need more than English reading and writing. *The importance of* listening and speaking abilities *cannot be overemphasized*. Without this all-around ability in English, how can we get more involved with the world?

This is a major undertaking that requires government help. Your ministry took a giant leap forward with the introduction of the GEPT in 1999 for both students and workers. *However*, this is not enough. Many of our students are well trained in what is stressed on exams, *that is*, to read and write English. What they really lack are chances to interact with native speakers. They are in urgent need of opportunities to practice listening to, *and above all*, speaking English. *Therefore*, we truly hope that the policy of placing foreign teachers in all schools will be implemented. They are not to replace the local English teachers, but to complement and strengthen the current training in English that students receive. *Furthermore*, schools or even communities should provide more English clubs, books or movies, and English-related activities for students and residents.

Moreover, the government should also put public service messages in English on TV, radio, and the Internet, and on the MRT, buses and billboards. Let English be seen everywhere and in every aspect of people's lives. Put everyone in touch with English. *Then* Taiwan can become more like the international place we want it to be.

Respectfully yours,

Sandra Tsai

【註】 minister〔ˈmɪnɪstɚ〕n. 部長　　aware〔əˈwɛr〕adj. 知道的
　　　latest〔ˈletɪst〕adj. 最新的　　survey〔ˈsɝve〕n. 調查
　　　score〔skor〕n. 成績　　rank〔ræŋk〕v. 位居
　　　wonder〔ˈwʌndɚ〕v. 想知道
　　　dedicated〔ˈdɛdəˌketɪd〕adj. 致力於…的 < to >
　　　perform〔pɚˈfɔrm〕v. 表現
　　　notoriously〔noˈtorɪəslɪ〕adv. 惡名昭彰地；衆所皆知地
　　　oriented〔ˈorɪˌɛntɪd〕adj. 以…爲取向的
　　　introduce〔ˌɪntrəˈdjus〕v. 引進
　　　fresh〔frɛʃ〕adj. 新鮮的；新的　　boost〔bust〕v. 促進

　　　tourism〔ˈturɪzəm〕n. 觀光業
　　　cannot be overemphasized 再怎麼強調也不爲過
　　　all-around〔ˈɔləˈraʊnd〕adj. 全面的
　　　involved〔ɪnˈvɑlvd〕adj. 有牽連的；有關係的
　　　major〔ˈmedʒɚ〕adj. 重要的
　　　undertaking〔ˌʌndɚˈtekɪŋ〕n. 工作
　　　require〔rɪˈkwaɪr〕v. 需要　　ministry〔ˈmɪnɪstrɪ〕n. 部
　　　giant〔ˈdʒaɪənt〕adj. 巨大的　　*a leap forward* 躍進；大變化
　　　introduction〔ˌɪntrəˈdʌkʃən〕n. 引進；提出
　　　stress〔strɛs〕v. 強調　　*that is* 也就是
　　　lack〔læk〕v. 缺乏　　interact〔ˌɪntɚˈækt〕v. 互動

　　　native speaker 說母語的人　　urgent〔ˈɝdʒnt〕adj. 迫切的
　　　above all 最重要的是　　place〔ples〕v. 使就任；使任職
　　　implement〔ˈɪmpləˌmɛnt〕v. 實施　　*be to V*. 表「預定」。
　　　replace〔rɪˈples〕v. 取代
　　　complement〔ˈkɑmpləˌmɛnt〕v. 補足
　　　strengthen〔ˈstrɛŋθən〕v. 加強
　　　community〔kəˈmjunətɪ〕n. 社會；社區
　　　club〔klʌb〕n. 社團　　resident〔ˈrɛzədənt〕n. 居民
　　　MRT 大衆捷運系統　　billboard〔ˈbɪlˌbord〕n. 廣告看板
　　　aspect〔ˈæspɛkt〕n. 方面　　respectfully〔rɪˈspɛktfəlɪ〕adv. 恭敬地
　　　Respectfully (yours)【信函結尾客套話】謹上

口說能力測驗詳解

PART 1 回答問題

1. Do you watch your weight? What do you do?

你有在注意你的體重嗎？你都怎麼做？

【回答範例 1】

As a matter of fact, I do.

I count my calorie intake carefully.

I'm afraid I'll get too fat.

I have a sweet tooth.

I also love to eat junk food.

That's why I have to keep an eye on
　　my weight.

I follow an exercise routine.

I play basketball several times a week.

It helps me stay slim and trim.

【中文翻譯】

事實上，我有。

我會仔細地計算我的卡路里攝取量。

我怕我會變得太胖。

我喜歡吃甜食。

我也愛吃垃圾食物。

這就是為什麼我必須注意我的體重。

我會做例行的運動。

我每個禮拜會打好幾次籃球。

它幫助我保持身材苗條。

** ————————————

watch〔watʃ〕v. 注意　　weight〔wet〕n. 體重

as a matter of fact　事實上（= *in fact*）

calorie〔'kælərɪ〕n. 卡路里

intake〔'ɪnˌtek〕n. 攝取量

have a sweet tooth　喜歡甜食

keep an eye on　注意　　follow〔'falo〕v. 遵循

routine〔ru'tin〕n. 例行公事；慣例

slim〔slɪm〕adj. 苗條的

trim〔trɪm〕adj. 苗條的

【回答範例 2】

I have no particular need to do so.
I'm not obsessed with looking perfect.
I just try to be natural.

I'm not too fat.
I'm not too skinny.
I'm somewhere in between.

Sometimes I eat like a horse.
Sometimes I eat like a bird.
I just eat what I enjoy.

【中文翻譯】

我不需要特別這麼做。

我不會一心追求要看起來很完美。

我只想要順其自然。

我不會太胖。

我不會太瘦。

我介於兩者之間。

有時我會大吃大喝。

有時我吃得很少。

我只吃我喜歡吃的。

** ————————————

have no need to V. 不必～；不需要～
obsess〔əb'sɛs〕*v.* 迷住；使著迷
skinny〔'skɪnɪ〕*adj.* 很瘦的；皮包骨的
somewhere in between 介於兩者之間
eat like a horse 大吃大喝   *eat like a bird* 吃得很少

2. **Do you think of yourself as an optimistic person?**
   Why or why not?

   你認為你是個樂觀的人嗎？為什麼是或為什麼不是？

【回答範例 1】

I'm an extremely optimistic person.

I always look on the bright side
   of things.

I have a cheerful outlook on life.

I owe my good attitude to my parents.

They raised me in a very supportive way.

My philosophy is that my cup is always
   half full.

I'm grateful for every opportunity
   I have.

If I fail, instead of whining, I try harder.

I truly believe tomorrow will be a
   better day.

【中文翻譯】

我是個非常樂觀的人。

我總是看事情的光明面。

我有快樂的人生觀。

我能有良好的心態，都要歸功於我的父母。

他們以很支持我的方式來養育我。

我的人生哲學是，我的杯子一直是半滿的。

我很感激我擁有的每一次機會。

如果我失敗了，我不會發牢騷，而是會更努力。

我真的相信明天會更好。

** ——————————————————

optimistic〔͵ɑptə'mɪstɪk〕*adj.* 樂觀的

（↔ *pessimistic adj.* 悲觀的）

extremely〔ɪk'strimlɪ〕*adv.* 非常（= *very*）

outlook〔'aut͵luk〕*n.* 看法；觀點

outlook on life 人生觀　　owe〔o〕*v.* 將…歸功於

owe sth. to sb. 把某事歸功於某人

attitude〔'ætə͵tjud〕*n.* 心態　　raise〔rez〕*v.* 養育

supportive〔sə'portɪv〕*adj.* 有支持力的

philosophy〔fə'lɑsəfɪ〕*n.* 人生哲學；人生觀

my cup is always half full 我的杯子一直是半滿的【一杯水
在你面前，你看到的是半杯有水，還是半杯空掉？悲觀的人會認
為是半空（half empty），樂觀的人會認為是半滿（half full）】

grateful〔'gretfəl〕*adj.* 感激的　　***instead of*** 不…而～

whine〔hwaɪn〕*v.* 發牢騷　　***try hard*** 盡力而為

【回答範例2】

I have to admit that I'm not a positive person.

I've had too many discouraging and disappointing experiences.

I would describe myself as a pessimist.

There is too much evil, greed and hate in our world.

There are too many corrupt people.

It is frustrating to read the newspaper every day.

Look at the countless disasters around the world.

Look at the deteriorating moral values in society.

I really feel gloomy about the future.

【中文翻譯】

我必須承認我不是個樂觀的人。

我已經有太多令人氣餒和失望的經驗了。

我會把我自己形容成是一個悲觀者。

我們的世界有太多罪惡、貪婪和憎恨。

有太多墮落的人。

每天看報紙都會令人沮喪。

看看全世界無數的災難。

看看社會上惡化的道德價值觀。

我真的對未來感到憂鬱。

** ——————————————————

admit〔əd'mɪt〕v. 承認

positive〔'pɑzətɪv〕adj. 積極的；樂觀的 (= optimistic)

discouraging〔dɪs'kɝɪdʒɪŋ〕adj. 令人氣餒的

disappointing〔‚dɪsə'pɔɪntɪŋ〕adj. 令人失望的

describe〔dɪ'skraɪb〕v. 描述；形容

pessimist〔'pɛsəmɪst〕n. 悲觀者　evil〔'ivl̩〕n. 罪惡

greed〔grid〕n. 貪婪　corrupt〔kə'rʌpt〕adj. 墮落的

frustrating〔'frʌstretɪŋ〕adj. 令人沮喪的

countless〔'kaʊntlɪs〕adj. 無數的

disaster〔dɪz'æstə〕n. 災難

deteriorate〔dɪ'tɪrɪə‚ret〕v. 惡化

moral values 道德價值觀

gloomy〔'glumɪ〕adj. 憂傷的；悲觀的

3. **What was the happiest thing you did last year?**
   Why did it bring you joy?

   你在去年做過最快樂的事情是什麼？爲什麼它能帶給
   你快樂？

【回答範例 1】

> My most joyful memory was our family
> 　vacation.
>
> *We* took a trip to a Southeast Asian island.
>
> *We* felt like we were in paradise.
>
>
> *We* swam and sunbathed on the beach.
>
> *We* went fishing and scuba diving.
>
> *We* left all our worries and problems
> 　behind.
>
>
> *The* trip was out of this world!
>
> *The* scenery, the food and the activities
> 　were terrific.
>
> Every day was like a dream come true.

【中文翻譯】

我最快樂的回憶是我們全家去渡假。

我們到東南亞的島嶼旅行。

我們覺得像是在天堂一樣。

我們在海邊游泳和做日光浴。

我們去釣魚和潛水。

我們把我們所有的煩惱及問題拋在腦後。

這趟旅行真是太棒了！

風景、食物和活動都很棒。

每天就像是美夢成真。

** ───────────────

joyful〔ˈdʒɔɪfəl〕*adj.* 快樂的

Southeast Asian 東南亞的

paradise〔ˈpærəˌdaɪs〕*n.* 天堂

sunbathe〔ˈsʌnˌbeð〕*v.* 做日光浴

scuba〔ˈskubə〕*n.* 水肺

diving〔ˈdaɪvɪŋ〕*n.* 潛水

scuba diving 水肺潛水

out of this world 極好的；很棒的

scenery〔ˈsinərɪ〕*n.* 風景

terrific〔təˈrɪfɪk〕*adj.* 很棒的

a dream come true 夢想的實現；美夢成真

【回答範例2】

I think it was when I received
　　an award.

I won a competition at my school.

My teachers praised me and presented
　　a certificate to me.

There was a special ceremony.

Everybody clapped and cheered
　　for me.

I felt like I was on top of the world.

My family went out for a feast
　　to celebrate.

Even my little brother gave me
　　a card.

It felt great to make my parents proud
　　of me.

【中文翻譯】

我想是我領獎的時候。

我在學校贏了一場比賽。

我的老師稱讚我,並頒給我一張證書。

有一場很特別的典禮。

每個人為我鼓掌歡呼。

我高興得心情飄飄然。

我們全家出去吃大餐慶祝。

甚至連我的弟弟也給了我一張卡片。

能讓父母以我為榮,我覺得很棒。

** ————————————————

receive 〔 rɪˈsiv 〕 *v.* 得到;領受

award 〔 əˈwɔrd 〕 *n.* 獎

competition 〔 ˌkɑmpəˈtɪʃən 〕 *n.* 比賽

praise 〔 prez 〕 *v.* 稱讚

present 〔 prɪˈzɛnt 〕 *v.* 贈送;授予

certificate 〔 səˈtɪfəkɪt 〕 *n.* 證書

ceremony 〔 ˈsɛrəˌmonɪ 〕 *n.* 典禮

clap 〔 klæp 〕 *v.* 鼓掌　　cheer 〔 tʃɪr 〕 *v.* 歡呼

on top of the world 得意洋洋的

feast 〔 fist 〕 *n.* 盛宴

proud 〔 praʊd 〕 *adj.* 感到光榮的

be proud of 以～為榮

4. **Describe one of your bad habits and what makes you do this?**

描述你的一個壞習慣，以及是什麼原因使你這麼做？

【回答範例】

I have a bad habit of biting my fingernails.

I often do it subconsciously.

I do it when my hands are free.

I don't know when I started this habit
  or why I do it.

I will do it whenever I am pondering
  something.

It just happens that my fingernails are
  soft, too.

Experts say that many people have
  such a habit.

Those who do it seem to be a little
  self-conscious.

This kind of behavior indicates a
  sense of insecurity.

【中文翻譯】

我有咬指甲的壞習慣。
我常常下意識地這麼做。
當我的手閒著時，我就會這麼做。

我不知道我從什麼時候開始這個習慣，或
我為什麼要這麼做。
每當我在沉思某件事情時，就會這麼做。
剛好我的指甲也是很柔軟。

專家說很多人都有這種習慣。
會這樣做的人似乎有一點害羞。
這種行為表示沒有安全感。

**　＊＊**　————————————————

bite〔baɪt〕*v.* 咬
fingernail〔'fɪŋgɚ‚nel〕*n.* 指甲
subconsciously〔sʌb'kɑnʃəslɪ〕*adv.* 下意識地
free〔fri〕*adj.* 有空的　　ponder〔'pɑndɚ〕*v.* 沉思
It happens that~ 碰巧~　　expert〔'ɛkspɝt〕*n.* 專家
self-conscious〔'sɛlf'kɑnʃəs〕*adj.* 害羞的
behavior〔bɪ'hevjɚ〕*n.* 行為
indicate〔'ɪndə‚ket〕*v.* 表示　　sense〔sɛns〕*n.* 感覺
insecurity〔‚ɪnsɪ'kjurətɪ〕*n.* 不安
a sense of insecurity 不安全感

5. **What is an ideal trip in your opinion?**

依你看來，怎樣才是一個理想的旅行？

【回答範例 1】

I love to be close to Mother Nature.

So I enjoy traveling in a pristine area.

A place with unspoiled natural scenery
suits me well.

Urban prosperity doesn't appeal to me.

I am not interested in shopping or
theme parks.

I would rather choose a less developed
place.

Hiking and camping in the mountains
would do.

A few days at a beach would be great.

Doing something thrilling like diving
would be best of all.

【中文翻譯】

我很喜歡接近大自然。

所以我喜歡在原始的地區旅遊。

一個自然風景未遭受破壞的地方就很適合我。

都市的繁榮並不吸引我。

我對購物或主題樂園沒興趣。

我寧願選擇一個低度開發的地方。

在山區健行和露營也可以。

在海邊待個幾天也很棒。

做些像是跳水這種刺激的事情是最棒的。

** ——————————————

Mother Nature 大自然

pristine〔ˋprɪstin〕*adj.* 原始的；純樸的；自然狀態的

unspoiled〔ʌnˋspɔɪld〕*adj.* 未受破壞的

suit sb. well 很適合某人　　urban〔ˋɝbən〕*adj.* 都市的

prosperity〔prɑsˋpɛrətɪ〕*n.* 繁榮

appeal to 吸引（= *attract*）

theme park 主題樂園　　*would rather* 寧願

developed〔dɪˋvɛləpt〕*adj.* 已開發的

hiking〔ˋhaɪkɪŋ〕*n.* 健行

camping〔ˋkæmpɪŋ〕*n.* 露營

do〔du〕*v.* 行；可以　　thrilling〔ˋθrɪlɪŋ〕*adj.* 刺激的

diving〔ˋdaɪvɪŋ〕*n.* 跳水

【回答範例 2】

I don't care for less developed areas.

Their lack of hygiene and security
　　worry me.

I feel insecure if I go to these places.

I love to go to a modern place.

My ideal trip would be to Japan, the U.S.,
　　or Europe.

All of them are clean, have beautiful
　　sights, and world-class facilities.

I can enjoy their rich culture
　　and history.

I can enjoy their delicious and
　　safe foods.

These places offer a lot for me to see
　　and to do without worrying.

【中文翻譯】

我不喜歡低度開發的地區。

它們缺乏衛生及安全會使我擔心。

如果我去這些地方，我會感到不安。

我喜歡去現代化的地方。

我理想的旅行會是去日本、美國，或歐洲。

這些地方都很乾淨、有漂亮的風景，和世
界級的設施。

我可以欣賞它們豐富的文化和歷史。

我可以享受它們美味而且安全的食物。

這些地方提供我很多可看可做的事，不
用煩惱。

** ─────────────────

care for 喜歡　　lack〔 læk 〕*n.* 缺乏

hygiene〔 ˈhaɪdʒin 〕*n.* 衛生

security〔 sɪˈkjʊrətɪ 〕*n.* 安全

insecure〔 ˌɪnsɪˈkjʊr 〕*adj.* 感到不安的

sight〔 saɪt 〕*n.* 風景

world-class〔 ˈwɝldˈklæs 〕*adj.* 世界級的

facilities〔 fəˈsɪlətɪz 〕*n. pl.* 設施

rich〔 rɪtʃ 〕*adj.* 豐富的

6. **Have you ever been a tutor or taught anyone anything? Describe your experience(s).**
你曾經當過家教或教過任何人任何東西嗎？描述一下你的經驗。

【回答範例】

Sure, I've coached others before.

In junior high I tutored my two younger
　　cousins.

I helped them for a year with math
　　and science.

During senior high, I taught my neighbor's
　　kids English.

It felt great to work and earn money.

I felt my own English improved a lot
　　as well.

In college, I got a part-time job at a
　　cram school.

I instructed elementary students in English.

It was a challenging yet very rewarding
　　experience.

【中文翻譯】

當然，我之前指導過別人。

在國中時，我教過我的兩位堂弟。

我協助他們的數學和科學一年。

高中期間，我教我鄰居的小孩英文。

工作和賺錢的感覺很棒。

我覺得我自己的英文也進步很多。

大學時，我在補習班打工。

我教國小學生英文。

它是一個具挑戰性但很值得的經驗。

** ─────────────────────

tutor〔'tutɚ〕 n. 家庭教師　v. 教

coach〔kotʃ〕 v. 指導

cousin〔'kʌzn̩〕 n. 表（堂）兄弟姊妹

improve〔ɪm'pruv〕 v. 改善；進步

as well 也（ = too ）

part-time〔'part'taɪm〕 adj. 兼差的

cram school 補習班

instruct〔ɪn'strʌkt〕 v. 教

challenging〔'tʃælɪndʒɪŋ〕 adj. 具挑戰性的

yet〔jɛt〕 conj. 但是

rewarding〔rɪ'wɔrdɪŋ〕 adj. 值得的

7. **What are the advantage(s) and disadvantage(s) of being the only child in the family? Please explain.**
身為家中獨生子（女）的優缺點是什麼？請說明。

【回答範例】

It seems great to be the only child in
the family.

The family has more resources to
offer to a single child.

The only child receives all the attention.

The main disadvantage would be
loneliness.

It would be sad having no siblings.

It would be a boring, solitary existence.

Parents might spoil an only child.

Or, the child might be exceptionally
mature.

It depends on the relationship between
the parents and the kid.

【中文翻譯】

身為家中的獨生子（女）似乎很好。

家裡有更多的資源可以提供給獨生子（女）。

獨生子（女）可以得到所有的關注。

主要的缺點是寂寞。

沒有兄弟姊妹會很可悲。

那會是無聊而且孤獨的生活。

父母可能會寵壞獨生子（女）。

或者，這個小孩可能會特別成熟。

這要視父母與孩子之間的關係而定。

** ————————————————

advantage〔əd'væntɪdʒ〕n. 優點

disadvantage〔,dɪsəd'væntɪdʒ〕n. 缺點

resource〔rɪ'sors〕n. 資源

single〔'sɪŋgḷ〕adj. 單一的

receive〔rɪ'siv〕v. 受到；獲得

attention〔ə'tɛnʃən〕n. 注意；關照

siblings〔'sɪblɪŋz〕n. pl. 兄弟姊妹

solitary〔'salə,tɛrɪ〕adj. 孤獨的

existence〔ɪg'zɪstəns〕n. 生活

spoil〔spɔɪl〕v. 寵壞

exceptionally〔ɪk'sɛpʃənḷɪ〕adv. 特別地

mature〔mə'tʃʊr〕adj. 成熟的　　***depend on*** 視…而定

8. **Your American friend asks you about dragon boat racing. Tell him or her something about it**.

你的美國朋友向你詢問關於龍舟競賽的問題。告訴他(她)一些關於它的事情。

【回答範例】

Dragon boat racing comes from a story.

A patriotic poet named Chu Yuan drowned
　　himself to protest his king's tyranny.

People rowed their boats into the river,
　　trying to save him.

They also dropped rice dumplings into the
　　river to keep the fish from eating him.

That's why we hold dragon boat races and
　　eat chung-tze, rice dumplings, during the
　　Dragon Boat Festival today.

The holiday is also called The Poet's Day,
　　in memory of Chu Yuan.

The boat races are very colorful and exciting.

Most major cities hold their own competitions.

Even teams from abroad participate in the
　　competitions now.

【中文翻譯】

龍舟競賽源自一個故事。

有位名叫屈原的愛國詩人,他投水自盡來抗議君
王的暴政。

人們划船到河中,試著要救他。

他們也把粽子丟到河裡,爲了讓魚不要吃他。

這就是爲什麼我們現在會在端午節舉行龍舟競賽
和吃粽子。

爲了紀念屈原,這個節日也叫作「詩人節」。

龍舟競賽非常精采刺激。

大多數的主要都會城市會舉行他們自己的比賽。

現在甚至還有外國隊伍參加比賽。

**

---

dragon boat racing 龍舟競賽

patriotic〔͵petrɪˈɑtɪk〕*adj.* 愛國的　　poet〔ˈpo‧ɪt〕*n.* 詩人

drown〔draʊn〕*v.* 使淹死　　*drown oneself* 投水自盡

protest〔prəˈtɛst〕*v.* 抗議　　tyranny〔ˈtɪrənɪ〕*n.* 暴政

row〔ro〕*v.* 划　　dumpling〔ˈdʌmplɪŋ〕*n.* 蒸或煮的麵糰

rice dumpling 粽子 (= *chung-tze*)

hold〔hold〕*v.* 舉行　　race〔res〕*n.* 競賽

Dragon Boat Festival 端午節　　*in memory of* 紀念

colorful〔ˈkʌləfəl〕*adj.* 精采的　　major〔ˈmedʒə〕*adj.* 主要的

competition〔͵kɑmpəˈtɪʃən〕*n.* 比賽

from abroad 來自國外的

participate〔parˈtɪsə͵pet〕*v.* 參加 < *in* >

PART 2 看圖敘述

1. **What is this place?** 這是什麼地方？

   This is a picture of a park in a Western country.

   這是一張西方國家的公園照片。

2. **What kind of occasion do you think it is?**

   你認為這是什麼場合？

   I think this is a picnic. The people may be
   co-workers or classmates.

   我想這是野餐。這些人可能是同事或同學。

** ————————————————————

   occasion〔ə'keʒən〕n. 場合
   co-worker〔ko'wɝkɚ〕n. 同事

3. **What are the people in the picture doing?**

照片裡的人在做什麼？

They are socializing. They are talking in small groups and some of them are having a drink. Others are standing and it looks like someone is barbecuing.

他們正在參加交際。他們一小群人在講話，其中有些人正在喝飲料。有些人站著，看起來像是有人在烤肉。

4. **Have you ever joined in an activity like this before?**

你曾經參加過這樣的活動嗎？

I myself have joined in such an activity. I once had a picnic with my class in high school. We went to a park and everyone brought something to eat or drink. We had a good time that day.

我自己參加過這種活動。我曾經在高中時和全班同學一起野餐。我們去一座公園，每個人都帶吃的或喝的。我們那天玩得很開心。

5. **If you still have time, please describe the picture in as much detail as you can.**

如果你還有時間，請儘可能描述照片中的細節。

** ————————————

socialize〔'soʃə,laɪz〕 v. 參加社交活動；交際
barbecue〔'bɑrbɪ,kju〕 v. 烤肉 n. 烤肉架
have a good time 玩得愉快

This is a very spacious park with large trees. There are two groups of young people sitting or standing in the shade. In front, four people are sitting on chairs. Each is having a drink and the only man is smoking a cigarette. In the background several more people are standing near what looks like a table of food or perhaps a barbecue. They are all casually dressed and it looks like they are having a good time.

這是一座廣闊的公園，裡面有高大的樹。有兩群年輕人坐或站在樹蔭下。前方有四個人坐在椅子上。每個人都在喝飲料，唯一的男生在抽煙。背後還有好幾個人，站在看起來像一桌子食物或可能是烤肉架的旁邊。他們都穿得很休閒，而且看起來玩得很愉快。

** ───────────────────────────

spacious〔'speʃəs〕*adj.* 廣闊的　　shade〔ʃed〕*n.* 樹蔭
in front 在前面　　smoke〔smok〕*v.* 抽（煙）
cigarette〔ˌsɪgə'rɛt〕*n.* 香煙
background〔'bæk͵graʊnd〕*n.* 背景
casually〔'kæʒʊəlɪ〕*adv.* 休閒地；簡便地
be casually dressed 穿得很休閒

PART 3　申述題

What kind of boy or girl will catch your attention? Name some physical features or personal traits that attract you to a boy or girl. Please explain.

什麼樣的男（女）生可以吸引你的注意？舉出一些可以吸引你的男（女）生的外在特徵或個人特質。請說明。

【回答範例1】

Like most people, I notice attractive people. *So* a tall, handsome boy is sure to catch my attention. He does not have to be very well dressed, but he should be neat because that means he cares about his appearance and the impression that he makes on others. *On the other hand*, he should not be too fashionably dressed because that might mean he is self-centered or vain.

Appearance is not everything, of course. It is more important that he be kind and intelligent. A sense of humor also helps. And he must have a smile on his face. *After all*, who wants to talk to someone who looks gloomy all the time?

【中文翻譯】

我像大多數人一樣，會注意有吸引力的人。所以高大、英俊的男生一定可以吸引我的注意。他不需要穿得很體面，但他應該要看起來整潔，因爲那代表他在意自己的外表以及他給人的印象。另一方面，他不應該穿得太時髦，因爲那可能意味著他以自我爲中心，或很虛榮。

　　當然外表不是一切。善良和聰明是更加重要的。幽默感也是有用的。而且他必須臉上掛著笑容。畢竟，誰想要跟一個看起來一直很憂鬱的人講話呢？

** ─────────────────

catch〔kætʃ〕v. 吸引（注意力）　　name〔nem〕v. 提出；舉出

physical〔ˋfɪzɪkḷ〕adj. 身體的；外在的　　feature〔ˋfitʃɚ〕n. 特性

trait〔tret〕n. 特點　　notice〔ˋnotɪs〕v. 注意

attractive〔əˋtræktɪv〕adj. 有吸引力的

neat〔nit〕adj. 乾淨的；整齊的　　appearance〔əˋpɪrəns〕n. 外表

impression〔ɪmˋprɛʃən〕n. 印象　　**on the other hand** 另一方面

fashionably〔ˋfæʃənəblɪ〕adv. 時髦地

self-centered〔ˋsɛlfˋsɛntɚd〕adj. 自我中心的

vain〔ven〕adj. 虛榮心強的

intelligent〔ɪnˋtɛlədʒənt〕adj. 聰明的　　humor〔ˋhjumɚ〕n. 幽默

a sense of humor 幽默感　　**after all** 畢竟

gloomy〔ˋglumɪ〕adj. 憂鬱的　　**all the time** 一直；始終

【回答範例 2】

　　A beautiful girl is sure to catch my attention. *However*, I will pay special attention to a girl's outfit. Knowing how to dress properly is very important for a girl. She doesn't have to wear fancy or fashionable clothes, but she must have her own style. A girl's clothing and even the accessories she chooses reveal her sense of beauty. *Besides*, it is important for her to wear something that fits the occasion.

Appearance is not everything, of course. It is more
important that she be kind and intelligent. A sense of
humor also helps. And she must have a smile on her
face. ***After all***, who wants to talk to someone who looks
gloomy all the time?

【中文翻譯】

一個漂亮的女生一定可以吸引我的注意。不過,我會特別注意一個女生的服裝。知道如何適當地穿著對女生是很重要的。她不用穿著華麗或流行的衣服,但她必須要有她自己的風格。一個女生的服裝,甚至她選擇的配件,都會透露出她的審美眼光。此外,她穿戴的東西是否符合場合也是很重要的。

當然外表不是一切。善良和聰明是更加重要的。幽默感也是有用的。而且她必須臉上掛著笑容。畢竟,誰想要跟一個看起來一直很憂鬱的人講話呢?

**　―――――――――――――――――――

outfit〔'aʊt,fɪt〕*n.* 服裝　　properly〔'prɑpɚlɪ〕*adv.* 適當地
fancy〔'fænsɪ〕*adj.* 華麗的
fashionable〔'fæʃənəbl̩〕*adj.* 流行的
accessory〔æk'sɛsərɪ〕*n.* 配件
reveal〔rɪ'vil〕*v.* 透露　　sense〔sɛns〕*n.* 感覺能力
a sense of beauty 美感;審美的眼光
fit〔fɪt〕*v.* 適合;符合　　occasion〔ə'keʒən〕*n.* 場合

座位號碼：＿＿＿＿＿＿＿＿＿＿＿　　　　試題別：＿＿＿＿＿＿＿＿

第一部份請由本頁第1行開始作答，請勿隔行書寫。第二部份請翻至第2頁作答。

5

10

15

20

25

寫作口說能力測驗②

寫作能力測驗

Part I: Chinese-English Translation (40%)

Translate the following Chinese passage into an English passage, and write your answer on the Writing Test Answer Sheet.

你晚上睡覺會失眠嗎？當你擔心無法入睡、輾轉反側，想找一個舒適的姿勢時，你其實會使心跳加速，更難放鬆。所以在失眠的夜晚裡，你該做什麼呢？別碰安眠藥，因為安眠藥只會使你的問題更加惡化。你可以在睡前喝些熱牛奶、吃起司或鮪魚。這些食物中所含有的某些物質會幫助你容易入睡、睡得好。

Part II: Guided Writing (60%)

Write an essay of **150-180 words** in an appropriate style on the following topic. Write your answer on the Writing Test Answer Sheet.

Nowadays, online shopping has become very popular. Have you ever bought anything online? How do you feel about this means of purchasing? Please state your opinions and reasons.

口説能力測驗

Please read the self-introduction sentence.

My seat number is （複試座位號碼）, and my

registration number is （初試准考證號碼）.

Part I: Answering Questions

You will hear 8 questions. Each question will be spoken once. Please answer the question immediately after you hear it.

For questions 1 to 4, you will have 15 seconds to answer each question.

For questions 5 to 8, you will have 30 seconds to answer each question.

Part II: Picture Description

Look at the picture, think about the questions below for 30 seconds, and then record your answers for 1 ½ minutes.

1. What is this place?

2. Who do you think these people, including the adults, are?

3. What is the female who is kneeling on the right side of the picture doing?

4. What do you suppose the two kids with helmets are going to do?

5. If you still have time, please describe the picture in as much detail as you can.

Part III: Discussion

Think about your answer(s) to the question(s) below
for 1 ½ minutes, and then record your answer(s) for
1 ½ minutes.

You may use your test paper to make notes and
organize your ideas.

Nearly everyone has collections of some sort or other.
Please describe what you collect, how you get them,
and with whom you always share them.

Please read the self-introduction sentence again.

My seat number is （複試座位號碼）, and my
registration number is （初試准考證號碼）.

寫作口説能力測驗 ② 詳解

寫作能力測驗詳解

PART 1 中譯英 (40%)

　　你晚上睡覺會失眠嗎？當你擔心無法入睡、輾轉反側，想找一個舒適的姿勢時，你其實會使心跳加速，更難放鬆。所以在失眠的夜晚裡，你該做什麼呢？別碰安眠藥，因為安眠藥只會使你的問題更加惡化。你可以在睡前喝些熱牛奶、吃起司或鮪魚。這些食物中所含有的某些物質會幫助你容易入睡、睡得好。

Do you have difficulty sleeping at night? When you worry about not being able to fall asleep and toss and turn trying to find a comfortable position, you actually increase your heart rate and make it harder to relax. So what should you do on those sleepless nights? Don't touch sleeping pills, because they only make your problem worse. You can drink some hot milk or eat cheese or tuna fish before you go to bed. Certain substances in these foods can help you get to sleep more easily and have a good night's sleep.

【註】　***have difficulty (in) + V-ing*** 很難～　　***fall asleep*** 入睡
toss and turn 輾轉反側　　position〔pə'zıʃən〕*n.* 姿勢
rate〔ret〕*n.* 速度　　relax〔rı'læks〕*v.* 放鬆
sleepless〔'sliplıs〕*adj.* 失眠的　　pill〔pıl〕*n.* 藥丸
sleeping pill 安眠藥　　tuna〔'tunə〕*n.* 鮪魚（= *tuna fish*）
certain〔'sɝtṇ〕*adj.* 某些　　substance〔'sʌbstəns〕*n.* 物質

PART 2 引導寫作 (60%)

Nowadays, online shopping has become very popular. Have you ever bought anything online? How do you feel about this means of purchasing? Please state your opinions and reasons.

現在線上購物已經變得非常受歡迎。你曾經在網路上買過任何東西嗎？你對這種購買方式有什麼看法？請陳述你的看法和理由。

【作文範例 1】

Online Shopping

Shopping is a popular pastime, but not everyone enjoys pushing their way through a crowded store. Now there is an alternative—online shopping. I have bought several items this way and I feel very positive about the experience.

Online shopping has several advantages. *First of all*, I don't have to leave my home. That means I don't spend time in traffic just getting to the store. *In addition*, I can find a wide variety of goods on the Internet. That makes it easy to compare prices and features. *Finally*, after I make a purchase, I only have to wait for it to be delivered. I don't have to carry any heavy items home with me.

Of course, there are some drawbacks to this method, *too*. I am very careful to buy only from reputable merchants. *Otherwise*, my credit information could be stolen. With a little common sense, I think this means of purchasing is safe enough. *Overall*, I find shopping from home convenient and comfortable.

【註】 online〔'ɑn,laɪn〕*adj.* 線上的
pastime〔'pæs,taɪm〕*n.* 消遣
push one's way 推開前進；擠　　*push through* 擠過去
crowded〔'kraʊdɪd〕*adj.* 擁擠的
alternative〔ɔl'tɝnətɪv〕*n.* 可選擇的事物
item〔'aɪtəm〕*n.* 物品
positive〔'pɑzətɪv〕*adj.* 肯定的
advantage〔əd'væntɪdʒ〕*n.* 優點
a variety of 各式各樣的　　goods〔gʊdz〕*n. pl.* 商品
compare〔kəm'pɛr〕*v.* 比較

feature〔'fitʃɚ〕*n.* 特色　　purchase〔'pɝtʃəs〕*n.* 購買
drawback〔'drɔ,bæk〕*n.* 缺點
method〔'mɛθəd〕*n.* 方法
reputable〔'rɛpjətəbḷ〕*adj.* 有聲譽的
merchant〔'mɝtʃənt〕*n.* 商人
otherwise〔'ʌðɚ,waɪz〕*adv.* 否則
credit〔'krɛdɪt〕*n.* 信用
information〔,ɪnfɚ'meʃən〕*n.* 資料
common sense 常識　　means〔minz〕*n.* 方法
overall〔,ovɚ'ɔl〕*adv.* 就整體來說

【作文範例 2】

Online Shopping

Who in this world has not heard of Amazon.com? If you haven't, you must be living in a cave. It is the world's largest online retailer. The diversity of goods and services it offers is amazing. Now millions of other retailers also do business online and this model is growing like crazy.

The Pros: *Firstly*, you can shop conveniently from your own home, whenever it suits you, day or night, 365 days a year. You are not confined to store hours. *Secondly*, you save time and energy plus all the expenses connected with traveling back and forth to shop. *Third*, there are no pushy, rude, or otherwise unpleasant salespeople to deal with. *Finally*, you get to see or browse through a much wider selection than you ever could in a store, and there are even special, deeper discounts for online customers only.

The Cons: *First*, seeing photos of goods is just not the same as being able to touch them. Although quality assurance is now standard operating procedure for online shopping, when it comes to items like clothing, the size, fit, and even color may just not be up to your expectations. Returning and exchanging goods is a hassle, too. *And finally*, and perhaps most importantly, the chance of identity theft increases dramatically when you shop online.

In the final analysis, the pros of online shopping easily outweigh the cons, and the whole process continues to improve as it becomes more and more commonplace.　It's the wave of the present and the tsunami of the future.　Online shopping is an irresistible force.

【註】Amazon〔'æmə,zɑn〕*n.* 亞馬遜　　cave〔kev〕*n.* 洞穴
　　　retailer〔'ritelə〕*n.* 零售商　　diversity〔də'vɜsətɪ〕*n.* 多樣性
　　　amazing〔ə'mezɪŋ〕*adj.* 驚人的
　　　online〔'ɑn,laɪn〕*adv.* 在網路上　　model〔'mɑdḷ〕*n.* 模式
　　　like crazy 拼命地　　pro〔pro〕*n.* 贊成的論點
　　　suit〔sut〕*v.* 適合　　confine〔kən'faɪn〕*v.* 限制
　　　hours〔aʊrz〕*n. pl.* 營業時間　　plus〔plʌs〕*prep.* 加上
　　　expense〔ɪk'spɛns〕*n.* 費用　　*be connected with* 與～有關
　　　travel〔'trævḷ〕*v.* 移動　　*back and forth* 來回地
　　　pushy〔'pʊʃɪ〕*adj.* 咄咄逼人的　　rude〔rud〕*adj.* 無禮的

　　　otherwise〔'ʌðə,waɪz〕*adv.* 以別的方法；在其他狀態
　　　unpleasant〔ʌn'plɛzṇt〕*adj.* 令人討厭的　　*deal with* 應付
　　　browse〔braʊz〕*v.* 瀏覽
　　　selection〔sə'lɛkʃən〕*n.* 供選擇的範圍　　deep〔dip〕*adj.* 大的
　　　discount〔'dɪskaʊnt〕*n.* 折扣　　con〔kɑn〕*n.* 反對的論點
　　　assurance〔ə'ʃʊrəns〕*n.* 保證　　standard〔'stændəd〕*adj.* 標準的
　　　operating〔'ɑpəretɪŋ〕*adj.* 經營的
　　　procedure〔prə'sidʒə〕*n.* 程序　　*when it comes to* 一提到
　　　item〔'aɪtəm〕*n.* 物品；項目　　fit〔fɪt〕*n.* 合身
　　　up to 達到　　hassle〔'hæsḷ〕*n.* 麻煩

　　　identity〔aɪ'dɛntətɪ〕*n.* 身分　　theft〔θɛft〕*n.* 竊盜
　　　dramatically〔drə'mætɪkḷɪ〕*adv.* 顯著地；大大地
　　　in the final analysis 總之　　outweigh〔aʊt'we〕*v.* 勝過
　　　commonplace〔'kɑmən,ples〕*adj.* 普通的　　wave〔wev〕*n.* 波浪
　　　present〔'prɛzṇt〕*n.* 現在　　tsunami〔tsu'nɑmɪ〕*n.* 海嘯
　　　irresistible〔,ɪrɪ'zɪstəbḷ〕*adj.* 不能抵抗的

口說能力測驗詳解

PART 1 回答問題

1. **Have you gone shopping lately? Describe your experience.**

你最近有去購物嗎？描述一下你的經驗。

【回答範例 1】

I went shopping with my mom last weekend.

We went to a major department store.

We had an excellent time shopping.

We went to the store shortly after it opened.

The clerks seemed more attentive in the morning.

There were few customers and we got great
    service.

I bought myself a pair of shoes and for my
    nephew a stuffed animal as well as toy cars.

After we had lunch at the food court,
    the crowds grew larger.

So we went home because I don't enjoy being
    in crowds.

【中文翻譯】

上週末我和媽媽去購物。

我們去一家大型的百貨公司。

我們買得很開心。

我們在它開始營業之後不久就去了。

店員在早上的時候似乎比較親切。

客人很少，於是我們得到很棒的服務。

我買一雙鞋給自己，一隻填充玩具動物和玩具

車給我的姪子。

我們在美食街吃完午餐後，人變多了。

因為我不喜歡人擠人，所以我們就回家了。

** ————————————

lately〔'letlɪ〕 adv. 最近

major〔'medʒɚ〕 adj. 較大的

clerk〔klɜk〕 n. 店員

attentive〔ə'tɛntɪv〕 adj. 專注的；親切的

nephew〔'nɛfju〕 n. 姪子；外甥

stuffed〔stʌft〕 adj. 填塞的

stuffed animal 填充玩具動物　　**as well as** 以及

food court 美食街　　crowd〔kraud〕 n. 人群

grow〔gro〕 v. 變得　　enjoy〔ɪn'dʒɔɪ〕 v. 喜歡

【回答範例2】

Last Sunday I went bargain hunting
   in the shopping district.

I enjoyed haggling with the
   storekeepers.

I was good at it, too.

I searched for sales and discounts
   everywhere.

Negotiating over the price was fun
   and saved money.

My hard work paid off with some
   super buys.

I bought a pair of sneakers at half price.

I bought some cool shirts at three for
   the price of two.

I also received some new promotional
   products for free.

【中文翻譯】

上禮拜天，我在購物區找尋便宜的東西。

我喜歡和商店老板殺價。

我對這一點也很內行。

我到處尋找特價和折扣。

議價很有趣，還能省錢。

我的努力成功買到一些很棒而且很便宜的東西。

我用半價買了一雙運動鞋。

我用買二送一的價格買了一些很酷的襯衫。

我還免費拿到一些新的促銷產品。

＊＊ ──────────

bargain〔'bɑrgɪn〕n. 特價品；便宜的東西

hunt〔hʌnt〕v. 找尋　　　district〔'dɪstrɪkt〕n. 地區

haggle〔'hægḷ〕v. 討價還價；殺價

storekeeper〔'stor͵kipɚ〕n. 商店老板

negotiate〔nɪ'goʃɪ͵et〕v. 談判；協商

pay off 得到好結果；取得成功

super〔'supɚ〕adj. 極好的

buy〔baɪ〕n. 買得的東西；便宜貨

sneakers〔'snikɚz〕n. pl. 運動鞋

cool〔kul〕adj. 酷的

promotional〔prə'moʃənḷ〕adj. 促銷的

for free 免費地

2. **When your family eats out, what kind of cuisine do you usually choose and why?**

當你們全家外出用餐時，你們通常會選擇哪一種菜？
爲什麼？

【回答範例】

Actually we have tried various kinds of cuisine.

Taiwan is a paradise for food.

We hope to taste as many kinds of food as
　　we can.

If it is a usual family get-together, we go to a
　　Chinese restaurant and eat Cantonese,
　　Sichuan, or Taiwanese dishes.

For one thing, it is usually reasonably priced.

For another, it is suitable for my grandparents.

If we have something special to celebrate,
　　we will choose to have foreign food,
　　such as Japanese or French.

What is better is that we go to an all-you-can-eat
　　restaurant that serves all kinds of dishes.

Everyone can enjoy a pleasant atmosphere
　　and eat whatever he or she likes.

【中文翻譯】

事實上我們嚐過各種不同的菜。

台灣是個美食天堂。

我們希望能儘可能品嚐多種食物。

如果是平常的家庭聚會，我們會去中國餐廳吃廣東菜、

四川菜，或台灣菜。

一是因為它的價格合理。

二是因為它比較適合我的祖父母。

如果我們有特別的事情要慶祝，我們會選擇吃外國食

物，例如日本料理或法國菜。

去吃到飽的餐廳更好，那裡提供各種菜餚。

每個人都能享受愉快的氣氛，並且吃自己喜歡的食物。

** ————————————————

cuisine〔kwɪ'zin〕*n.* 菜餚
actually〔'æktʃʊəlɪ〕*adv.* 事實上
various〔'vɛrɪəs〕*adj.* 各種不同的
paradise〔'pærə,daɪs〕*n.* 天堂　　taste〔test〕*v.* 品嚐
as…as one can 儘可能　　get-together〔'gɛttʊ,gɛðɚ〕*n.* 聚會
Cantonese〔,kæntən'iz〕*adj.* 廣東的
Sichuan〔'sitʃwɑn〕*adj.* 四川的　　dish〔dɪʃ〕*n.* 菜餚
for one thing…for another ～　一來…二來；一則…再則
reasonably〔'riznəblɪ〕*adv.* 合理地
price〔praɪs〕*v.* 給…定價　　suitable〔'sutəbl〕*adj.* 適合的
all-you-can-eat *adj.* 吃到飽的　　serve〔sɝv〕*v.* 供應
pleasant〔'plɛznt〕*adj.* 令人愉快的
atmosphere〔'ætməs,fɪr〕*n.* 氣氛

3. **How often do you clean your house? How do you do it?**

你多久打掃一次房子？你會怎麼打掃？

【回答範例】

We do a light cleaning every day.

This includes making our beds and
  sweeping the floors.

Of course we also do the dishes, wipe
  the counters and take out the trash.

In addition, we do the laundry every
  two or three days.

We mop the floors, dust, and wipe
  all the tables.

My father washes his car weekly.

Once a month, we do a thorough
  cleaning.

We air out the pillows and blankets.

We wash the windows and scrub the
  whole bathroom.

【中文翻譯】

我們每天都會做個簡單的打掃。

包括整理床鋪和掃地。

當然我們也有洗碗盤、擦長餐檯和倒垃圾。

此外，我們每兩三天會洗一次衣服。

我們會拖地、撣去所有桌子的灰塵然後擦拭。

我的爸爸每個禮拜會洗一次車。

我們每個月會有一次大掃除。

我們會曬枕頭和毯子。

我們會清洗窗戶和刷洗整間浴室。

** ───────────────────

light〔laɪt〕 adj. 輕微的；少量的

make one's bed 整理床鋪　　sweep〔swip〕v. 掃

do the dishes 洗碗盤　　wipe〔waɪp〕v. 擦

counter〔'kaʊntɚ〕n. 長餐檯　　trash〔træʃ〕n. 垃圾

laundry〔'lɔndrɪ〕n. 待洗的衣服

do the laundry 洗衣服

mop〔mɑp〕v. 用拖把拖（地板）

dust〔dʌst〕v. 撣去…的灰塵

weekly〔'wiklɪ〕adv. 每週一次地

thorough〔'θɝo〕adj. 徹底的

air〔ɛr〕v. 晾曬　　pillow〔'pɪlo〕n. 枕頭

blanket〔'blæŋkɪt〕n. 毯子　　scrub〔skrʌb〕v. 刷洗

4. **If you heard one of your friends speaking ill of another person, what would you do?**

如果你聽到你的一個朋友說別人的壞話，

你會怎麼做？

【回答範例 1】

I don't approve of those who gossip.

I also feel it's wrong to speak ill

of another.

However, I think I wouldn't do

anything.

I wouldn't like to confront my friend.

And I think it's not my responsibility

to correct my friend.

If I did, my friend might feel offended.

I would simply keep silent.

I would pretend I heard nothing.

I would just let the mean remark pass.

【中文翻譯】

我不贊同那些講閒話的人。

我也覺得說別人的壞話是不對的。

不過，我想我什麼都不會做。

我不想和我的朋友對峙。

而且我認為糾正我的朋友不是我的責任。

如果我這麼做，我的朋友可能會覺得生氣。

我只會保持沉默。

我會假裝我什麼都沒聽到。

我會讓惡意的評論就這樣過去。

**　————————————

speak ill of 說…的壞話

approve〔ə'pruv〕v. 贊同 < of >

gossip〔'gɑsəp〕v. 說閒話

confront〔kən'frʌnt〕v. 對抗

responsibility〔rɪ,spɑnsə'bɪlətɪ〕n. 責任

correct〔kə'rɛkt〕v. 糾正

offended〔ə'fɛndɪd〕adj. 被激怒的

simply〔'sɪmplɪ〕adv. 只　　silent〔'saɪlənt〕adj. 沉默的

pretend〔prɪ'tɛnd〕v. 假裝　　mean〔min〕adj. 惡意的

remark〔rɪ'mɑrk〕n. 評論；話

pass〔pæs〕v. 離去；消失

【回答範例 2】

I don't approve of those who gossip.

I also feel it's wrong to speak ill of
    another.

So I would immediately tell my
    friend to stop.

I'd explain that I'm not comfortable
    hearing that.

I'd tell my friend it is not polite.

I'd ask my friend not to do it again.

I'd say, "A wonderful person like
    you shouldn't talk like that.

Criticizing others only belittles you.

Please try to get rid of this bad habit."

【中文翻譯】

我不贊同那些講閒話的人。

我也覺得說別人的壞話是不對的。

所以我會立刻叫我的朋友停止。

我會解釋我聽到那些話會覺得不舒服。

我會告訴我的朋友那是不禮貌的。

我也會要求我的朋友不要再這樣做了。

我會說：「像你這麼好的人不應該那樣說話。

批評別人只會貶低你自己。

請試著改掉這個壞習慣。」

** ────────────

immediately〔 ɪˋmidɪɪtlɪ 〕*adv.* 立刻

polite〔 pəˋlaɪt 〕*adj.* 有禮貌的

criticize〔ˋkrɪtəˏsaɪz 〕*v.* 批評

belittle〔 bɪˋlɪtl̩ 〕*v.* 貶低

get rid of 除去；擺脫

habit〔ˋhæbɪt 〕*n.* 習慣

5. **In addition to your English textbooks and testing materials, have you ever read any other English publications? Please describe your experiences.**

除了你的英文課本和考試資料外，你還曾經閱讀過任何其他英文刊物嗎？請描述你的經驗。

【回答範例1】

My dad gets an English newspaper daily.

I often browse through it.

The sports section is my favorite.

I subscribe to a monthly magazine called "Studio Classroom."

It's interesting, informative and extremely useful.

I study it nearly every day.

My sister also has a monthly subscription to "Reader's Digest."

Sometimes I will borrow it from her.

I enjoy the stories and the many articles concerned with the latest health research.

【中文翻譯】

我的爸爸每天都有買英文報紙。
我常常瀏覽它。
體育版是我的最愛。

我有訂月刊,叫作「空中英語教室」。
它很有趣、有教育性,也非常有用。
我幾乎每天都會讀它。

我姐姐也有訂「讀者文摘」的月刊。
有時我會跟她借。
我喜歡裡面的故事,和許多關於最新健康研究的文章。

** ———————————————————

textbook〔'tɛkst,bʊk〕n. 課本;教科書
material〔mə'tɪrɪəl〕n. 資料
publication〔,pʌblɪ'keʃən〕n. 刊物　daily〔'delɪ〕adv. 每天
browse〔braʊz〕v. 瀏覽　sports〔sports〕adj. 運動的
section〔'sɛkʃən〕n. (報紙、雜誌的) 版
subscribe〔səb'skraɪb〕v. 訂閱 < to >
monthly〔'mʌnθlɪ〕adj. 每月的
studio〔'stjudɪ,o〕n. 廣播室
informative〔ɪn'fɔrmətɪv〕adj. 提供知識的;有敎育性的
extremetly〔ɪk'strimlɪ〕adv. 非常
subscription〔səb'skrɪpʃən〕n. 訂閱
digest〔'daɪdʒɛst〕n. 文摘　article〔'ɑrtɪkḷ〕n. 文章
concerned〔kən'sɝnd〕adj. 有關的
latest〔'letɪst〕adj. 最新的

【回答範例 2】

No, I have to admit I haven't.

My English ability is not good enough.

My English comprehension is
very poor.

The lessons in my textbooks alone are
too much for me.

Worse yet, I also have a lot of testing
materials.

I struggle with my poor English every
day.

Sometimes I feel like giving up.

I just don't have the aptitude for
learning languages.

I study English only for the sake
of exams.

【中文翻譯】

不，我必須承認我沒有。

我的英文能力不夠好。

我的英文理解力很差。

光是課本的課程對我來說就太多了。

更糟的是，我也有很多考試資料。

我每天都要和我的破英文搏鬥。

有時我會想要放棄。

我就是沒有學習語言的才能。

我學英文只是爲了考試。

** ——————————

admit〔əd'mɪt〕v. 承認

comprehension〔͵kɑmprɪ'hɛnʃən〕n. 理解力

poor〔pʊr〕adj. 差勁的

alone〔ə'lon〕adv. 僅；單單

yet〔jɛt〕adv.【強調比較級】更加

worse yet 更糟的是

struggle〔'strʌg!〕v. 搏鬥

feel like + V-ing 想要～　　***give up*** 放棄

aptitude〔'æptə͵tjud〕n. 才能 < *for* >

for the sake of 爲了…的緣故

6. **Christmas is not an official holiday in Taiwan; however, more and more people, and especially department stores and shops, celebrate it. Please describe what you have seen or your own celebrations of Christmas.**

在台灣，聖誕節不是國定假日；不過，越來越多人，尤其是百貨公司和店家，會慶祝它。請描述你看過或你自己的聖誕節慶祝活動。

【回答範例 1】

In Taiwan, Christmas is a big commercial event.
Many merchants use Christmas to increase profits.
Celebrating Christmas is an effective way to
　　expand sales.

Hotels, stores and clubs all commemorate
　　this holiday.
Restaurants have special Christmas feasts.
Even schools have Christmas decorations
　　everywhere.

We all know Christmas falls on December 25.
It celebrates the birth of Jesus Christ.
Does anyone remember that December 25 is
　　also Taiwan's Constitution Day?

【中文翻譯】

在台灣，聖誕節是一個大型的商業活動。

很多商人利用聖誕節增加收益。

慶祝聖誕節是擴大銷售額的一個有效方法。

飯店、商店和俱樂部全都會慶祝這個節日。

餐廳會有特別的聖誕大餐。

甚至連學校到處都有聖誕裝飾。

我們都知道聖誕節是十二月二十五日。

那天是要慶祝耶穌基督的誕生。

有人記得十二月二十五日也是台灣的行憲紀念日嗎？

** ——————————————

official 〔ə'fɪʃəl〕 *adj.* 正式的；官方的
official holiday 國定假日
commercial 〔kə'mɝʃəl〕 *adj.* 商業的
event 〔ɪ'vɛnt〕 *n.* 事件；活動
merchant 〔'mɝtʃənt〕 *n.* 商人
profit 〔'prɑfɪt〕 *n.* 利潤；收益
effective 〔ɪ'fɛktɪv〕 *adj.* 有效的
expand 〔ɪk'spænd〕 *v.* 擴大　　sales 〔selz〕 *n. pl.* 銷售額
commemorate 〔kə'mɛmə,ret〕 *v.* 慶祝
feast 〔fist〕 *n.* 盛宴　　decoration 〔,dɛkə'reʃən〕 *n.* 裝飾
fall on 適逢　　birth 〔bɝθ〕 *n.* 誕生
Jesus Christ 耶穌基督
constitution 〔,kɑnstə'tjuʃən〕 *n.* 憲法
Constitution Day 行憲紀念日

【回答範例 2】

My family celebrates Christmas even though we are not Christians.

We place a Christmas tree in the living room.

We decorate it with many cute, little ornaments.

Christmas is not a holiday here, but each of us manages to come home for dinner on Christmas Eve.

My mother often prepares a special Christmas feast.

Sometimes our relatives join us, too.

We buy and exchange gifts.

We also give each other cards expressing our loving feelings.

Christmas is a time for us to share love and thanks together.

【中文翻譯】

雖然我們不是基督徒，但是我家會慶祝聖誕節。

我們會在客廳放一棵聖誕樹。

我們會用很多可愛的小裝飾品裝飾它。

聖誕節在這裡不是假日，但是我們每個人都會設
法在聖誕夜回家吃晚餐。

我的媽媽常常會準備特別的聖誕大餐。

有時我們的親戚也會加入我們。

我們會購買並交換禮物。

我們也會給彼此卡片來表達我們充滿愛的感情。

聖誕節是讓我們一起分享愛及感謝的時刻。

** ———————————————————————

even though 即使

Christian〔'krɪstʃən〕 *n.* 基督徒

place〔ples〕 *v.* 放置

decorate〔'dɛkə,ret〕 *v.* 裝飾

ornament〔'ɔrnəmənt〕 *n.* 裝飾品

manage〔'mænɪdʒ〕 *v.* 設法

Christmas Eve 聖誕夜　　relative〔'rɛlətɪv〕 *n.* 親戚

exchange〔ɪks'tʃendʒ〕 *v.* 交換

loving〔'lʌvɪŋ〕 *adj.* 充滿著愛的

feelings〔'filɪŋz〕 *n. pl.* 感情　　share〔ʃɛr〕 *v.* 分享

thanks〔θæŋks〕 *n. pl.* 感謝

7. Who is your role model and why?

誰是你的榜樣？爲什麼？

【回答範例 1】

My father is my hero.

He was born poor so he barely finished high school.

He started working in a factory when he was 18.

Though he doesn't hold a high-ranking position, he works very hard to support my family.

He doesn't want me to get the highest scores on exams but he does ask me to be a nice person.

Though he is not well-educated, he teaches me a lot.

He doesn't pressure me to study all the time.

Instead, he encourages me to develop some interesting hobbies.

I feel lucky to have a father like him.

【中文翻譯】

我的父親是我的英雄。

他出生窮困，所以他僅能完成高中學業。

他十八歲的時候，就開始在工廠上班。

即使他的工作職位不高，他還是很努力工作來扶
養我們全家。

他不會要我考試拿到最高分，但是他要求我要做
個好人。

雖然他沒有受過良好的教育，但是他教我很多事情。

他不會一直強迫我唸書。

他反而鼓勵我培養一些有趣的嗜好。

我覺得很幸運，能有像他這樣的父親。

** ———————————

role model 榜樣；典範　　hero〔'hɪro〕*n.* 英雄

barely〔'bɛrlɪ〕*adv.* 僅　　factory〔'fæktərɪ〕*n.* 工廠

hold〔hold〕*v.* 擁有

high-ranking〔'haɪ'ræŋkɪŋ〕*adj.* 高級的；職位高的

position〔pə'zɪʃən〕*n.* 職位

support〔sə'port〕*v.* 扶養　　score〔skor〕*n.* 分數

well-educated〔'wɛl'ɛdʒəˌketɪd〕*adj.* 受過良好教育的

pressure〔'prɛʃɚ〕*v.* 強迫　　*all the time* 一直

instead〔ɪn'stɛd〕*adv.* 取而代之

develop〔dɪ'vɛləp〕*v.* 培養　　hobby〔'habɪ〕*n.* 嗜好

【回答範例 2】

My big brother is my role model.

I admire him for his versatility.

He is almost perfect in my eyes.

He is excellent in academics.

He is a straight A student.

He is extremely intelligent yet
　　modest.

Besides, he is always cheerful
　　and easy to get along with.

He also has a great sense of humor
　　and enjoys helping others.

I hope I can be as nice as he, with a
　　high IQ and EQ.

【中文翻譯】

我的大哥是我的榜樣。

我佩服他的多才多藝。

在我的眼中，他近乎完美。

他在學業方面很優秀。

他是一位成績全部甲等的學生。

他非常聰明但很謙虛。

此外，他總是很開朗也很好相處。

他也很有幽默感，還喜歡幫助別人。

我希望我能變得跟他一樣好，有高智商和高情緒

智商。

＊＊ ───────────

admire〔əd'maɪr〕*v.* 佩服

versatility〔͵vɝsə'tɪlətɪ〕*n.* 多才多藝

excellent〔'ɛksl̩ənt〕*adj.* 極好的

academics〔͵ækə'dɛmɪks〕*n. pl.* 學業；學科（= *academic
subjects*）

straight A〔'stret'e〕*adj.*（學業成績）全部甲等的

intelligent〔ɪn'tɛlədʒənt〕*adj.* 聰明的

yet〔jɛt〕*conj.* 但是　　modest〔'mɑdɪst〕*adj.* 謙虛的

cheerful〔'tʃɪrfəl〕*adj.* 開朗的　　***get along with*** 相處

humor〔'hjumɚ〕*n.* 幽默　　***a sense of humor*** 幽默感

IQ 智商（= *intelligence quotient*）

EQ 情緒商數（= *emotional quotient*）

8. **What do you think are the reasons for the high crime rate in today's society?** 你認為現今社會高犯罪率的原因是什麼？

【回答範例】

I think many factors contribute to this problem.
The breakdown of traditional families is one cause.
Many kids of divorced parents fall into delinquency.

Society has become so materialistic.
People have become alienated and confused.
Morality has declined as a result.

Schools seem to lack the ability to instill moral values.
The educational system stresses academics too heavily.
Ethics, public service, and patriotism are often
    neglected.

Our government is to blame.
The poor economic conditions lead many to crime.
The lack of honest policemen and upright officials is
    another cause.

The media also contribute to the high crime rate.
They sensationalize criminals and their ill-gotten gains.
Program content on TV also glorifies criminal leaders
    and their luxurious lifestyles.

【中文翻譯】

我認為有很多原因造成這個問題。

傳統家庭的瓦解是一個原因。

很多父母離婚的小孩會犯罪。

社會變得很重視物質享受。

大家變得疏遠而且困惑。

因此道德感就降低了。

學校似乎缺乏灌輸道德價值觀的能力。

教育制度過度強調學業。

道德倫理、社會服務和愛國心，常常會被忽視。

我們的政府應該負責任。

貧困的經濟狀況導致許多人犯罪。

缺乏誠實的警察和正直的官員是另一個原因。

媒體也會造成高犯罪率。

他們會渲染犯罪者以及他們的不義之財。

電視節目的內容也會美化犯罪首領和他們奢侈
的生活方式。

** ─────────────

crime〔kraɪm〕*n.* 犯罪　　rate〔ret〕*n.* 比率
contribute〔kən'trɪbjut〕*v.* 促成 < *to* >
breakdown〔'brek͵daun〕*n.* 崩潰；瓦解
cause〔kɔz〕*n.* 原因

divorced〔dəˈvɔrst〕adj. 離婚的　　**fall into** 陷入

delinquency〔dɪˈlɪŋkwənsɪ〕n. 罪行；不法行為

materialistic〔məˌtɪrɪəlˈɪstɪk〕adj. 物質主義的

alienated〔ˈeljənˌetɪd〕adj. 疏遠的

confused〔kənˈfjuzd〕adj. 困惑的

morality〔mɔˈrælətɪ〕n. 道德

decline〔dɪˈklaɪn〕v. 下降

as a result 因此；結果　　lack〔læk〕v. n. 缺乏

instill〔ɪnˈstɪl〕v. 灌輸

moral values 道德價值觀　　stress〔strɛs〕v. 強調

academics〔ˌækəˈdɛmɪks〕n. pl. 學科；學業

ethics〔ˈɛθɪks〕n. pl. 道德；倫理

public service 公共服務；社會服務

patriotism〔ˈpetrɪətɪzəm〕n. 愛國心

neglect〔nɪˈglɛkt〕v. 忽視

be to blame 應受責備；應負責任

lead sb. **to V**. 使某人～

upright〔ˈʌpˌraɪt〕adj. 正直的

official〔əˈfɪʃəl〕n. 官員

media〔ˈmidɪə〕n. pl. 媒體

sensationalize〔sɛnˈseʃənlˌaɪz〕v. 渲染；使聳人聽聞

criminal〔ˈkrɪmənl〕n. 罪犯　　adj. 犯罪的

ill-gotten〔ˈɪlˈgɑtn̩〕adj. 非法獲得的

gains〔genz〕n. pl. 利潤

ill-gotten gains 不當的利潤；不義之財

glorify〔ˈglorəˌfaɪ〕v. 美化

leader〔ˈlidə〕n. 領導者；首領

luxurious〔lʌgˈʒurɪəs〕adj. 奢侈的

PART 2 看圖敘述

1. **What is this place?** 這是什麼地方？

   This is a kindergarten classroom. 這裡是幼稚園的教室。

2. **Who do you think these people, including the adults, are?**

   你認為這些人，包括大人，是誰？

   The kids are students and the adults are teachers. Some
   of them may be visiting teachers because this looks like
   a special safety class. 小孩是學生，大人是老師。其中有些人
   可能是上門授課的教師，因為這看起來像是一堂特殊安全講習。

   ＊＊────────────

   kindergarten〔ˈkɪndɚˌgartn̩〕*n.* 幼稚園
   visiting〔ˈvɪzɪtɪŋ〕*adj.* 上門提供短時間服務的
   visiting teacher 上門授課教師

3. **What is the female who is kneeling on the right side of the picture doing?**

在照片右方跪著的女性在做什麼？

The kneeling woman is helping a girl put on some kneepads. I think the woman next to her is doing the same thing.

這位跪著的女士在幫一位女孩穿上某種護膝。我想她旁邊的女士也在做同樣的事情。

4. **What do you suppose the two kids with helmets are going to do?**

你認為這兩位戴著安全帽的小孩將要做什麼？

Perhaps they are going to learn how to skate or ride a bike. It is hard to imagine that they will do this in the classroom, so maybe they are just learning how to wear protective equipment.

可能他們將要學習如何溜冰或騎腳踏車。很難想像他們會在這間教室裡做這件事，所以也許他們只是在學習如何穿戴護具。

** ─────────────

female〔'fimel〕n. 女性
kneel〔nil〕v. 跪下　　***put on***　穿上；戴上
kneepad〔'ni,pæd〕n. 護膝墊
suppose〔sə'poz〕v. 認為　　helmet〔'hɛlmɪt〕n. 安全帽
skate〔sket〕v. 溜冰　　imagine〔ɪ'mædʒɪn〕v. 想像
protective〔prə'tɛktɪv〕adj. 防護的
equipment〔ɪ'kwɪpmənt〕n. 裝備；全套器具

5. **If you still have time, please describe the picture in as much detail as you can.**

如果你還有時間，請儘可能描述照片中的細節。

This is a picture of a classroom for young children. There are pictures and a map on the walls and low tables around the sides of the room. Several children are seated on the floor in a semicircle and one woman is sitting behind them on a chair. There is another woman sitting on a chair near the stage. On the stage are three other women. Two of them are helping children put on kneepads. The children are already wearing helmets.

這是一張幼兒教室的照片。牆上有照片和一張地圖，教室周邊有矮桌。有幾位小孩圍成半圓形坐在地上，在他們後面有一位女士坐在椅子上。有另一位女士坐在靠近講台的椅子上。講台上還有三位女士。其中兩位在幫小孩穿護膝。小孩都戴著安全帽。

** _____

seat〔sit〕v. 使就座　　semicircle〔'sɛmə,sɝkl̩〕n. 半圓形
stage〔stedʒ〕n. 講台

PART 3 申述題 ●─────────────────●

Nearly everyone has collections of some sort or other. Please describe what you collect, how you get them, and with whom you always share them.

幾乎每個人都有某種收藏。請描述你收藏什麼、你如何取得它們，以及你總是和誰分享它們。

【回答範例】

　　I collect dolls from different countries. Each of them is dressed in the traditional clothes of his or her country. I began collecting the dolls as a child. When I was seven, my parents took me to Japan and I brought back my first doll. She is wearing a traditional kimono and I still have her. Since then, I have purchased a doll every time I visit a new country. I have also received dolls as gifts from relatives and friends who travel. I display them on some shelves in my room and share them with my family and friends. They remind me of all the places I have seen and of how diverse the world is. Perhaps someday I will give them to my daughter.

【中文翻譯】

　　我收集來自不同國家的娃娃。每一個都穿著他(她)的國家的傳統服飾。我從小開始收集娃娃。當我七歲的時候,我的父母帶我去日本,然後我帶回我的第一個娃娃。她穿著傳統的和服,而且我現在還留著她。在那時起,我每次去遊覽一個新的國家,我就會買一個娃娃。從去旅行的親戚或朋友那裡,我也會收到當作禮物的娃娃。我把它們陳列在我房間的一些架子上,並且會和我的家人及朋友分享它們。它們會使我想起所有我曾經參觀過的地方,也想起這世界上的人有多麼不同。也許將來有一天,我會把它們給我的女兒。

**　　——————————————————

traditional〔trəˈdɪʃənḷ〕adj. 傳統的
kimono〔kəˈmonə〕n. 和服　　　purchase〔ˈpɝtʃəs〕v. 購買
relative〔ˈrɛlətɪv〕n. 親戚　　　display〔dɪˈsple〕v. 陳列;展示
shelf〔ʃɛlf〕n. 架子　　　remind〔rɪˈmaɪnd〕v. 使想起
diverse〔dəˈvɝs , daɪ-〕adj. 多種的;不同的

座位號碼：_____　　　試題別：_____

第一部份請由本頁第1行開始作答，請勿隔行書寫。第二部份請翻至第2頁作答。

_____
_____
_____
_____
_____
_____
_____
_____
_____
_____
_____
_____
_____
_____
_____
_____
_____
_____
_____
_____
_____
_____
_____

55

60

65

70

寫作口説能力測驗 ③

寫作能力測驗

Part I: Chinese-English Translation (40%)

Translate the following Chinese passage into an English passage, and write your answer on the Writing Test Answer Sheet.

　　成功的人是一個能以幽默感面對挫折的人。世上無人能永遠成功，也沒有人總是失敗。要成功，通常先要歷經一連串失敗的考驗。換言之，能輸得起的人就有贏的希望。持續不斷的努力是你致勝的關鍵。但是必定要記住，勝不驕、敗不餒。被一時的勝利沖昏了頭，你就和你的成功說再見了。

Part II: Guided Writing (60%)

Write an essay of **150-180 words** in an appropriate style on the following topic. Write your answer on the Writing Test Answer Sheet.

There are now many universities and businesses requiring their applicants to pass some kind of English proficiency test, like the one you are taking now. Do you agree or disagree with such a policy? Please state your opinions and reasons.

口說能力測驗

Please read the self-introduction sentence.

My seat number is ＿(複試座位號碼)＿, and my
registration number is ＿(初試准考證號碼)＿.

Part I: Answering Questions

You will hear 8 questions. Each question will be
spoken once. Please answer the question immediately
after you hear it.

For questions 1 to 4, you will have 15 seconds to
answer each question.

For questions 5 to 8, you will have 30 seconds to
answer each question.

Part II: Picture Description

Look at the picture, think about the questions below for 30 seconds, and then record your answers for 1 ½ minutes.

1. What is this place?

2. What are these people doing?

3. What is the difference between the woman on the left and the others?

4. If you still have time, please describe the picture in as much detail as you can.

Part III: Discussion

Think about your answer(s) to the question(s) below
for 1 ½ minutes, and then record your answer(s) for
1 ½ minutes.
You may use your test paper to make notes and
organize your ideas.

There are more and more foreigners coming to
Taiwan either for sightseeing or for work. What
attractions do we have to bring them here? What else
should we do to encourage more to come? Please
explain.

Please read the self-introduction sentence again.

My seat number is （複試座位號碼）, and my
registration number is （初試准考證號碼）.

寫作口說能力測驗 ③ 詳解

寫作能力測驗詳解

PART 1 中譯英 (40%)

　　成功的人是一個能以幽默感面對挫折的人。世上無人能永遠成功，也沒有人總是失敗。要成功，通常先要歷經一連串失敗的考驗。換言之，能輸得起的人就有贏的希望。持續不斷的努力是你致勝的關鍵。但是必定要記住，勝不驕、敗不餒。被一時的勝利沖昏了頭，你就和你的成功說再見了。

A successful person is one who can face frustration with a sense of humor. No one in the world can succeed all the time, nor will one always fail. To succeed, one will usually go through the ordeal of a series of failures first. In other words, a person who takes defeat well stands a chance of winning. Constant effort is the key to victory. However, make sure to remember that you mustn't be overly proud when you win and that you shouldn't be discouraged when you lose. Let an instant triumph go to your head, and you are saying goodbye to your success.

【註】frustration〔frʌˈtreʃən〕n. 挫折

　　　humor〔ˈhjumɚ〕n. 幽默　　*a sense of humor* 幽默感

　　　all the time 一直　　　fail〔fel〕v. 失敗

　　　go through 經歷　　ordeal〔ɔrˈdil〕n. 嚴酷的考驗

　　　a series of 一連串的　　failure〔ˈfeljɚ〕n. 失敗

　　　in other words 換言之　　defeat〔dɪˈfit〕n. 失敗；輸

　　　take defeat well 坦然接受失敗　　stand〔stænd〕v. 有

　　　stand a chance of 有…的希望

　　　constant〔ˈkɑnstənt〕adj. 不斷的

　　　effort〔ˈɛfɚt〕n. 努力　　key〔ki〕n. 關鍵 < to >

　　　victory〔ˈvɪktərɪ〕n. 勝利

　　　make sure to + V. 一定要…

　　　overly〔ˈovɚlɪ〕adv. 過度地

　　　proud〔praʊd〕adj. 驕傲的

　　　discourage〔dɪsˈkɝɪdʒ〕v. 使氣餒

　　　instant〔ˈɪnstənt〕adj. 立即的；短暫的

　　　triumph〔ˈtraɪəmf〕n. 勝利

　　　go to one's head 使某人驕傲自滿

PART 2　引導寫作 (60%)

There are now many universities and businesses requiring their applicants to pass some kind of English proficiency test, like the one you are taking now. Do you agree or disagree with such a policy? Please state your opinions and reasons.

現在有很多大學和企業要求他們的申請人和應徵者要通過某種英語能力測驗，就像你現在所做的英語能力測驗。你同不同意這種政策？請陳述你的意見和理由。

【作文範例】

English Proficiency Test

　　Many businesses now require their employees to speak English and universities expect incoming students to have a reasonable command of the language. In order to ensure a certain level of proficiency, they require prospective workers or students to take a test. I agree with this policy, but I don't believe that it should be the only factor in the hiring or admission decision.

　　Companies and schools need an efficient way to narrow down their number of applicants. If English is an important part of the job or course, then an entrance examination makes sense. It will not only tell the decision makers that the applicant is able to communicate in English but also that he or she is able to prepare well and to handle stressful situations. *Moreover*, a basic test is a fair way to distinguish among the applicants.

　　However, since English ability is not the only thing that qualifies a person for a position, other factors must be considered. Each person's general intelligence, achievements and personality should also be taken into account. *After all*, if an applicant is good in other areas, it stands to reason that he or she could improve in English.

【註】proficiency〔prə'fɪʃənsɪ〕n. 精通

English proficiency test 英語能力測驗

require〔rɪ'kwaɪr〕v. 要求

employee〔ˌɛmplɔɪ'i〕n. 員工

incoming〔'ɪnˌkʌmɪŋ〕adj. 新來的

reasonable〔'riznəbl〕adj. 合理的；適度的

command〔kə'mænd〕n. 運用自如的能力；精通

ensure〔ɪn'ʃʊr〕v. 確保　certain〔'sʒtn̩〕adj. 某種

level〔'lɛvl̩〕n. 程度

prospective〔prə'spɛktɪv〕adj. 未來的；可能的

policy〔'pɑləsɪ〕n. 政策　factor〔'fæktɚ〕n. 因素

hire〔haɪr〕v. 雇用

admission〔əd'mɪʃən〕n. 入學（許可）

efficient〔ə'fɪʃənt〕adj. 有效率的

narrow〔'næro〕v. 縮減 < *down* >

applicant〔'æpləkənt〕n. 申請人；應徵者

entrance〔'ɛntrəns〕n. 入學；就業

make sense 合理　handle〔'hændl̩〕v. 處理

stressful〔'strɛsfəl〕adj. 緊張的；壓力大的

fair〔fɛr〕adj. 公平的　distinguish〔dɪ'stɪŋgwɪʃ〕v. 分辨

qualify〔'kwɑləˌfaɪ〕v. 使有資格；使適任

position〔pə'zɪʃən〕n. 職位

consider〔kən'sɪdɚ〕v. 考慮

general〔'dʒɛnərəl〕adj. 一般的

intelligence〔ɪn'tɛlədʒəns〕n. 智力

achievements〔ə'tʃivmənts〕n. pl. 成就

personality〔ˌpʒsn̩'ælətɪ〕n. 個性

take into account 考慮到

after all 畢竟　area〔'ɛrɪə〕n. 領域

stand to reason 合乎情理；理所當然

improve〔ɪm'pruv〕v. 改善；進步

口說能力測驗詳解

PART 1 回答問題

1. **When a show that you are looking forward to is canceled, what do you say?**

當一個你期待的表演取消了，你會說什麼？

【回答範例】

Oh, no, I can't believe it.

It's happened to me again.

The show has been canceled.

Why am I so unlucky?

I think I wanted it too much.

I feel like I've been cursed.

Well, there's nothing that can be done
  about it.

We'll have to figure out something
  else for the night.

Maybe we can find a decent movie
  instead.

【中文翻譯】

喔，不，我真不敢相信。

我又遇到這種事了。

表演取消了。

為什麼我這麼倒楣啊？

我想是我太想看到它。

我覺得我被詛咒了。

算了，對於這種事，也沒辦法做什麼。

我們必須想出其他晚上可以做的事。

也許我們可以找到一部不錯的電影代替。

** ——————————————

show〔ʃo〕*n.* 表演

look forward to 期待

cancel〔'kænsḷ〕*v.* 取消

curse〔kɝs〕*v.* 詛咒　　***figure out*** 想出

decent〔'disṇt〕*adj.* 不錯的

instead〔ɪn'stɛd〕*adv.* 作為代替

2. **What do you usually do for English practice?**
你通常會做什麼來練習英文？

【回答範例】

I listen to ICRT every day.

I also enjoy listening to English songs.

I improve my listening ability in this
way.

Besides, I read English newspapers
a lot.

I enjoy comic books in English.

I often practice writing English essays.

Most of all, I think it is great to
converse face to face with foreigners.

I never pass up any chance to speak
English.

Whenever I go to a McDonald's or
Starbucks, I try to strike up a
conversation with a native speaker.

【中文翻譯】

我每天聽 ICRT。

我也喜歡聽英文歌曲。

我是用這種方式來改善自己的聽力。

除此之外，我常看英文報紙。

我喜歡英文漫畫書。

我常常練習寫英文文章。

最重要的是，我覺得和外國人面對面交談是
很棒的。

我絕不會放過說英文的機會。

每當我去麥當勞或星巴克時，我都會試著和
以英文為母語的人交談。

**

ICRT 台北國際社區廣播電台

  (= *International Community Radio Taipei*)

a lot 常常　　***comic book*** 漫畫書

essay〔ˋɛse〕*n.* 文章；論文

most of all 更重要的是

converse〔kənˋvɝs〕*v.* 交談　　***face to face*** 面對面

pass up 放過　　***strike up*** 開始

strike up a conversation with *sb.* 開始與某人交談

native speaker 說母語的人

3. **Have you ever thought about studying abroad?**
   Why or why not?

   你曾經想過要到國外唸書嗎？為什麼有或為什麼沒有？

【回答範例 1】

Of course, I've thought about studying
  abroad.

What student hasn't?

I would love to study in America.

American universities offer a wide
  range of courses.

The facilities are state-of-the-art.

The professors are tops in their fields.

Above all, I enjoy the liberal
  atmosphere on American campuses.

Besides, I'll get immersed in American
  culture.

I can take advantage of the opportunity
  to travel around the States at the
  same time.

【中文翻譯】

當然，我想過要到國外唸書。
有哪個學生沒有想過？
我想在美國唸書。

美國大學提供的課程範圍很廣泛。
那裡的設備是最先進的。
教授都是各自領域中最頂尖的。

最重要的是，我喜歡美國校園自由的氣氛。
此外，我可以沉浸在美國文化中。
我同時可以利用機會遊覽美國各地。

**

abroad〔əˋbrɔd〕 adv. 到國外
facilities〔fəˋsɪlətɪz〕 n. pl. 設施
state-of-the-art adj. 最先進的
field〔fild〕 n. 領域　　　*above all* 最重要的是
liberal〔ˋlɪbərəl〕 adj. 自由的
atmosphere〔ˋætməsˏfɪr〕 n. 氣氛
campus〔ˋkæmpəs〕 n. 校園
immerse〔ɪˋmɝs〕 v. 使沉浸在
take advantage of 利用

【回答範例 2】

There's no way I can study abroad.

It's a total fantasy.

First of all, my English isn't good
　enough.

In addition, there's also the question
　of money.

It costs a fortune to study overseas.

My parents just couldn't afford it.

Besides, I am a homebody.

Just the thought of living in a
　foreign environment makes me
　feel ill at ease.

It would be hard for me to get used
　to life away from home.

【中文翻譯】

我絕不會去國外唸書。

這完全是一個幻想。

首先,我的英文能力不夠好。

此外,也有金錢方面的問題。

到國外唸書要花一大筆錢。

我的父母無法負擔。

此外,我是個喜歡留在家裡的人。

光是想到住在國外的環境裡,就讓我覺得不自在。

對我來說,要習慣離開家的生活是很難的。

** ————————————————————

no way 絕不　　total〔ˈtotl̩〕*adj.* 完全的

fantasy〔ˈfæntəsɪ〕*n.* 幻想

in addition 此外

fortune〔ˈfɔrtʃən〕*n.* 財富;大筆錢

overseas〔ˌovɚˈsiz〕*adv.* 到國外

afford〔əˈford〕*v.* 負擔得起

homebody〔ˈhomˌbɑdɪ〕*n.* 喜歡待在家裡的人

foreign〔ˈfɔrɪn〕*adj.* 國外的;陌生的

ill at ease 不自在　　hard〔hɑrd〕*adj.* 困難的

get used to 習慣於

4. **Are you a rational or emotional person?**

你是一個理性或感性的人？

【回答範例 1 】

I am a believer in Descartes.

My motto is "I think, therefore I am."

I try to make every decision rationally.

I analyze before and after I do
　everything.

I make it a habit to get things
　organized.

That's why I got the nickname "Robot"
　from my friends.

Perhaps they think I am a little boring.

However, when they're in trouble,
　it's me they come to for advice
　or help.

They know they can always count
　on me.

【中文翻譯】

我是笛卡爾的信徒。

我的座右銘是「我思故我在。」

我做每個決定都很理性。

我做每件事的前後都會分析。

我養成讓事情有條理的習慣。

這就是為什麼我會被朋友取了「機器人」的綽號。

或許他們覺得我有點無聊。

然而，當他們有困難時，他們會來找我尋求忠告

或幫助。

他們知道他們總是可以依賴我。

** ─────────────

rational〔ˈræʃənḷ〕adj. 理性的

emotional〔ɪˈmoʃənḷ〕adj. 情緒化的

believer〔bɪˈlivɚ〕n. 相信的人；信徒

Descartes〔deˈkɑrt〕n. 笛卡爾【1596-1650，法國哲學家及數學家】

motto〔ˈmɑto〕n. 座右銘

I think, therefore I am. 我思故我在。

rationally〔ˈræʃənḷɪ〕adv. 理性地

analyze〔ˈænḷˌaɪz〕v. 分析

make it a habit to V. 養成…習慣

organized〔ˈɔrgənˌaɪzd〕adj. 有組織的；有條理的

nickname〔ˈnɪkˌnem〕n. 綽號　　　robot〔ˈrobət〕n. 機器人

advice〔ədˈvaɪs〕n. 忠告　　　***count on*** 依賴

【回答範例 2】

I am an emotional person.

I get touched very easily.

Just a good movie or a nice song
may move me to tears.

I believe in following my heart.

I like to be spontaneous.

I'm happiest when I say and do what
I am feeling.

If I were less sensitive, I wouldn't
get hurt as much as I do.

But it wouldn't be me.

Besides, I'd have missed virtually all
of my most memorable experiences.

【中文翻譯】

我是個感性的人。

我很容易受感動。

只要是一部好電影或一首好歌，就可能讓我感動落淚。

我認為要跟著心走。

我喜歡自然一點。

當我說的和做的都是心裡所想的，我覺得最快樂。

如果我不那麼敏感，就不會像現在一樣受那麼多傷害。

但這樣就不是我了。

此外，我也就會錯過幾乎所有我最難忘的經驗。

** ─────────────────

touch〔tʌtʃ〕v. 感動　　move〔muv〕v. 感動

believe in 認為…有益

spontaneous〔spɑnˊtenɪəs〕*adj.* 自然的

sensitive〔ˊsɛnsətɪv〕*adj.* 敏感的

get hurt 受到傷害　　miss〔mɪs〕v. 錯過；失去

virtually〔ˊvɝtʃʊəlɪ〕*adv.* 幾乎

memorable〔ˊmɛmərəb!〕*adj.* 難忘的

5. **Please describe one of your frustrating experiences.**

請描述一個令你沮喪的經驗。

【回答範例 1】

I love American basketball, especially
　　the NBA.

A couple of years back a famous NBA
　　star was invited to Taipei.

He came for only one day to demonstrate
　　his skills and then answer questions.

With great difficulty, my friend and I
　　got tickets for the exhibition.

We were so excited.

We started counting down the days
　　from 100.

And then it happened.

My sister fell in love and got married
　　in the blink of an eye.

You guessed it—the marriage took place
　　on what should have been my NBA day.

【中文翻譯】

我愛美國職籃,尤其是 NBA。

幾年前,一位有名的 NBA 明星受邀到台北來。

他只來一天,要示範他的球技,然後回答問題。

我和我的朋友非常不容易才拿到表演的門票。

我們非常興奮。

我們從前一百天就開始倒數。

然後事情發生了。

我的姊姊墜入愛河,然後閃電結婚。

你猜的沒錯——婚禮在我應該要去看 NBA 明星的那天舉行。

** ————————————————

frustrating〔ˈfrʌstretɪŋ〕*adj.* 令人沮喪的

NBA 全美籃球協會 (= *National Basketball Association*)

a couple of years back 回顧幾年前

demonstrate〔ˈdɛmənˌstret〕*v.* 示範

skill〔skɪl〕*n.* 技巧　　***with difficulty*** 困難地;好不容易地

exhibition〔ˌɛksəˈbɪʃən〕*n.* 展覽會;表演

count down 倒數　　***fall in love*** 墜入愛河

blink〔blɪŋk〕*n.* 眨眼　　***in the blink of an eye*** 在一瞬間

guess〔gɛs〕*v.* 說中;猜對

marriage〔ˈmærɪdʒ〕*n.* 婚姻;婚禮　　***take place*** 舉行

【回答範例2】

I've been interested in math since elementary school.

I was at the top of the class in math.

I even won a math competition in my school.

I was confident that I could get high scores in math.

I had thought it would not be a problem at all in the college entrance exam.

However, when the college entrance exam did come, I read the test paper and my mind went blank.

I failed to answer several questions.

I felt extremely frustrated after the test.

It turned out that I got a relatively low score.

【中文翻譯】

我從小學開始就對數學有興趣。

我的數學是班上第一名。

我甚至在學校的數學比賽中獲勝。

我確信我的數學能拿到高分。

我認為在大學入學考試中我的數學完全不會有問題。

然而，當大學入學考試真的來臨時，我看到考試卷時，腦筋就一片空白。

我有好幾題都沒回答。

考完試後，我覺得非常挫敗。

結果是我拿到相當低的分數。

** ——————————————————

competition〔͵kɑmpə'tɪʃən〕*n.* 競賽

confident〔'kɑnfədənt〕*adj.* 有信心的；確信的

score〔skor〕*n.* 分數

entrance〔'ɛntrəns〕*n.* 進入；入學

test paper 考卷　　go〔go〕*v.* 變得

blank〔blæŋk〕*adj.* 空白的

fail to V. 未能～

extremely〔ɪk'strimlɪ〕*adv.* 非常

frustrated〔'frʌstretɪd〕*adj.* 受挫的

turn out 結果是

relatively〔'rɛlətɪvlɪ〕*adv.* 相對地；比較上

6. **Would you prefer being at the bottom of an excellent class or at the top of an ordinary class? Please state the reasons for your choice.**

你比較喜歡當資優班的最後一名，還是普通班的第一名？請為你的選擇闡述理由。

【回答範例1】

I'd much prefer to be at the bottom
　　of an excellent class.
I would be perpetually forced to strive.
I would be constantly seeking to improve.

Being in this position would keep me
　　on my toes.
Yes, it would be difficult at times.
But the rewards would be tremendous.

I'm sure I would make great progress.
Even if I remained at the bottom,
　　my absolute improvement would
　　be significant.
I'm sure with diligence I would make
　　my parents and myself proud.

【中文翻譯】

我比較喜歡當資優班的最後一名。

我會不斷地被迫要努力。

我會不斷地追求進步。

在這個位置會讓我保持警覺。

是的，有時候會很辛苦。

但是報酬是很大的。

我確定我會有大幅的進步。

即使我停留在最後一名，但是我進步的幅度是相當
大的。

我確定用功的話，就會使我的父母和我自己感到驕傲。

** ————————————————

much prefer 寧願　　bottom〔ˋbɑtəm〕*n.* 底部；最後一名

ordinary〔ˋɔrdn͵ɛrɪ〕*adj.* 普通的

perpetually〔pɚˋpɛtʃʊəlɪ〕*adv.* 不斷地

force〔fors〕*v.* 強迫　　strive〔straɪv〕*v.* 努力

constantly〔ˋkɑnstəntlɪ〕*adv.* 不斷地　　seek〔sik〕*v.* 尋求

position〔pəˋzɪʃən〕*n.* 位置　　***on one's toes*** 警覺的

at times 有時候；偶爾　　reward〔rɪˋwɔrd〕*n.* 報酬；獎賞

tremendous〔trɪˋmɛndəs〕*adj.* 巨大的

progress〔ˋprɑgrɛs〕*n.* 進步　　remain〔rɪˋmen〕*v.* 停留

absolute〔ˋæbsə͵lut〕*adj.* 絕對的；完全的（= *total*）

significant〔sɪgˋnɪfəkənt〕*adj.* 相當大的

diligence〔ˋdɪlədʒəns〕*n.* 勤勉；用功

proud〔praʊd〕*adj.* 驕傲的

【回答範例 2】

I would rather be at the top of an
　　ordinary class.

I believe that would be less pressure.

I would feel less stressed out.

I wouldn't feel inferior to others.

I wouldn't feel frustrated all
　　the time.

That way I would be a happier person.

I could enjoy studying more.

I could enjoy a sense of
　　accomplishment.

I'd be in a position to be helpful
　　to both my classmates and my
　　teachers.

【中文翻譯】

我寧願當普通班的第一名。

我相信這樣壓力會比較小。

我會覺得沒那麼緊張。

我不會覺得自己比別人差。

我不會一直覺得挫敗。

這樣的話，我會比較快樂。

我會更喜歡念書。

我可以享受成就感。

我可以對同學和老師都有幫助。

** ───────────────────

pressure〔ˈprɛʃ⋋〕n. 壓力

stressed out 緊張的；感到有壓力的

inferior〔ɪnˈfɪrɪ⋋〕adj. 較差的 < *to* >

accomplishment〔əˈkamplɪʃmənt〕n. 成就

position〔pəˈzɪʃən〕n.（做…的）立場

7. **Your American friend is going to visit you and you are planning to show him around. Which place will you take him to and why?**

你的美國朋友將要來拜訪你，你計畫要帶他到處參觀。你會帶他去哪個地方？爲什麼？

【回答範例 1】

When my friend comes to Taipei, I will first take
　　him to the latest hot spot in town, Taipei 101.
I decided on this place for a number of reasons.
Right now, right here in our nation's capital,
　　we have one of the tallest buildings in the
　　whole world.

It is something we Taiwanese can be proud of,
　　our latest and greatest landmark.
It's in a definite Chinese style, suggesting a
　　bamboo stalk.
The observation deck affords a magnificent view
　　of the city and its environs.

After the manmade masterpiece, I will take him to
　　appreciate the natural beauty of Yangmingshan.
We can enjoy the fresh air and maybe a hot
　　spring bath there.
We can totally relax ourselves.

【中文翻譯】

當我的朋友來到台北，我會先帶他到市區最新的熱門景
點，台北 101。

我決定這個地方有幾個理由。

現在，就在我們國家的首都，有全世界最高的建築物之一。

這是我們台灣人可以引以為榮的，它是我們最新且最棒
的地標。

它有明確的中國風格，使人聯想到竹幹。

觀景台能提供台北市和其近郊壯麗的景色。

參觀完人造的傑作之後，我會帶他去欣賞陽明山的自然
美景。

我們可以享受新鮮的空氣，而且可能會在那裡泡溫泉。

我們可以完全放鬆自己。

**　——————————

show sb. around 帶領某人到處參觀　latest〔ˋletɪst〕adj. 最新的
spot〔spɑt〕n. 地點　　**decide on** 選定
capital〔ˋkæpətḷ〕n. 首都　　landmark〔ˋlænd͵mɑrk〕n. 地標
definite〔ˋdɛfənɪt〕adj. 明確的
suggest〔səgˋdʒɛst〕v. 使人聯想到　　bamboo〔bæmˋbu〕n. 竹子
stalk〔stɔk〕n. 莖　　observation〔͵ɑbzɚˋveʃən〕n. 觀察；觀測
deck〔dɛk〕n. 層；露天平台　　afford〔əˋford〕v. 給予；供給
magnificent〔mægˋnɪfəsṇt〕adj. 壯麗的
environs〔ɪnˋvaɪrənz〕n. pl.（都市的）周圍；近郊
manmade〔ˋmæn͵med〕adj. 人造的
masterpiece〔ˋmæstɚ͵pis〕n. 傑作
appreciate〔əˋpriʃɪ͵et〕v. 欣賞　　**a hot spring bath** 泡溫泉

【回答範例 2】

My favorite place in Taiwan for a visit
　　is Tainan.

It is the fourth largest city in Taiwan.

It is also the oldest city on the island
　　and full of history.

You can say it is the Kyoto of Taiwan.

The Confucius Temple is the oldest
　　of its kind in the country.

There are many famous historic sites,
　　such as the Chikhan Tower, the Anping
　　Fort, and the Eternal Castle.

Besides, Tainan is also called "the city
　　of snacks."

There are many delicious and special
　　foods available, like eel noodles
　　and coffin toast.

I think I would also take him to Cheng
　　Kung University.

【中文翻譯】

在台灣，我最喜歡遊覽的地方是台南。

它是台灣第四大都市。

它也是這個島上最古老的城市，並充滿歷史。

你可以說它是台灣的京都。

這裡的孔廟是全國最古老的孔廟。

這裡有很多有名的歷史古蹟，像是赤坎樓、安平古堡，和億載金城。

此外，台南也被稱為「小吃城」。

可以買到很多美味和特別的食物，像是鱔魚麵和棺材板。

我想我也會帶他去成功大學。

** ——————————————————————

be full of 充滿了　　Kyoto〔ˋkjoto〕*n.* 京都

Confucius〔kənˋfjuʃəs〕*n.* 孔子

temple〔ˋtɛmpl〕*n.* 寺廟　　*of one's kind* 和～同一類的

site〔saɪt〕*n.* 遺跡　　*historic site* 歷史古蹟

tower〔ˋtauɚ〕*n.* 高樓　　fort〔fort〕*n.* 堡壘；城堡

eternal〔ɪˋtɝnl〕*adj.* 永恆的；不朽的

castle〔ˋkæsl〕*n.* 城堡　　snack〔snæk〕*n.* 小吃

available〔əˋveləbl〕*adj.* 可獲得的；買得到的

eel〔il〕*n.* 鰻魚；鱔魚　　noodle〔ˋnudl〕*n.* 麵

coffin〔ˋkɔfɪn〕*n.* 棺材　　toast〔tost〕*n.* 土司

coffin toast 棺材板【台南傳統美食，厚片麵包中間挖洞填料】

【回答範例 3】

　　I will take him to the east coast
　　　of Taiwan, Hualien.

　　First of all, we can go to the Taroko
　　　Gorge.

　　I think it is the most spectacular
　　　view in Taiwan.

　　Second, white water rafting on the
　　　Hsiukuluan River is very popular.

　　I think we can give it a try.

　　It must be a thrilling thing to do.

　　We will definitely go to the new
　　　Ocean Park there.

　　We can enjoy the sea lion and dolphin
　　　shows.

　　Getting close to the dolphins and even
　　　swimming with them is fantastic.

【中文翻譯】

我會帶他去台灣的東海岸，花蓮。

首先，我們可以去太魯閣峽谷。

我覺得它是台灣最壯觀的景色。

其次，秀姑巒溪的泛舟是非常受歡迎的。

我想我們可以試試看。

那一定很刺激。

我們一定會去那裡新開的海洋公園。

我們可以欣賞海獅和海豚的表演。

能接近海豚，甚至可以和牠們一起游泳，是很

棒的事。

＊＊ ─────────────

coast〔kost〕n. 海岸　　gorge〔gɔrdʒ〕n. 峽谷

spectacular〔spɛk'tækjələ〕adj. 壯觀的

view〔vju〕n. 景色　　*white water* 浪花

raft〔ræft〕v. 搭乘筏子航行

white water rafting 泛舟

thrilling〔'θrɪlɪŋ〕adj. 刺激的

definitely〔'dɛfənɪtlɪ〕adv. 一定　　*sea lion* 海獅

dolphin〔'dɑlfɪn〕n. 海豚　　show〔ʃo〕n. 表演

fantastic〔fæn'tæstɪk〕adj. 很棒的

8. **What's your opinion of having so many beer and alcohol advertisements on TV?**

對於電視上有這麼多啤酒和酒類的廣告，你有什麼看法？

【回答範例】

In my opinion, the last thing young people
　　need are beer and alcohol advertisements.

They give our youth a false impression.

They mislead the youth into thinking that
　　it is cool to drink beer and alcohol.

Stars from the movies, TV and music sing
　　its praises.

They glamorize alcohol consumption.

But I think it only undermines our health.

I suggest that the government should
　　restrict the TV hours of these ads.

They had better not be aired in prime time.

Celebrities should not set a bad example,
　　either.

【中文翻譯】

我認為，年輕人最不需要的，就是啤酒和酒類的
廣告。
它們會給我們的年輕人錯誤的印象。
它們會使年輕人誤以為喝啤酒和酒是很酷的事。

電影、電視和音樂裡的明星都在高度讚揚它。
他們使喝酒變得有魅力。
但我認為它只會逐漸損害我們的健康。

我建議政府應該限制這些廣告的電視播出時間。
它們最好不要在黃金時段播送。
名人也不應該樹立壞榜樣。

**

alcohol〔'ælkə,hɔl〕n. 酒
in my opinion 依我之見；我認為
last〔læst〕adj. 最不…的　　youth〔juθ〕n. 年輕人
false〔fɔls〕adj. 錯誤的　　impression〔ɪm'prɛʃən〕n. 印象
mislead〔mɪs'lid〕v. 使誤解　　praise〔prez〕n. 讚美的話
sing one's praises 高度讚揚某人
glamorize〔'glæməraɪz〕v. 使有魅力
consumption〔kən'sʌmpʃən〕n. 消耗；吃；喝
undermine〔ˌʌndə'maɪn〕v. 逐漸損害
restrict〔rɪ'strɪkt〕v. 限制　　hours〔aurz〕n. pl. 時間
air〔ɛr〕v. 播送　　prime〔praɪm〕adj. 主要的
prime time 黃金時段　　celebrity〔sə'lɛbrətɪ〕n. 名人
set〔sɛt〕v. 樹立（榜樣）　　example〔ɪg'zæmpl〕n. 榜樣

PART 2　看圖敘述

1. **What is this place?**　這是什麼地方？

   This is a stage. It might be in an auditorium or in
   some outdoor place like a park.

   這是一個舞台。它可能是在禮堂或某個戶外場地，像是
   公園。

2. **What are these people doing?**

   這些人在做什麼？

   The people are playing music. They are members
   of a band.　這些人在演奏音樂。他們是樂團的成員。

   ** ────────────

   stage〔stedʒ〕 *n.* 舞台
   auditorium〔͵ɔdə'torɪəm〕 *n.* 禮堂
   outdoor〔'aut͵dor〕 *adj.* 戶外的

3. **What is the difference between the woman on the left and the others?**

左邊的女士和其他人有什麼不同？

The woman on the left is singing while the others are not. They are the musicians and she is the vocalist.

左邊的女士在唱歌，而其他人沒有在唱。他們是樂手，而她是歌手。

4. **If you still have time, please describe the picture in as much detail as you can.**

如果你還有時間，請儘可能描述照片中的細節。

It is a picture of a band on a stage. There are four people in the band, three women and one man. One of the women is a singer and the other two are playing instruments, a guitar and a drum. The man is also playing a guitar. They are wearing casual clothes and there are microphones and music stands in front of them. They are probably giving a performance, taking part in a contest, or auditioning.

這是一張樂團在舞台上的照片。這個樂團有四個人，三女一男。其中一位女士是歌手，其他兩個在演奏樂器，吉他和鼓。那位男士也在彈吉他。他們穿著便服，他們的前方有麥克風和樂譜架。他們可能正在表演、參加比賽，或是試唱。

** ——————————————

vocalist〔'vokḷɪst〕n. 歌手　instrument〔'ɪnstrəmənt〕n. 樂器
drum〔drʌm〕n. 鼓　casual〔'kæʒuəl〕adj. 休閒的；非正式的
microphone〔'maɪkrə͵fon〕n. 麥克風
music stand 樂譜架　performance〔pə'fɔrməns〕n. 表演
take part in 參加　contest〔'kɑntɛst〕n. 比賽
audition〔ɔ'dɪʃən〕v. 試唱；試奏

PART 3　申述題

There are more and more foreigners coming to Taiwan either for sightseeing or for work. What attractions do we have to bring them here? What else should we do to encourage more to come? Please explain.

有越來越多的外國人來台灣觀光或工作。我們有什麼吸引人的事物使他們來這裡？我們應該另外做些什麼鼓勵更多人來？請說明。

【回答範例】

Taiwan is attracting more foreign visitors these days because it offers several advantages to them. *However*, with improvements in certain areas, the island could attract even more.

Taiwan has many wonderful features. Most visitors appreciate its natural beauty and friendly people. They also like the convenience of good transportation and communication systems. The country is also politically stable and safe. This all makes doing business and sightseeing here both easier and more enjoyable.

Although the island has many fascinating sights, many potential visitors lack information about them. *Therefore*, I think we could do more to promote Taiwan abroad and to help visitors discover its unique beauty once they arrive.

【中文翻譯】

　　最近台灣吸引更多外國觀光客，因為台灣提供他們很多好處。然而，如果某些地方能有改善，這座島可以吸引更多人。

　　台灣有許多很棒的特色。大部分的觀光客都很欣賞台灣的自然美景和友善的民眾。他們也喜歡良好的交通運輸和通訊系統的便利。這個國家的政治也很穩定而且安全。這些都使得到這裡做生意和觀光變得更容易而且更令人愉快。

　　雖然這座島上有許多迷人的風景，但是很多潛在的觀光客缺乏相關資訊。因此，我認為我們可以多做一點努力，將台灣推銷到國外，而且一旦觀光客來，就幫他們去發現台灣獨特的美。

** ─────────────────────

these days 最近

advantage〔əd'væntɪdʒ〕 *n.* 優點；好處

certain〔'sɝtn̩〕 *adj.* 某些　　area〔'ɛrɪə〕 *n.* 領域

feature〔'fitʃɚ〕 *n.* 特色　　appreciate〔ə'priʃɪ‚et〕 *v.* 欣賞

transportation〔‚træspɚ'teʃən〕 *n.* 運輸工具

communication〔kə‚mjunə'keʃən〕 *n.* 通訊

politically〔pə'lɪtɪkl̩ɪ〕 *adv.* 政治上

stable〔'stebl̩〕 *adj.* 穩定的　　sightseeing〔'saɪt‚siɪŋ〕 *n.* 觀光

enjoyable〔ɪn'dʒɔɪəbl̩〕 *adj.* 令人愉快的

fascinating〔'fæsn̩‚etɪŋ〕 *adj.* 迷人的　　sight〔saɪt〕 *n.* 風景

potential〔pə'tɛnʃəl〕 *adj.* 潛在的　　lack〔læk〕 *v.* 缺乏

promote〔prə'mot〕 *v.* 推銷

unique〔ju'nik〕 *adj.* 獨特的　　once〔wʌns〕 *adv.* 一旦

全民英語能力分級檢定測驗
中高級寫作能力測驗答案紙

座位號碼：＿＿＿＿＿＿＿＿＿＿＿＿＿＿＿　　　試題別：＿＿＿＿＿＿＿＿

第一部份請由本頁第 1 行開始作答，請勿隔行書寫。第二部份請翻至第 2 頁作答。

_____

_____

_____

_____

_____

_____

_____

_____

_____

_____

_____

_____

_____

_____

_____

_____

_____

_____

_____

_____

_____

_____

55

60

65

70

寫作口說能力測驗④

寫作能力測驗

Part I: Chinese-English Translation (40%)

Translate the following Chinese passage into an English passage, and write your answer on the Writing Test Answer Sheet.

現代社會中，許多人經常忙到忽略了年長的父母或祖父母。有些人不得不將老人送到安養中心，在那裡他們可以找到同伴。但事實上，老人家所需要的不只是同伴，還有家人的親情及關懷。老年人奉獻了青春及一生的努力，給他們的家庭及社會，因此年輕的一代應該要心存感激，幫助他們過安祥愉快的生活。

Part II: Guided Writing (60%)

Write an essay of **150-180 words** in an appropriate style on the following topic. Write your answer on the Writing Test Answer Sheet.

When you encounter a difficult question in studying, will you turn to your teacher or your classmate for help, or do you try to solve the problem on your own? On the other hand, if your classmate asks you to help with his or her studying, what will you do?

口説能力測驗

Please read the self-introduction sentence.

My seat number is ＿（複試座位號碼）＿, and my

registration number is ＿（初試准考證號碼）＿.

Part I: Answering Questions

You will hear 8 questions. Each question will be
spoken once. Please answer the question immediately
after you hear it.

For questions 1 to 4, you will have 15 seconds to
answer each question.

For questions 5 to 8, you will have 30 seconds to
answer each question.

Part II: Picture Description

Look at the picture, think about the questions below for 30 seconds, and then record your answers for 1 ½ minutes.

1. What is this place?

2. Who are the people in the picture?　What makes you think so?

3. Have you ever been to such a place?

4. If you still have time, please describe the picture in as much detail as you can.

Part III: Discussion

Think about your answer(s) to the question(s) below for 1 ½ minutes, and then record your answer(s) for 1 ½ minutes.

You may use your test paper to make notes and organize your ideas.

It is true that the computer brings us a lot of benefits, but there is a growing trend toward computer addiction, which is harmful not only to the computer addicts themselves but also to the whole society. Describe your views about the use of the computer.

Please read the self-introduction sentence again.

My seat number is （複試座位號碼）, and my registration number is （初試准考證號碼）.

寫作口說能力測驗 ④ 詳解

寫作能力測驗詳解

PART 1 中譯英 (40%)

　　現代社會中，許多人經常忙到忽略了年長的父母或祖父母。有些人不得不將老人送到安養中心，在那裡他們可以找到同伴。但事實上，老人家所需要的不只是同伴，還有家人的親情及關懷。老年人奉獻了青春及一生的努力，給他們的家庭及社會，因此年輕的一代應該要心存感激，幫助他們過安祥愉快的生活。

　　In modern society, many people are so busy that they ignore their aged parents or grandparents. Some of them have no choice but to send the aged to nursing homes, where they can find companions. But actually, what the elderly need is not only companions but also the affection and concern of their family. Senior citizens have devoted their youth and lifelong efforts to their families and the society; therefore, the younger generation should be grateful and help them lead a peaceful and pleasant life.

【註】ignore〔ɪg'nor〕v. 忽視　　aged〔edʒd〕adj. 年長的

have no choice but to V. 不得不～

nursing〔'nɜsɪŋ〕n. 看護；照顧病人

nursing home 療養院

companion〔kəm'pænjən〕n. 同伴

actually〔'æktʃuəlɪ〕adv. 事實上

elderly〔'ɛldəlɪ〕adj. 年長的　　*the elderly* 老人

affection〔ə'fɛkʃən〕n. 愛

concern〔kən'sɜn〕n. 關懷　　senior〔'sinjə〕adj. 年長的

citizen〔'sɪtəzn̩〕n. 公民；人民　　*senior citizen* 老人

devote〔dɪ'vot〕v. 奉獻　　youth〔juθ〕n. 青春

lifelong〔'laɪf'lɔŋ〕adj. 一生的　　effort〔'ɛfət〕n. 努力

generation〔ˌdʒɛnə'reʃən〕n. 世代

grateful〔'gretfəl〕adj. 感激的　　lead〔lid〕v. 過著

peaceful〔'pisfəl〕adj. 平靜的

pleasant〔'plɛznt̩〕adj. 令人愉快的

PART 2 引導寫作 (60%)

When you encounter a difficult question in studying, will you turn to your teacher or your classmate for help, or do you try to solve the problem on your own? On the other hand, if your classmate asks you to help with his or her studying, what will you do?

當你在課業上碰到困難時，你會向你的老師或同學求救，或是試著靠自己解決問題？另一方面，如果你的同學請教你課業問題，你會怎麼做？

【作文範例】

Overcoming Difficulties in Studying

　　When I am studying and I run into difficulty, firstly I will try to figure it out by myself because I think it is important to be self-sufficient. I also believe that I will remember the answer better if I work it out on my own. *However*, if I am not successful, I will turn to a classmate or my teacher for help. And I prefer to ask my teacher because I want to be certain that I get the correct answer.

　　Sometimes my classmates will ask me for help with their studies, too. *In that case*, I always do my best to teach them. I have found that teaching is the best way of learning. Tutoring somebody else helps me to remember and reinforce what I have learned better. *Besides*, it also gives me a chance to help out a friend, which makes me feel great and definitely strengthens our relationship. Perhaps my classmate will return the favor one day.

【註】overcome〔͵ovə'kʌm〕v. 克服
　　　run into 遭遇　　*figure out* 解決
　　　self-sufficient〔͵sɛlfsə'fɪʃənt〕adj. 能自給自足的
　　　work out 解決　　*turn to* 求助於
　　　in that case 那樣的話　　tutor〔'tutɚ〕v. 教
　　　reinforce〔͵riɪn'fors〕v. 加強　　*help out* 幫助
　　　definitely〔'dɛfənɪtlɪ〕adv. 一定
　　　strengthen〔'strɛŋθən〕v. 加強；使堅固
　　　return〔rɪ't3n〕v. 回報　　favor〔'fevɚ〕n. 幫忙；恩惠

口說能力測驗詳解

PART 1 回答問題

1. Do you agree with students working part-time?

你贊成學生打工嗎？

【回答範例 1】

I am in favor of students working part-time.

It introduces them to the adult world.

It helps them develop relationships outside
of school.

They learn about responsibility.
Punctuality becomes a serious issue.
So does having a proper appearance at work.

Most importantly, they can earn extra
pocket money.
It's never too soon to learn the value
of a buck.
They learn to appreciate their hard-earned
money.

【中文翻譯】

我贊成學生打工。

它能引領學生進入成人世界。

它能幫學生發展校外關係。

他們能學會負責任。

守時會成為一個重要的問題。

在工作場所有適當的外表也是一樣。

最重要的是，他們可以賺到額外的零用錢。

認識一塊錢的價值絕不會嫌太早。

他們能學會重視自己辛苦賺來的錢。

** ————————————————

part-time〔ˈpɑrtˈtaɪm〕adv. 兼差地

be in favor of 贊成

introduce〔ˌɪntrəˈdjus〕v. 引領

punctuality〔ˌpʌŋktʃʊˈælətɪ〕n. 守時

serious〔ˈsɪrɪəs〕adj. 重要的；重大的

issue〔ˈɪʃʊ〕n. 問題

proper〔ˈprɑpɚ〕adj. 適當的

appearance〔əˈpɪrəns〕n. 外表

extra〔ˈɛkstrə〕adj. 額外的

pocket money 零用錢　　buck〔bʌk〕n. 一美元

appreciate〔əˈpriʃɪˌet〕v. 欣賞；重視

hard-earned〔ˈhɑrdˈɝnd〕adj. 辛苦賺得的

【回答範例 2】

I am opposed to the idea of students working part-time.

It will distract students from their studying.

It surely has a negative effect on their school performance.

A student's chief obligation is to study.

School days are the prime time for learning.

Fail to make the best of this golden opportunity, and you will be sorry.

Besides, a student working part-time is easily affected by the real, ugly world.

He may become materialistic.

He may get infected with the evils of society sooner.

【中文翻譯】

我反對學生打工的想法。

它會使學生不能專心讀書。

它對學生的在校表現一定會有負面的影響。

學生主要的責任是讀書。

上學的日子是最重要的學習時間。

如果不能善用這個寶貴的機會，你將會覺得遺憾。

此外，打工的學生很容易被現實且醜陋的世界影響。

他可能會變得重視物質享受。

他可能會提早沾染上社會的惡行。

**　——————————————

be opposed to 反對　　distract〔dɪˋstrækt〕v. 使分心

negative〔ˋnɛɡətɪv〕adj. 負面的　　effect〔ɪˋfɛkt〕n. 影響

performance〔pɚˋfɔrməns〕n. 表現

chief〔tʃif〕adj. 主要的

obligation〔͵ɑbləˋgeʃən〕n. 義務；責任

prime〔praɪm〕adj. 最重要的

fail to V. 未能～　　**make the best of** 善用

golden〔ˋgoldn̩〕adj. 寶貴的　　ugly〔ˋʌglɪ〕adj. 醜陋的

materialistic〔mə͵tɪrɪəlˋɪstɪk〕adj. 物質主義的

infect〔ɪnˋfɛkt〕v. 使沾染；使受（惡習）影響

evil〔ˋivl̩〕n. 惡事；邪惡

2. **Do you prefer watching a movie at a movie theater or on a DVD at home?**

你比較喜歡在電影院看電影，還是在家看 DVD？

【回答範例 1】

I'll admit that I'm a bit old-fashioned.

I much prefer watching a movie at the cinema.

There's still something magical when the
lights go off.

I love the collective hush of anticipation in the
audience as the film begins.

There is something special about sharing the
experience with hundreds of strangers.

In a movie theater, I can enjoy the film with
undivided attention.

Furthermore, today's blockbuster action films
require a large screen.

The special effects, especially through the
professional sound system, are amazing on
the big screen.

On a DVD at home, too much is lost.

【中文翻譯】

我會承認自己有點過時。

我比較喜歡在電影院看電影。

燈光熄滅的時候，仍然會有神奇的感覺。

我喜歡電影開始時，觀眾因為期待而全都安靜下來。

和數百位陌生人共享這種體驗是很特別的。

在電影院裡，我可以專心欣賞電影。

而且，現在耗費鉅資拍攝的動作片需要大銀幕。

特效，尤其是經過專業的音響設備，在大銀幕上

是很驚人的。

在家看 DVD，便會失色許多。

** _____

admit〔əd'mɪt〕v. 承認　　***a bit*** 有點

old-fashioned〔'old'fæʃənd〕adj. 過時的

cinema〔'sɪnəmə〕n. 電影院

magical〔'mædʒɪkḷ〕adj. 神奇的　　***go off*** 熄滅

collective〔kə'lɛktɪv〕adj. 集體的　　hush〔hʌʃ〕n. 安靜

anticipation〔æn,tɪsə'peʃən〕n. 期待

undivided〔,ʌndə'vaɪdɪd〕adj. 專心的

undivided attention 專心一意

blockbuster〔'blɑk,bʌstɚ〕n. 耗費鉅資拍攝的電影

require〔rɪ'kwaɪr〕v. 需要　　screen〔skrin〕n. 銀幕

special effect 特效　　professional〔prə'fɛʃənḷ〕adj. 專業的

sound system 音響設備　　amazing〔ə'mezɪŋ〕adj. 驚人的

【回答範例 2】

I prefer watching a movie on DVD at home any day.

I have many reasons to support my feelings.

For starters, I have every comfort within reach in my own living room.

I can watch it with exactly the people I want to be there.

I can eat a messy dessert, have a beer or an apple—whatever I please.

I'm not confined to overpriced popcorn and empty calorie soft drinks.

If I need to use the facilities, I just press the pause button.

In a movie theater, I'd have to miss part of the movie.

Besides, I don't like the acoustics in a movie theater because I feel they are too loud and noisy.

【中文翻譯】

我比較喜歡隨時在家看 DVD。

我有許多理由來支持我的看法。

首先，在我自己的客廳裡，每樣東西都伸手可及。

我可以和完全是自己想要的人一起看電影。

我可以吃會弄得一團亂的甜食、喝啤酒或吃蘋果——喜歡吃什麼就吃什麼。

我不會受限於定價過高的爆米花，和無營養卡路里的飲料。

如果我必須去上廁所，我只要按暫停鍵。

在電影院，我必須錯過一段電影。

此外，我不喜歡電影院的音響效果，因為我覺得它們太大聲又吵。

** ————————————————————

any day 任何日子；隨時　　feeling〔ˈfilɪŋ〕*n.* 看法

for starters 首先　　comfort〔ˈkʌmfət〕*n.* 使生活舒適的東西

reach〔ritʃ〕*n.* 伸手可及的範圍

exactly〔ɪgˈzæktlɪ〕*adv.* 完全地　　messy〔ˈmɛsɪ〕*adj.* 雜亂的

dessert〔dɪˈzɜt〕*n.* 甜食　　please〔pliz〕*v.* 喜歡

confine〔kənˈfaɪn〕*v.* 限制

overpriced〔ˌovəˈpraɪst〕*adj.* 定價過高的

popcorn〔ˈpɑpˌkɔrn〕*n.* 爆米花

empty〔ˈɛmptɪ〕*adj.* 空的；無用的　　calorie〔ˈkælərɪ〕*n.* 卡路里

empty calorie 無營養卡路里【營養含量極低，或根本無營養價值的食物】

soft drink （不含酒精的）清涼飲料

facilities〔fəˈsɪlətɪz〕*n. pl.* 廁所　　pause〔pɔz〕*n.* 暫停

button〔ˈbʌtṇ〕*n.* 按鈕　　acoustics〔əˈkustɪks〕*n. pl.* 音響效果

3. **In a movie theater, a man's cell phone keeps ringing and distracts you. Please tell him of your complaint.**

在電影院，有位男士的手機一直響，讓你無法專心。
請告訴他你的不滿。

【回答範例】

Excuse me, sir.

Your constantly ringing cell phone
   is annoying.

The rest of us are here to see the movie.

The first time I let it go.

Ditto the second.

But this is too much.

Please put your phone on vibrate.

I don't want to hear it again.

If it does ring, I'll be forced to call
   the manager.

【中文翻譯】

不好意思，先生。

你那支響個不停的手機很煩人。

我們其他人都在這裡看電影。

第一次就算了。

第二次也一樣。

但這真的太過分了。

請將你的手機開成震動。

我不想再聽到它響。

如果它再響，我就不得不叫經理了。

**　——————————

distract〔dɪˋstrækt〕v. 使分心

complaint〔kəmˋplent〕n. 抱怨；不滿

constantly〔ˋkɑnstəntlɪ〕adv. 不斷地

ring〔rɪŋ〕v.（鈴）響

annoying〔əˋnɔɪɪŋ〕adj. 煩人的

rest〔rɛst〕n. 其餘的人　　*let~go* 對~不予理會

ditto〔ˋdɪto〕adv. 同樣地　　*too much* 太過分

put〔put〕v. 使處於（特定狀態）

vibrate〔ˋvaɪbret〕v. 震動

force〔fors〕v. 強迫；使不得不

4. **Your friend is not confident about a promotion. Encourage him to work hard for it.**

你的朋友對升遷不太有信心。鼓勵他更努力。

【回答範例】

I believe in you.

You have all the necessary skills.

You don't need to be afraid or worried.

You are an experienced worker.

I'm certain you can handle the
　job well.

I'm sure you will be an excellent
　manager.

Just keep up your hard work.

You deserve the promotion.

It's yours for the asking.

【中文翻譯】

我相信你。

所有必要的技能你都有了。

你不需要害怕或擔心。

你是個經驗豐富的員工。

我確定這個工作你可以處理得很好。

我確定你將會成為優秀的經理。

只要你繼續努力。

你就應該要升遷。

如果你要，它就會是你的。

** ─────────────────

confident〔ˈkɑnfədənt〕adj. 有信心的

promotion〔prəˈmoʃən〕n. 升遷

believe in 信任　　skill〔skɪl〕n. 技能

experienced〔ɪkˈspɪrɪənst〕adj. 經驗豐富的

handle〔ˈhændl̩〕v. 處理　　*keep up* 持續

hard work 努力　　deserve〔dɪˈzɝv〕v. 應得

for the asking 只需詢問（或要求）一下便可

5. **Who in your family are you closest to and why?**

你和家裡的誰最親近？為什麼？

【回答範例 1】

I'm closest to my mother.

We two are much alike.

I resemble my mother not only in
　　appearance but also in character.

We have similar attitudes and opinions.

She always understands what I think
　　and vice versa.

Whenever I am in trouble, she is always
　　there for me.

Sure, she spoils me, but only a little.

When she thinks I need a reproach or
　　even a full lecture, she doesn't hesitate.

I never doubt for a second how deeply
　　she loves me.

【中文翻譯】

我和我媽媽最親近。

我們兩個很相像。

我不僅外表像我媽，個性也很像。

我們的看法和意見很類似。

她總是知道我在想什麼，而我也知道她在想什麼。

每當我有困難，她總是在我身邊。

當然，她會溺愛我，但只有一點點。

當她認為我需要責備或強而有力的訓誡時，

她不會猶豫。

我從未片刻懷疑過她愛我有多深。

** ─────────────

close〔klos〕*adj.* 親近的　　alike〔ə'laɪk〕*adj.* 相像的

resemble〔rɪ'zɛmbl̩〕*v.* 像

character〔'kærɪktɚ〕*n.* 性格

attitude〔'ætə,tjud〕*n.* 態度；看法

opinion〔ə'pɪnjən〕*n.* 意見　　***vice versa*** 反之亦然

spoil〔spɔɪl〕*v.* 寵壞；溺愛

reproach〔rɪ'protʃ〕*n.* 責備

full〔fʊl〕*adj.* 強有力的　　lecture〔'lɛktʃɚ〕*n.* 訓誡

hesitate〔'hɛzə,tet〕*v.* 猶豫　　doubt〔daʊt〕*v.* 懷疑

second〔'sɛkənd〕*n.* 片刻；瞬間

【回答範例 2 】

I am closest to my youngest sister.

She is four years my junior.

However, sometimes she acts very
    maturely, as if she were the
    big sister.

She joins my class gatherings very
    often.

So she knows my friends very well.

There's nothing we haven't talked
    about.

We share a lot of common interests
    and topics.

We have always confided in each
    other very openly.

I'm sure no matter where our lives
    take us, we will always remain tight.

【中文翻譯】

我和我最小的妹妹最親近。

她比我小四歲。

然而，有時她表現得很成熟，好像她是姊姊一樣。

她常常參加我們班的聚會。

所以她跟我的朋友很熟。

我們什麼都聊。

我們會分享很多共同的興趣和話題。

我們總是很坦率地把秘密告訴對方。

我確定無論我們的生活中會發生什麼事，我們依舊
會緊緊相連。

** —————————————————

junior〔ˈdʒunjɚ〕n. 較年輕者

four years my junior 比我小四歲

maturely〔məˈtʃʊrlɪ〕adv. 成熟地　　**as if** 就好像

gathering〔ˈgæðərɪŋ〕n. 聚會　　share〔ʃɛr〕v. 分享

common〔ˈkɑmən〕adj. 共同的

confide〔kənˈfaɪd〕v. 吐露秘密

openly〔ˈopənlɪ〕adv. 坦率地

no matter where our lives take us 無論我們的生活中會
發生什麼事（= *no matter what happens in our lives*）

remain〔rɪˈmen〕v. 依然；依舊

tight〔taɪt〕adj. 親密的；緊密聯合的

6. **When planning a trip, would you consider a package tour or would you prefer traveling on your own? Please explain.**

規劃旅行時，你會考慮套裝行程還是比較喜歡自助旅行？
請說明。

【回答範例 1】

I like to travel on group tours.

This is the way to get the best deal.

I pay less for the flights, hotels, food
　　and tours than when I travel on my own.

Secondly, there is no wasted time.

The group tour always includes all the
　　must-see places.

It is convenient to travel from place to
　　place on a tour bus.

Everything from transportation to
　　accommodations is well taken care of.

You are assured of good hotels
　　and reputable restaurants.

You don't have to worry about quality.

【中文翻譯】

我喜歡跟團旅行。

這是能撿到便宜的方法。

我花在機票、旅館、食物和觀光上的錢，

會比自助旅行少。

其次，不會浪費時間。

跟團旅行通常包括所有必看的景點。

搭遊覽車到處旅行很方便。

從交通到住宿的大小事都有人處理得很好。

保證你會有好的旅館和聲譽好的餐廳。

你不必擔心品質。

** ————————————————

package tour （由旅行社代辦一切手續的）套裝行程

the best deal 最划算的交易　　flight〔flaɪt〕n. 班機

wasted〔'westɪd〕adj. 浪費掉的

must-see〔'mʌst'si〕adj. 必看的

travel〔'trævḷ〕v. 旅行；行進　　**tour bus** 遊覽車

transportation〔ˌtrænspɚ'teʃən〕n. 交通運輸

accommodations〔əˌkɑmə'deʃənz〕n. pl. 住宿設備

take care of 處理　　assure〔ə'ʃur〕v. 向～保證

reputable〔'rɛpjətəbḷ〕adj. 聲譽好的

【回答範例2】

I would like to try traveling on my own.

An independent trip has great appeal
for me.

I can tour the place at my own pace.

I can go to any place that comes to
my mind.

I can sit at an outdoor café sipping
a latte.

I don't have to follow the program
of a package tour.

Besides, I have more chances of
meeting local people.

I can sample the native cuisine.

I may bump into people or things by
accident and have some memorable
experiences.

【中文翻譯】

我會想要嘗試自助旅行。

自助旅行對我有很大的吸引力。

我可以依照自己的步調遊覽該地。

我可以去任何一個浮現在腦海裡的地方。

我可以坐在露天咖啡座啜飲拿鐵。

我不必照著套裝行程的計畫走。

此外，我有比較多認識當地人的機會。

我可以品嚐當地的菜餚。

我可能會意外遇到一些人或事物，而有難忘

的經驗。

** ——————————————————

independent trip 白助旅行（= *independent travel*）

appeal〔ə'pil〕*n.* 吸引力　　tour〔tur〕*v.* 遊覽

pace〔pes〕*n.* 步調　　*at one's own pace* 以自己的步調

café〔kə'fe〕*n.* 咖啡廳

outdoor café 露天咖啡廳　　sip〔sɪp〕*v.* 啜飲

latte〔lɑ'te〕*n.* 拿鐵　　follow〔'fɑlo〕*v.* 遵循

program〔'progræm〕*n.* 計畫；預定表

sample〔'sæmpḷ〕*v.* 品嚐　　native〔'netɪv〕*adj.* 當地的

cuisine〔kwɪ'zin〕*n.* 菜餚　　*bump into* 偶然遇到

by accident 偶然地；意外地

memorable〔'mɛmərəbḷ〕*adj.* 令人難忘的

7. **Have you ever had something lost or stolen and how? Please describe your experience.**

你曾經搞丟東西或東西被偷嗎？如何發生的？
請描述你的經驗。

【回答範例 1】

My bicycle was stolen when I was in
    junior high.

I had no one to blame but myself.

I was too lazy to lock it.

My mom asked me to go to the 7-Eleven
    to pick up some ice cream after dinner.

I thought it would only take a minute.

I ran in, bought it and got my change,
    and ran out.

When I got outside, I couldn't believe
    my eyes.

I was completely at a loss.

My beloved bicycle was gone.

【中文翻譯】

在我國中時，我的腳踏車被偷。
我只能怪自己。
我太懶惰，沒把它上鎖。

吃完晚餐後，我媽媽叫我去 7-11 買一些冰淇淋。
我想只需要一下子的時間。
我跑進去，買完冰淇淋，並拿了找的錢，然後
就跑出來。

當我到外面時，我無法相信自己的眼睛。
我完全不知所措。
我心愛的腳踏車不見了。

** ————————————————

blame〔blem〕v. 責怪　　but〔bʌt〕prep. 除了
lazy〔'lezɪ〕adj. 懶惰的　　lock〔lɑk〕v. 鎖
pick up 買　　**a minute** 一下子
change〔tʃendʒ〕n. 零錢；找回的零錢
completely〔kəm'plitlɪ〕adv. 完全地
at a loss 茫然；不知所措
beloved〔bɪ'lʌvɪd〕adj. 心愛的
gone〔gɔn〕adj. 消失的

【回答範例2】

I am a forgetful person.

I often misplace things and then they
　　are gone.

Worse yet, I was once robbed.

On that drizzling night, I walked
　　home alone after a busy and tiring day.

I was kind of distracted and didn't pay
　　much attention to what was going on
　　around me.

Suddenly a man came out of nowhere
　　and grabbed at my handbag.

I struggled to protect my stuff but
　　in vain.

He ran away with my bag after all.

I reported it to the police but received
　　no results.

【中文翻譯】

我是個健忘的人。

我常把東西亂擺,之後它們就不見了。

更糟的是,我曾經被搶過。

一個下著毛毛雨的夜晚,在忙碌且累人的一天

過後,我獨自走回家。

我有點心不在焉,沒有注意我周遭發生的事。

突然有個不知道哪裡來的男子,抓住我的手提包。

我掙扎著要保護我的東西,但是沒有用。

他最後拿著我的包包跑走了。

我向警方報案,但是沒有結果。

** ——————————————

forgetful〔fəˈgɛtfəl〕 adj. 健忘的

misplace〔mɪsˈples〕 v. 將…放錯位置

yet〔jɛt〕 adv.【強調比較級】更加　　***worse yet*** 更糟的是

once〔wʌns〕 adv. 曾經　　rob〔rɑb〕 v. 搶劫

drizzle〔ˈdrɪzl̩〕 v. 下毛毛雨　　tiring〔ˈtaɪrɪŋ〕 adj. 累人的

kind of 有一點　　distracted〔dɪˈstræktɪd〕 adj. 分心的

go on 發生　　nowhere〔ˈnoˌhwɛr〕 n. 無人知道的地方

come out of nowhere 不知來自何處

grab〔græb〕 v. 抓　　handbag〔ˈhændˌbæg〕 n. 手提包

struggle〔ˈstrʌgl̩〕 v. 掙扎　　stuff〔stʌf〕 n. 東西

in vain 徒勞無功　　***after all*** 終究

8. **Youngsters nowadays enjoy many more comforts and advantages than did their parents' generation. However, they have lost a lot as well. Please compare the gains and losses.**

現在的年輕人比他們的父母那一代擁有更多舒適的設備和有利條件。然而，他們也失去很多。請比較得與失。

【回答範例】

Youngsters' lives today are so different
from those of their parents' generation.

On the surface it appears their lives are
better in every way.

But have they really only improved?

Certainly in material terms, there is no
comparison.

Parents spare no effort to give whatever
they can afford to their children.

It seems like every kid has his own cell
phone, computer and scooter.

Moreover, youngsters grow up in a better developed and more democratic environment.

They have abundant resources and information to learn from.

Kids now are a lot more intelligent than their counterparts in the past.

However, kids nowadays experience the darker side of society earlier and become mature earlier.

They tend to lose the innocence of childhood.

They also lose a lot of chances to experience a simple life.

In addition, the divorce rate is much higher than before.

More children than before come from broken families.

More youngsters easily go astray without proper discipline.

【中文翻譯】

現在年輕人的生活和他們父母那一代的生活
大不相同。
表面上，他們的生活好像各方面都比較好。
但是他們真的只有變得更好嗎？

從物質上的觀點來看，一定是無法比較的。
父母會不遺餘力地給孩子任何他們買得起的
東西。
似乎每個小孩都有自己的手機、電腦，和摩
托車。

而且，年輕人在一個較為開發和民主的環境
中成長。
他們有豐富的資源和資訊可以學習。
現在的小孩比以前的小孩聰明很多。

然而，現在的小孩提早體驗社會較黑暗的
一面，變得早熟。
他們容易失去孩童的天真。
他們也會失去很多體驗簡單生活的機會。

此外，離婚率也比以前高很多。

來自破碎家庭的小孩比以前多。

沒有適當的教養，會有更多年輕人容易誤入歧途。

** ───────────────

youngster〔'jʌŋstɚ〕*n.* 年輕人

nowadays〔'naʊə,dez〕*adv.* 現今

comfort〔'kʌmfɚt〕*n.* 使生活舒適的東西

advantage〔əd'væntɪdʒ〕*n.* 優點；有利條件

as well 也　　compare〔kəm'pɛr〕*v.* 比較

gain〔gen〕*n.* 獲得　　loss〔lɔs〕*n.* 損失

surface〔'sɝfɪs〕*n.* 表面　　*on the surface* 在表面上

appear〔ə'pɪr〕*v.* 似乎；好像

certainly〔'sɝtn̩lɪ〕*adv.* 一定；當然

material〔mə'tɪrɪəl〕*adj.* 物質上的　　terms〔tɝmz〕*n. pl.* 觀點

comparison〔kəm'pærəsn̩〕*n.* 比較；相似之處

there is no comparison 無相似之處；相差懸殊

spare〔spɛr〕*v.* 吝惜　　*spare no effort* 不遺餘力

afford〔ə'ford〕*v.* 負擔得起　　*cell phone* 手機

scooter〔'skutɚ〕*n.* 摩托車

democratic〔,dɛmə'krætɪk〕*adj.* 民主的

abundant〔ə'bʌndənt〕*adj.* 豐富的　　resource〔rɪ'sors〕*n.* 資源

intelligent〔ɪn'tɛlədʒənt〕*adj.* 聰明的

counterpart〔'kaʊntɚ,part〕*n.* 對應的人或物

mature〔mə'tʃʊr〕*adj.* 成熟的　　*tend to V.* 易於～；傾向於～

innocence〔'ɪnəsns〕*n.* 天眞

experience〔ɪk'spɪrɪəns〕*v.* 經歷；體驗

divorce〔də'vors〕*n.* 離婚　　astray〔ə'stre〕*adv.* 離開正道

go astray 誤入歧途　　discipline〔'dɪsəplɪn〕*n.* 紀律；教養

PART 2　看圖敘述

1. **What is this place?**　這是什麼地方？

   This is most likely a convention room, possibly in a hotel.

   這很可能是一間會議室，可能是在旅館內。

2. **Who are the people in the picture? What makes you think so?**

   照片裡的人是誰？是什麼讓你這麼想的？

   I think they are business people attending a convention or a seminar, because most of them are dressed in business attire, they are wearing ID badges and there are displays set up in the room.

我想他們是商人，在參加一場會議或研討會，因爲大部分
的人都穿著上班族服裝，他們配帶識別證，而且室內有
設置展示品。

3. **Have you ever been to such a place?**

你曾經去過這樣的地方嗎？

I have never attended a business convention, but
I did go to an education fair last year. Many
universities set up booths to give students
information about their programs.

我從未參加過商業會議，但我去年有去教育博覽會。
許多大學有設立攤位，提供課程資訊給學生。

** ─────────────

convention〔kənˈvɛnʃən〕*n.* 代表大會；定期會議

attend〔əˈtɛnd〕*v.* 參加

seminar〔ˈsɛməˌnɑr〕*n.* 研討會

attire〔əˈtaɪr〕*n.* 服裝

ID〔ˈaɪˈdi〕*n.* 身份證明（= *identification*）

badge〔bædʒ〕*n.* 徽章；證章

display〔dɪˈsple〕*n.* 展示品　　***set up*** 設置

fair〔fɛr〕*n.* 博覽會　　booth〔buθ〕*n.* 攤位

program〔ˈprogræm〕*n.* 課程

4. **If you still have time, please describe the picture in as much detail as you can.**

如果你還有時間，請儘可能描述照片中的細節。

This is a picture of a corner of a room in which three tables with displays on them are visible. On the left is a temporary dividing wall with part of the name of a firm of solicitors. This makes me think the convention might be in England or perhaps Australia. There are three people in front of the table. A woman is taking a brochure from the table and two men are talking. Behind them is another display and there are several more people grouped around it.

這張照片是房間的一個角落，可以看到有三張桌子，上面有展示品。左邊是臨時的分隔牆，有一部分律師的公司名稱。這讓我認為這場會議可能是在英國或澳洲。有三個人在桌子前面。一位女士從桌上拿起一本小冊子，兩位男士正在說話。在他們後面是另一個展示品，而且有好幾個人聚集在那裡。

** ───────────

temporary〔'tɛmpə,rɛrɪ〕*adj.* 暫時的；臨時的
dividing〔də'vaɪdɪŋ〕*adj.* 起分隔作用的
firm〔fɜm〕*n.* 公司
solicitor〔sə'lɪsətə〕*n.* (英國的) 初級律師；
　事務律師 (= *lawyer*)
brochure〔bro'ʃʊr〕*n.* 小冊子
group〔grup〕*v.* 聚集

PART 3　申述題

It is true that the computer brings us a lot of benefits, but there is a growing trend toward computer addiction, which is harmful not only to the computer addicts themselves but also to the whole society. Describe your views about the use of the computer.

電腦的確帶給我們很多好處，但是電腦上癮的趨勢卻逐漸增加，這不僅對電腦上癮者本身有害，對整個社會也有害。請描述你對使用電腦的看法。

【回答範例】

I believe that the computer is an important and necessary tool. Without a computer, it would be difficult to keep up with others in business or education. So it is better for people to become computer literate. *However*, the computer also offers such distractions as online gaming, chat rooms and so on. Some users become so crazy about these things that they neglect their study, work, friends and family, which in turn causes society to suffer. To prevent this, computer users themselves should exercise self-discipline. Parents can also keep the family computer in the living room, not in their child's bedroom. Then they will know how much time the child spends on the computer and what he or she does. Or parents can be present while their child uses the computer, increasing the interaction with their kid at the same time.

【中文翻譯】

　　我相信電腦是很重要而且不可或缺的工具。如果沒有電腦，在商業或教育上要跟上其他人是很難的。所以，知道怎麼使用電腦對大家會比較好。然而，電腦也能提供娛樂，如線上遊戲、聊天室等。有些使用者太熱衷於這些東西，以致於忽略他們的學業、工作、朋友和家庭，這必然會使整個社會受害。為了預防這一點，電腦使用者本身應該要發揮自制力。父母也可以把家中的電腦放在客廳，而不是小孩的臥室。那麼他們就能知道小孩花多少時間在電腦上，也知道他們在做些什麼。或者小孩用電腦時，父母可以在場，同時也可以增加和孩子的互動。

**

addiction〔ə'dɪkʃən〕*n.* 上癮　　addict〔'ædɪkt〕*n.* 上癮者
keep up with 跟上　　literate〔'lɪtərɪt〕*adj.* 通曉的
distraction〔dɪ'strækʃən〕*n.* 使人分心的事物；娛樂
crazy〔'krezɪ〕*adj.* 熱衷的 < *about* >
neglect〔nɪ'glɛkt〕*v.* 忽略　　study〔'stʌdɪ〕*n.* 學業
in turn 必然也　　cause〔kɔz〕*v.* 使
suffer〔'sʌfə〕*v.* 受苦　　prevent〔prɪ'vɛnt〕*v.* 預防
exercise〔'ɛksə,saɪz〕*v.* 運用；發揮
self-discipline〔'sɛlf'dɪsəplɪn〕*n.* 自我約束；自制
present〔'prɛznt〕*adj.* 在場的
interaction〔,ɪntə'ækʃən〕*n.* 互動

座位號碼：_____   試題別：_____

第一部份請由本頁第 1 行開始作答，請勿隔行書寫。第二部份請翻至第 2 頁作答。

_____

_____

_____

_____

_____

_____

_____

_____

_____

_____

_____

_____

_____

_____

_____

_____

_____

_____

_____

_____

_____

55

60

65

70

寫作口說能力測驗 ⑤

寫作能力測驗

Part I: Chinese-English Translation (40%)

Translate the following Chinese passage into an English passage, and write your answer on the Writing Test Answer Sheet.

　　資源回收是處理垃圾最有用的方法之一。首先，資源回收有助於減少我們每天丟棄的垃圾量。其次，當我們做資源回收，我們就不必蓋那麼多的焚化爐。焚化爐在哪裡都不受居民的歡迎。此外，因為台灣人現在回收大約總垃圾量的百分之十三，政府就可節省必須用在垃圾處理上的大筆金錢。

Part II: Guided Writing (60%)

Write an essay of **150-180 words** in an appropriate style on the following topic. Write your answer on the Writing Test Answer Sheet.

　　When you see beggars on the street, do you help them? Why or why not? Please state your reasons.

口說能力測驗

Please read the self-introduction sentence.

My seat number is （複試座位號碼）, and my registration number is （初試准考證號碼）.

Part I: Answering Questions

You will hear 8 questions. Each question will be spoken once. Please answer the question immediately after you hear it.

For questions 1 to 4, you will have 15 seconds to answer each question.

For questions 5 to 8, you will have 30 seconds to answer each question.

Part II: Picture Description

Look at the picture, think about the questions below for 30 seconds, and then record your answers for 1 ½ minutes.

1. What is this place?

2. What do the people in the picture do?

3. What are they doing with the dolphins?

4. Would you like to go to this place?

5. If you still have time, please describe the picture in as much detail as you can.

Part III: Discussion

Think about your answer(s) to the question(s) below for 1 ½ minutes, and then record your answer(s) for 1 ½ minutes.

You may use your test paper to make notes and organize your ideas.

If you could have a vacation of a whole month, what would you like to do? Would you want to go abroad to travel or study, or just stay at home and spend the time with your family, or something else? Please explain.

Please read the self-introduction sentence again.

My seat number is （複試座位號碼）, and my registration number is （初試准考證號碼）.

寫作口說能力測驗 ⑤ 詳解

寫作能力測驗詳解

PART 1 中譯英 (40%)

　　資源回收是處理垃圾最有用的方法之一。首先，資源回收有助於減少我們每天丟棄的垃圾量。其次，當我們做資源回收，我們就不必蓋那麼多的焚化爐。焚化爐在哪裡都不受居民的歡迎。此外，因為台灣人現在回收大約總垃圾量的百分之十三，政府就可節省必須用在垃圾處理上的大筆金錢。

　　Recycling is one of the most useful ways to dispose of garbage. To begin with, it helps reduce the amount of trash we throw away every day. Next, when we recycle, we don't have to build so many incinerators, which are unpopular with residents everywhere. What's more, because people in Taiwan now recycle about thirteen percent of their total garbage, the government can save a huge sum of money that would have to be spent on garbage disposal.

【註】recycling〔rɪ'saɪklɪŋ〕n. 回收
　　　dispose〔dɪ'spoz〕v. 處置 <of>
　　　to begin with 首先　　reduce〔rɪ'djus〕v. 減少
　　　recycle〔rɪ'saɪkḷ〕v. 回收
　　　incinerator〔ɪn'sɪnə,retɚ〕n. 焚化爐
　　　unpopular〔ʌn'pɑpjəlɚ〕adj. 不受歡迎的
　　　resident〔'rɛzədənt〕n. 居民　　***what's more*** 此外
　　　sum〔sʌm〕n. 金額　　disposal〔dɪ'spozḷ〕n. 處理

PART 2 引導寫作 (60%)

When you see beggars on the street, do you help them? Why or why not? Please state your reasons.

當你在街上看到乞丐，你會幫助他們嗎？為什麼會或為什麼不會？請闡述你的理由。

【作文範例 1】

Beggars Deserve Some Kindness

These days I often see poor people begging on the street. I feel sorry for them and I always try to help them out if I can. Some people claim that giving to beggars will only encourage more begging, but I don't agree.

Most of the poor people we see on the streets would rather not be there. Many are disabled and unable to hold a regular job. Perhaps they have no family or their family is very poor. ***Either way***, they have no choice but to beg for money. Although what I give is only a small amount, it is better than nothing. If enough people help them throughout the day, then they will have enough to live on.

Giving to beggars is also a way of recognizing their humanity and dignity. Too often they are ignored or despised by the people around them. Who knows what got them into their sad situation? Maybe it happened through no fault of their own. When we acknowledge them with a coin, some food or even just a smile, they will not feel so alone in the world. ***Therefore***, I will continue to try to help them.

【註】 beggar〔'bɛgɚ〕 *n.* 乞丐　 deserve〔dɪ'zɝv〕 *v.* 應得
kindness〔'kaɪndnɪs〕 *n.* 仁慈　 beg〔bɛg〕 *v.* 乞討
help sb. out 幫忙某人　 claim〔klem〕 *v.* 宣稱；主張
disabled〔dɪs'ebl̩d〕 *adj.* 殘障的　 hold〔hold〕 *v.* 擁有
regular〔'rɛgjəlɚ〕 *adj.* 固定的　 ***either way*** 無論怎樣
have no choice but to + V. 不得不…
throughout〔θru'aʊt〕 *prep.* 整…；在…期間
live on 繼續活下去　 recognize〔'rɛkəg,naɪz〕 *v.* 認清
humanity〔hju'mænətɪ〕 *n.* 人性　 dignity〔'dɪgnətɪ〕 *n.* 尊嚴
ignore〔ɪg'nor〕 *v.* 忽視　 despise〔dɪ'spaɪz〕 *v.* 輕視
get〔gɛt〕 *v.* 使　 through〔θru〕 *prep.* 由於
acknowledge〔ək'nɑlɪdʒ〕 *v.* 跟…打招呼

【作文範例2】

I Won't Be Fooled Again

Have you ever seen beggars on the street? They must touch your heart a little bit and at least sometimes you must think that there but for the grace of God go I. When you see these people, what do you do? *As far as I am concerned*, I choose to pass them by.

It is not because I am heartless or cruel *but because* I have been deceived a couple of times. *On top of that*, such con games are often reported in the news. Behind these poor people are some immoral ones, who abuse our sympathy and kindness and cheat us out of our money. *Worse yet*, some beggars are not real beggars at all. I once saw a fake crippled beggar walking away merrily after his "job" was over, with the money he had collected and his crutches in his hands. I was furious at the sight of that. I don't want to fall victim to these tricks any more. I don't want to be taken advantage of again.

　　Of course, I do like to help people in need. I will do this by giving donations to trustworthy charities. *Only* in this way *can I* be assured that my money will go to those who really deserve it.

【註】 fool〔ful〕*v.* 愚弄；欺騙

　　　　touch one's heart 感動某人的心　　*at least* 至少

　　　　but for 如果沒有　　grace〔gres〕*n.* 神的恩典

　　　　there but for the grace of God go I 如果沒有上帝的恩典，

　　　　　我可能也會是這種情況（ = *it could happen to anyone*;

　　　　　I'm lucky it didn't happen to me）

　　　　as far as…be concerned 就…而言

　　　　pass ~ by 忽視 ~　　*not A but B* 不是 A 而是 B

　　　　heartless〔'hɑrtlɪs〕*adj.* 無情的　　cruel〔'kruəl〕*adj.* 殘忍的

　　　　deceive〔dɪ'siv〕*v.* 欺騙　　*a couple of times* 幾次

　　　　on top of 除了…之外　　con〔kɑn〕*adj.* 詐欺的

　　　　con game 騙局　　immoral〔ɪ'mɔrəl〕*adj.* 不道德的

　　　　abuse〔ə'bjuz〕*v.* 濫用　　sympathy〔'sɪmpəθɪ〕*n.* 同情

　　　　cheat sb. (out) of 欺騙某人的…　　*worse yet* 更糟的是

　　　　fake〔fek〕*adj.* 假的　　crippled〔'krɪpl̩d〕*adj.* 跛腳的

　　　　merrily〔'mɛrɪlɪ〕*adv.* 快樂地　　collect〔kə'lɛkt〕*v.* 收集

　　　　crutch〔krʌtʃ〕*n.* 拐杖　　furious〔'fjurɪəs〕*adj.* 狂怒的

　　　　at the sight of 一看到　　victim〔'vɪktɪm〕*n.* 受害者

　　　　fall victim to 成為…的受害者　　trick〔trɪk〕*n.* 詭計；騙局

　　　　take advantage of 利用；欺騙

　　　　in need 在貧困中的　　donation〔do'neʃən〕*n.* 捐款

　　　　trustworthy〔'trʌst,wɝðɪ〕*adj.* 可信賴的

　　　　charity〔'tʃærətɪ〕*n.* 慈善機構

　　　　assured〔ə'ʃurd〕*adj.* 確信的；有把握的

　　　　go to 被給予；屬於　　deserve〔dɪ'zɝv〕*v.* 應得

口說能力測驗詳解

PART 1 回答問題

1. **If you could become any animal, which one would you choose and why?**

   如果你可以變成任何一種動物，你會選擇哪一種？為什麼？

【回答範例 1】

Without a doubt, I'd like to be the king
　of the jungle.

Yes, I'd choose to be a lion.

I would be the master of the animal kingdom.

Virtually every other animal would fear
　or at least respect me.

I would almost always get my way.

And lions are such noble-looking creatures.

Most of the time lions take it easy.

They enjoy themselves in the sun on the
　plains of Africa.

Hunting for prey must be really exciting.

【中文翻譯】

無疑地，我想變成叢林之王。

是的，我會選擇變成獅子。

我想變成動物王國的統治者。

幾乎其他每一隻動物都會怕我或至少會尊敬我。

我幾乎能總是想怎樣就怎樣。

而且獅子是看起來很高貴的動物。

大部分的時間獅子都很輕鬆。

牠們在非洲草原的陽光下過得很快樂。

尋找獵物一定很刺激。

** ─────────────

without a doubt 無疑地（= *without doubt*）

master〔ˋmæstə〕*n.* 主人；統治者

kingdom〔ˋkɪŋdəm〕*n.* 王國

virtually〔ˋvɝtʃʊəlɪ〕*adv.* 幾乎　　***at least*** 至少

get *one's* **(own)** ***way*** 想怎樣就怎樣；隨心所欲

noble〔ˋnobḷ〕*adj.* 高貴的

noble-looking〔ˋnobḷˋlʊkɪŋ〕*adj.* 看起來很高貴的

creature〔ˋkritʃə〕*n.* 生物；動物

most of the time 大部分的時間

take it easy 放鬆；休息　　***enjoy*** *oneself* 過得快樂

in the sun 在陽光下　　plain〔plen〕*n.* 平原

hunt for 尋找；搜尋　　prey〔pre〕*n.* 獵物

【回答範例 2】

I'd like to be a koala bear because it
is lazy, just like me.

I've been to the Taipei Zoo to see
koalas.
They are so cute.

Koalas only eat the leaves of the
eucalyptus tree.
They hardly move at all.
They sleep a lot.

It seems that their lives center on
sleeping and eating.
How I envy this kind of idle life.
I think this kind of life would suit
me perfectly.

【中文翻譯】

我想變成無尾熊，因為牠很懶散，就像我
一樣。
我去過台北動物園看無尾熊。
牠們好可愛。

無尾熊只吃尤加利樹的葉子。
牠們幾乎完全不動。
牠們經常在睡覺。

好像牠們的生活是以睡覺和吃東西為主。
我多麼羨慕這種遊手好閒的生活啊。
我認為這種生活會非常適合我。

** ——————————————

koala〔ko'alə〕*n.* 無尾熊（= *koala bear*）
lazy〔'lezɪ〕*adj.* 懶惰的
eucalyptus〔,jukə'lɪptəs〕*n.* 尤加利樹
hardly〔'hɑrdlɪ〕*adv.* 幾乎不
move〔muv〕*v.* 移動　　　*a lot* 常常
center on 集中於　　envy〔'ɛnvɪ〕*v.* 羨慕
idle〔'aɪdḷ〕*adj.* 懶惰的；遊手好閒的
suit〔sut〕*v.* 適合
perfectly〔'pɝfɪktlɪ〕*adv.* 非常

2. There are all kinds of cram schools in Taiwan. Do you have any experience of attending one? Please explain.

在台灣有各式各樣的補習班。你有任何補習的經驗嗎？請說明。

【回答範例 1】

Like almost every kid in Taiwan,
　　I've gone to cram school.
It's a must, especially for high school
　　seniors.
They have to prepare thoroughly for
　　the JUEE.

I attended a very big and famous
　　cram school.
There were literally thousands
　　of students.
It was like a factory assembly line.

I thought I'd be lost in the crowd.
But the teachers and materials were
　　excellent.
Most importantly, thanks to that school,
　　I did very well on the July exams.

【中文翻譯】

像台灣幾乎每個小孩一樣，我有補過習。
補習是必要的，尤其是高三的學生。
他們必須很認真地準備大學入學考試。

我去一間很大又有名的補習班補習。
眞的有幾千個學生。
那裡就像是工廠的裝配線。

我還以爲我會迷失在人群中。
但是老師和教材都很棒。
最重要的是，由於那家補習班，七月的考試
我考得很好。

** ————————————

cram school 補習班
attend〔ə'tɛnd〕*v.* 上（學）
must〔mʌst〕*n.* 必備之物；必須要做的事
senior〔'sinjɚ〕*n.* 最高年級的學生
thoroughly〔'θɝolɪ〕*adv.* 徹底地；極認眞地
JUEE 大學入學考試（= *Joint University Entrance
　Examination*）
literally〔'lɪtərəlɪ〕*adv.* 不誇張地；眞正地
assembly〔ə'sɛmblɪ〕*n.* 裝配
assembly line 裝配線
lost〔lɔst〕*adj.* 迷路的；迷失的
material〔mə'tɪrɪəl〕*n.* 教材；資料
thanks to 由於　　***do well*** 考得好

【回答範例 2】

Of course, I went to cram school.

There's no getting around it.

My parents gave me no choice.

Actually, I shouldn't say that.

Unlike most parents, they allowed
   me to choose which one.

And *unlike most* of my friends,
   I opted for a small one.

I got to know my teachers very well.

They gave me a lot of individual
   attention.

I made great progress and exceeded
   everybody's expectations on the
   exam.

【中文翻譯】

當然，我補過習。

要逃避補習是不可能的。

我的父母沒有給我選擇的權利。

事實上，我不應該那麼說。

不像大多數的父母，他們讓我選擇補哪一間。

而且不像我大部分的朋友，我選擇小間的補

習班。

我能和老師很熟。

他們給我很多個別的關照。

我有很大的進步，並在考試時出乎每個人的

預料。

** ────────────────

There is no + V-ing …是不可能的

　(= *It is impossible to V.*)

get around 逃避

opt〔ɑpt〕*v.* 選擇　　***get to*** 得以

individual〔͵ɪndə'vɪdʒʊəl〕*adj.* 個別的

attention〔ə'tɛnʃən〕*n.* 關照；照顧

progress〔'prɑgrɛs〕*n.* 進步

exceed〔ɪk'sid〕*v.* 超越

expectations〔͵ɛkspɛk'teʃənz〕*n. pl.* 預期

exceed *one's* ***expectations*** 出乎某人的預料

3. Do you enjoy your life now? Why or why not?

你喜歡你現在的生活嗎？爲什麼喜歡或爲什麼不喜歡？

【回答範例 1】

> *I am* not enjoying my life very much
> right now.
>
> *I am* in my senior year of senior
> high school.
>
> The whole year is devoted to studying
> for the JUEE.
>
> I have no time for my friends.
>
> They, of course, also have no time
> for me.
>
> My time seems never to be my own.
>
> *My* waking hours are filled with
> studying, studying and more studying.
>
> *My* parents are always on my back.
>
> I do, however, realize that my entire
> future depends on this exam.

【中文翻譯】

我不是很喜歡我現在的生活。

我目前是高中三年級。

這一整年都為了大學入學考試在專心唸書。

我沒時間陪我的朋友。

當然，他們也沒時間陪我。

我的時間似乎從來都不是自己的。

我醒著的時間都是在唸書，除了唸書還是
唸書。

我的父母一直煩我。

然而，我的確能理解，我全部的未來就靠這
場考試了。

**　**

** ——————————

senior〔ˈsinjɚ〕*adj.* 最高年級的
devoted〔dɪˈvotɪd〕*adj.* 專心於…的
be devoted to 致力於
waking〔ˈwekɪŋ〕*adj.* 醒著的
on *one's* **back** 煩擾某人
entire〔ɪnˈtaɪr〕*adj.* 全部的
depend on 依賴

【回答範例 2】

I couldn't be enjoying my life more.

Things are going great.

Everything is as it should be.

I have a wonderful family.

We are all extremely close.

We love to do many different kinds
  of activities together.

I find my job very rewarding.

In addition, I have plenty of free
  time.

That allows me to pursue my
  hobbies.

【中文翻譯】

我非常喜歡我的生活。

一切都很好。

每件事都很正常。

我有一個很棒的家庭。

我們都非常親近。

我們喜愛一起做許多不同種類的活動。

我覺得我的工作很值得做。

此外，我有很多空閒時間。

這讓我能做自己有興趣的事。

** ──────────────────

things〔θɪŋz〕*n. pl.* 情況

go〔go〕*v.* 進展

Everything is as it should be. 每件事都

　是它該有的樣子；每件事都很正常。

extremely〔ɪk'strimlɪ〕*adv.* 非常

find〔faɪnd〕*v.* 覺得

rewarding〔rɪ'wɔrdɪŋ〕*adj.* 值得的

plenty of 很多　　***free time*** 空閒時間

pursue〔pɚ'su〕*v.* 從事

hobby〔'hɑbɪ〕*n.* 嗜好；興趣

4. **What do you expect to do in the near future? Please explain.**

你預計不久的將來要做什麼？請說明。

【回答範例 1】

I am certainly going to continue my
　　formal education.

I am definitely going to attend university
　　next year.

I won't know which one until the JUEE
　　results are out.

My dream is, of course, to be accepted
　　at NTU.

That would be just the right start.

In any event, I'm really happy to be finished
　　with high school.

Now I'll be able to have a much more
　　well-rounded life.

I want to get back to taking guitar lessons.

Now I'll have some time to go out with
　　my friends to KTVs and the movies.

【中文翻譯】

我一定要繼續我的正規教育。

我明年一定要上大學。

直到大學入學考試成績公布，我才知道是哪

一所大學。

當然，我的夢想是被台大錄取。

那樣就會是好的開始。

無論如何，我很高興能唸完高中。

現在，我將可以擁有更多元的生活。

我想回去上吉他課。

現在，我將會有一些時間，能和朋友一起去

唱 KTV 和看電影。

**—————————————————

certainly〔'sɝtn̩lɪ〕 *adv.* 一定

formal education 正規教育

definitely〔'dɛfənɪtlɪ〕 *adv.* 一定

results〔rɪ'zʌlts〕 *n. pl.* 成績

out〔aut〕 *adv.* 出現；顯露

accept〔ək'sɛpt〕 *v.* 接受；接納

in any event 無論如何

finished〔'fɪnɪʃt〕 *adj.* 完成的；做完的

well-rounded〔'wɛl'raundɪd〕 *adj.* 涵蓋多方面的

【回答範例 2】

It's summer now.

For the first time in a few years I will
    have a real vacation.

My whole family is going to the USA.

We are basing ourselves in
    Los Angeles.

My uncle and his family live there.

We will see all the standard
    attractions.

I am most looking forward to visiting
    Universal Studios.

We will also make some weekend side
    trips to Las Vegas and San Francisco.

I can't wait to get going.

【中文翻譯】

現在是夏天。

在這幾年裡面，我將擁有第一個真正的假期。

我們全家要去美國。

我們會住在洛杉磯。

我的叔叔和他的家人都住在那裡。

我們將會遊覽所有大家都會去的景點。

我最期待去參觀環球影城。

我們週末也會順道去拉斯維加斯和舊金山

旅行。

我等不及要去了。

** ─────────────

base〔bes〕v. 以…為基地；以…為根據地

Los Angeles〔lɔsˈændʒələs〕n. 洛杉磯

standard〔ˈstændəd〕adj. 標準的；通常的

attraction〔əˈtrækʃən〕n. 有吸引力的地方

look forward to + V-ing 期待

Universal Studios 環球影城

side〔saɪd〕adj. 附帶的

side trip 附帶的順路旅行

Las Vegas〔lɑsˈvegəs〕n. 拉斯維加斯

San Francisco〔ˌsænfrənˈsɪsko〕n. 舊金山

5. **Describe your neighborhood. Do you like living there? Why or why not?**

描述你家附近一帶。你喜歡住在那裡嗎？為什麼喜歡或為什麼不喜歡？

【回答範例 1】

I live in a high-rise building in the heart
  of Taipei city.

It is just a few blocks from Taipei 101.

And it is also quite convenient to the Tong
  Hwa night market.

I love my neighborhood.

I have so many friends right in our building.

That's why I never mind rainy days.

I've lived my entire life in this neighborhood;
  in fact, in this very building.

I couldn't imagine living anywhere else.

I honestly think I could spend my entire life
  here quite happily.

【中文翻譯】

我住在台北市中心的一棟高層大樓裡。

離台北 101 只有幾條街。

而且到通化夜市也相當方便。

我愛我的鄰居。

我有很多朋友就住在我們的大樓裡。

這就是我從不介意下雨天的原因。

我一輩子都住在這一區；事實上，就是住在

這棟大樓。

我無法想像住在任何其他地方。

我真的認為我一輩子都會在這裡過得很快樂。

** ————————————————

neighborhood〔'nebə‚hud〕*n.* 附近地區；

　附近的鄰居；地區

high-rise〔'haɪ'raɪz〕*adj.* 高層的

heart〔hɑrt〕*n.* 中心（部分）

block〔blɑk〕*n.* 街區；一條街

night market 夜市

right〔raɪt〕*adv.* 正好；剛好

in fact 事實上　　very〔'vɛrɪ〕*adj.* 正是；就是

honestly〔'ɑnɪstlɪ〕*adv.* 的確；真地

【回答範例 2】

My family moved to a new neighborhood
 after my first year of senior high school.

At first, I felt completely lost.

I was like a fish out of water.

I was so settled in my former
 neighborhood.

I can no longer walk to school.

Now it takes me forty minutes by the
 MRT and then a bus.

Besides, it's inconvenient in almost every
 other respect.

It's so far from my favorite specialty
 supermarket.

But it saves my dad a lot of commuting
 time and that's most important.

【中文翻譯】

我在高一唸完後，我們全家就搬到一個新的地區。

一開始，我完全不知所措。

我就像是離開水的魚一樣。

我在以前的地區過得很安定。

我不能再走路上學了。

現在坐捷運再轉公車，要花掉我四十分鐘。

此外，幾乎其他每一方面都很不方便。

它離我最喜歡的販賣特別食品的超市也很遠。

但它能讓我爸爸節省很多通勤時間，而這是最
重要的。

** ————————————————————

completely〔kəmˋplitlɪ〕*adv.* 完全地

lost〔lɔst〕*adj.* 不知所措的

like a fish out of water 好像離水的魚；感到
　生疏（或不適應）

settled〔ˋsɛtl̩d〕*adj.* 安定的

former〔ˋfɔrmɚ〕*adj.* 以前的　　*no longer* 不再

MRT 捷運　　respect〔rɪˋspɛkt〕*n.* 方面

specialty〔ˋspɛʃəltɪ〕*n.* 特色食品；特產　*adj.* 特產的

specialty supermarket 有賣特別食品的超市

commute〔kəˋmjut〕*v.* 通勤

6. **Do you enjoy reading? What kind of stuff do you usually read?**

你喜歡閱讀嗎？你通常會看哪一種書？

【回答範例 1】

I love to read novels, not necessarily the current bestsellers.

I love novels with real character development.

I love to learn about genuine human nature.

I especially love twentieth century American novels.

Give me Faulkner, Fitzgerald and Hemingway anytime.

They are so insightful about people—their motives and tendencies.

It doesn't matter a bit that they wrote some eighty years ago.

The material world may have changed enormously.

But on matters of the heart people will always be people.

【中文翻譯】

我喜歡看小說，不一定是現在的暢銷書。

我喜歡有真實人格發展的小說。

我喜歡了解真正的人性。

我特別喜歡二十世紀的美國小說。

你隨時都可以給我福克納、費茲傑羅和海明威的作品。

他們對人類有很深刻的見解——人類的動機和傾向。

他們寫作的時間是在大約八十年前，那一點也沒有關係。

這個物質世界可能已經改變很多。

但是關於內心的問題，人始終是一樣。

**

stuff〔stʌf〕*n.* 東西　　***not necessarily*** 未必；不一定

current〔'kɝənt〕*adj.* 現在的

bestseller〔'bɛst'sɛlə〕*n.* 暢銷書

character〔'kærıktə〕*n.* 人格　　learn〔lɝn〕*v.* 得知

genuine〔'dʒɛnjuın〕*adj.* 真正的　　***human nature*** 人性

Faulkner〔'fɔknə〕*n.* 福克納【1897-1962，美國小說家，獲 1949
　年諾貝爾文學獎】

Fitzgerald〔fıts'dʒɛrəld〕*n.* 費茲傑羅【1896-1940，美國小說家】

Hemingway〔'hɛmıŋˌwe〕*n.* 海明威【1899-1961，美國小說家，
　獲 1954 年諾貝爾文學獎】

anytime〔'ɛnıˌtaım〕*adv.* 在任何時候

insightful〔'ınˌsaıtfəl〕*adj.* 具洞察力的；有深刻見解的

motive〔'motıv〕*n.* 動機　　tendency〔'tɛndənsı〕*n.* 傾向

matter〔'mætə〕*v.* 有關係　*n.* 問題　　***a bit*** 一點

some〔sʌm〕*adv.* 大約　　material〔mə'tırıəl〕*adj.* 物質的

enormously〔ı'nɔrməslı〕*adv.* 巨大地

【回答範例 2】

I'm not much of a reader.

I have so much required reading
　for school.

When I get a little free time, I want to
　do something very different.

That doesn't mean I never pick up
　a book.

When I do, it's usually a biography.

I like to learn about my great heroes
　in more detail.

For example, I just finished a biography
　of Thomas Edison.

What an amazing range of inventions
　he created!

He is responsible for so many things
　of which I was not aware, besides
　his notable inventions.

【中文翻譯】

我不是很愛閱讀的人。

我有很多學校規定要看的書。

當我有一些空閒時間時，我想要做很不一樣的事。

這不代表我不曾拿書來看。

當我要看書的時候，通常會看傳記。

我喜歡更詳細地知道我偉大的英雄。

例如，我正好看完湯瑪士‧愛迪生的傳記。

他創造的發明，範圍是很驚人的！

除了有名的發明之外，還有很多我不知道的

東西都是他的功勞。

** ————————————————

not much of a ~　不是什麼了不起的～；不是很好的～

reader〔ˈridɚ〕*n.* 愛好閱讀的人

required〔rɪˈkwaɪrd〕*adj.* 必須的；規定的

reading〔ˈridɪŋ〕*n.* 閱讀；閱讀量

biography〔baɪˈɑgrəfɪ〕*n.* 傳記　　***in detail*** 詳細地

Thomas Edison〔ˈtɑməs ˈɛdəsn̩〕*n.* 湯瑪士‧愛迪生

amazing〔əˈmezɪŋ〕*adj.* 驚人的

range〔rendʒ〕*n.* 範圍

invention〔ɪnˈvɛnʃən〕*n.* 發明

responsible〔rɪˈspɑnsəbl̩〕*adj.* 有功勞的

aware〔əˈwɛr〕*adj.* 知道的

notable〔ˈnotəbl̩〕*adj.* 有名的

7. **Do you have a lot of good friends? What have you learned from them?**

你有很多好朋友嗎？你有從他們身上學到了什麼嗎？

【回答範例 1】

I used to think I had a lot of good friends.

But lately I'm beginning to wonder.

I've been let down by them time and time again.

When a friend asks me for a favor, I do it as quickly as possible.

Recently I've asked some friends for some small favors.

For example, I asked one to give me a phone number and another to pick up a cold drink for me.

I didn't get either one.

From these minor negative experiences has come an important, positive lesson.

Can you count on someone in an important situation who lets you down in insignificant matters?

【中文翻譯】

我以前認為自己有很多好朋友。

但是最近我開始感到懷疑。

他們一再地讓我失望。

當朋友請我幫忙時，我會盡快去做。

最近，我請幾個朋友幫我一些小忙。

例如，我要求一個朋友告訴我一個電話號碼，以及
要求另一個朋友幫我買瓶冷飲。

這兩者我都沒得到。

從這些較小的負面經驗中，我得到很重要且正面的
教訓。

在重要的情況，你能依賴那些在小事情上讓你失望
的人嗎？

** ─────────────────

used to 以前　　lately〔'letlɪ〕*adv.* 最近

wonder〔'wʌndɚ〕*v.* 想知道；感到懷疑

let down 使失望　　*time and* (*time*) *again* 一再；屢次

ask sb. for a favor 請某人幫忙

pick up 買　　minor〔'maɪnɚ〕*adj.* 較小的

negative〔'nɛgətɪv〕*adj.* 負面的

positive〔'pazətɪv〕*adj.* 正面的；實用的

count on 依賴

insignificant〔ˌɪnsɪg'nɪfəkənt〕*adj.* 不重要的；微小的

【回答範例 2】

I don't have many good friends.

But the ones I have are really dependable.

There's nothing they wouldn't do for me,
　　and vice versa.

True friendship is indeed a two-way street.

You've got to give consistently if you
　　want to get.

When a friend needs a favor, it should
　　automatically never be a "bad" time.

Friends must be loyal and reliable.

You must be able to depend on them.

Friends should always stick up for
　　each other.

【中文翻譯】

我沒有很多好朋友。

但我所擁有的好朋友真的都很可靠。

他們肯為我做任何事，我也肯為他們做任何事。

真正的友誼其實是互相的。

如果你想得到真正的友誼，你就要常常付出。

當朋友需要幫忙時，就應該不會認為它是「不適當的」時機。

朋友必須要忠實可靠。

你一定可以依賴他們。

朋友應該要一直互相支持。

** —————————————

dependable〔dɪ'pɛndəbḷ〕*adj.* 可靠的
vice versa〔'vaɪsɪ'vɜsə〕*adv.* 反之亦然
indeed〔ɪn'did〕*adv.* 真正地；其實
two-way〔'tu'we〕*adj.* 雙向的
two-way street 雙向道；需要雙方合作的情形
give〔gɪv〕*v.* 付出；給予
consistently〔kən'sɪstəntlɪ〕*adv.* 經常；一直
automatically〔,ɔtə'mætɪkḷɪ〕*adv.* 自動地；必然地
loyal〔'lɔɪəl〕*adj.* 忠實的
reliable〔rɪ'laɪəbḷ〕*adj.* 可靠的
stick up for 支持

8. **Chinese Valentine's Day is coming. Do you have any plans for that day?**
　　七夕情人節要到了。你那天有任何計劃嗎？

【回答範例】

Chinese Valentine's Day is a very
　　romantic holiday.
So, of course, I will be taking my
　　girlfriend out for a special dinner.
She loves Italian food.

This year I am going to give her a
　　special treat.
I'm surprising her by taking her to an
　　Italian themed buffet.
There's a pasta bar where you can choose
　　from assorted pastas and sauces.

The appetizers are fantastic.
The choice of main dishes is amazing.
I think she will appreciate the change
　　from our usual Chinese feast.

【中文翻譯】

七夕情人節是一個很浪漫的節日。
所以，當然，我會帶我的女朋友出去吃一頓特別
的晚餐。
她愛義大利菜。

今年我要請她吃特別一點的。
我要帶她去義大利主題自助餐，給她一個驚喜。
那裡有義大利麵吧檯，有各式各樣的義大利麵和
醬汁供人選擇。

開胃菜都很棒。
主菜的選擇種類很驚人。
從我們平常吃的中國菜換成義大利菜，我想她會
很感激。

** ———————————————

Valentine's Day 情人節　　treat〔trit〕*n.* 款待；請客
themed〔θimd〕*adj.* 反映一定主題的
buffet〔buˈfe〕*n.* 自助餐
pasta〔ˈpɑstɑ〕*n.* 義大利麵　　bar〔bɑr〕*n.* 吧檯
assorted〔əˈsɔrtɪd〕*adj.* 各種各樣的
sauce〔sɔs〕*n.* 醬汁　　appetizer〔ˈæpə͵taɪzɚ〕*n.* 開胃菜
fantastic〔fænˈtæstɪk〕*adj.* 很棒的　　**main dish** 主菜
appreciate〔əˈpriʃɪ͵et〕*v.* 欣賞；感激
feast〔fist〕*n.* 盛宴

PART 2　看圖敘述

1. **What is this place?** 這是什麼地方？

   This is a water park where dolphins perform for people.

   這是一個水上樂園，那裡有海豚在為觀眾表演。

2. **What do the people in the picture do?**

   照片裡的人從事什麼行業？

   Because of what they're wearing, I think that they work at the park and are not visitors. I believe the people are dolphin trainers.

   因為他們的穿著，我想他們應該是在這個樂園裡面工作，而不是遊客。我認為這些人是訓練海豚的人。

** ——————————————————————

dolphin〔ˈdɑlfɪn〕*n.* 海豚

trainer〔ˈtrenɚ〕*n.* 訓練者

3. **What are they doing with the dolphins?**

他們在和海豚做什麼？

They are feeding the dolphins. Perhaps it is part of training them to do some tricks.

他們在餵海豚。或許這是訓練牠們做一些特技的一部分。

4. **Would you like to go to this place?**

你會想去這個地方嗎？

Yes, I like animals and I especially like to watch dolphins.

是的，我喜歡動物，而且我特別喜歡看海豚。

5. **If you still have time, please describe the picture in as much detail as you can.**

如果你還有時間，請儘可能描述照片中的細節。

There are three people in the picture, two men and one woman. They are sitting on the edge of a pool with their legs dangling in the water. They are wearing wetsuits and are feeding and interacting with three dolphins. The dolphins are in the water in front of them. Their heads are out of the water and they are being petted and fed by the trainers.

照片中有三個人，兩位男士，一位女士。他們坐在水池的邊緣，雙腳垂放在水中。他們穿著潛水衣，在餵三隻海豚並和牠們互動。海豚在他們前面的水中。牠們的頭在水面上，被訓練員撫摸和餵食。

** ───────────────

trick〔trɪk〕n. 特技　　edge〔ɛdʒ〕n. 邊緣
pool〔pul〕n. 水池
dangle〔'dæŋgl〕v. 懸擺；懸垂
wetsuit〔'wɛt,sut〕n. 潛水衣 (= *wet suit*)
interact〔,ɪntɚ'ækt〕v. 互動　　pet〔pɛt〕v. 撫摸

PART 3　申述題

If you could have a vacation of a whole month, what would you like to do? Would you want to go abroad to travel or study, or just stay at home and spend the time with your family, or something else? Please explain.

如果你可以有一整個月的假期，你會想做什麼？你想出國旅行還是念書？或只是待在家裡花時間陪家人？還是做其他的事？請說明。

【回答範例】

　　　If I could have a month-long vacation, I would travel abroad. Normally, it is difficult to get enough time off to travel for very long, so I would definitely take advantage of this opportunity. I wouldn't study formally while I traveled but I think I would learn a lot about other cultures by observing the local people and their way of life. There are many places that I would like to see, so it would be a difficult choice. I might start in Africa because it is very different from my own country. *However*, I would not go alone. I would go with my family or some good friends. That way we could enjoy the experience together.

【中文翻譯】

　　　如果我可以有長達一個月的假期，我會出國旅行。通常能夠有足夠的休假去長時間旅行是很困難的，所以我一定會利用這個機會。當我旅行的時候，我不會很正式地研究，但我認為藉由觀察當地的人民和他們的生活方式，我會學到許多其他國家的文化。我想去很多地方遊覽，所以這會是個很困難的選擇。我可能會從非洲開始，因為它和我自己的國家差異很大。然而，我不會自己一個人去。我會和家人或一些好朋友去。這樣我們就可以一起享有這個體驗。

＊＊ ─────────────────────

go abroad 到國外

normally〔'nɔrml̩ɪ〕*adv.* 通常

get off 獲准在（某天或某段時間）休假

definitely〔'dɛfənɪtlɪ〕*adv.* 一定

take advantage of 利用

study〔'stʌdɪ〕*v.* 研究

formally〔'fɔrml̩ɪ〕*adv.* 正式地

observe〔əb'zɝv〕*v.* 觀察

local〔'lokl̩〕*adj.* 當地的

alone〔ə'lon〕*adv.* 獨自地

全民英語能力分級檢定測驗
中高級寫作能力測驗答案紙

座位號碼：＿＿＿＿＿＿＿＿＿＿＿＿　　　試題別：＿＿＿＿＿＿＿

第一部份請由本頁第 1 行開始作答，請勿隔行書寫。第二部份請翻至第 2 頁作答。

55

60

65

70

寫作口說能力測驗 ⑥

寫作能力測驗

Part I: Chinese-English Translation (40%)

Translate the following Chinese passage into an English passage, and write your answer on the Writing Test Answer Sheet.

在現代人的生活裡，失眠似乎是個相當普遍的問題。失眠通常會發生在我們有煩惱、緊張或生氣的時候。以我為例，我就曾經失眠。身為一個學生，我過去常常在考試前夕，緊張到無法入睡。然後當我考試的時候，我會覺得昏昏欲睡，而表現得很差。但現在，我已學會儘量放輕鬆，我會努力不讓焦慮影響到我的睡眠。

Part II: Guided Writing (60%)

Write an essay of **150-180 words** in an appropriate style on the following topic. Write your answer on the Writing Test Answer Sheet.

Residents in many Taiwanese cities are required to observe the "keep garbage off the ground" policy. That is, they have to take out their garbage to the garbage trucks at designated time, rather than leave it in outdoor garbage bins. What do you think of this policy? Do you agree or disagree with it?

口說能力測驗

Please read the self-introduction sentence.

My seat number is （複試座位號碼）, and my
registration number is （初試准考證號碼）.

Part I: Answering Questions

You will hear 8 questions. Each question will be
spoken once. Please answer the question immediately
after you hear it.

For questions 1 to 4, you will have 15 seconds to
answer each question.

For questions 5 to 8, you will have 30 seconds to
answer each question.

Part II: Picture Description

Look at the picture, think about the questions below for 30 seconds, and then record your answers for 1 ½ minutes.

1. What is this place?

2. What do you suppose the people in the picture are doing?

3. Have you ever been to such a place? If not, why not?

4. If you still have time, please describe the picture in as much detail as you can.

Part III: Discussion

Think about your answer(s) to the question(s) below for 1 ½ minutes, and then record your answer(s) for 1 ½ minutes.
You may use your test paper to make notes and organize your ideas.

Do you read newspapers every day? What section(s) do you like best and what section(s) aren't you interested in? Please explain.

Please read the self-introduction sentence again.

　My seat number is （複試座位號碼）, and my registration number is （初試准考證號碼）.

寫作口說能力測驗 ⑥ 詳解

寫作能力測驗詳解

PART 1 中譯英 (40%)

　　在現代人的生活裡，失眠似乎是個相當普遍的問題。失眠通常會發生在我們有煩惱、緊張或生氣的時候。以我爲例，我就曾經失眠。身爲一個學生，我過去常常在考試前夕，緊張到無法入睡。然後當我考試的時候，我會覺得昏昏欲睡，而表現得很差。但現在，我已學會儘量放輕鬆，我會努力不讓焦慮影響到我的睡眠。

1. In $\left\{\begin{array}{l}\text{the lives of modern people}\\\text{modern people's lives}\end{array}\right\}$, $\left\{\begin{array}{l}\text{insomnia}\\\text{sleeplessness}\end{array}\right\}$

　seems to be $\left\{\begin{array}{l}\text{a rather}\\\text{quite a}\end{array}\right\}$ $\left\{\begin{array}{l}\text{widespread}\\\text{prevalent}\\\text{common}\end{array}\right\}$ problem.

2. Insomnia usually $\left\{\begin{array}{l}\text{occurs}\\\text{happens}\end{array}\right\}$ when we are

$\left\{\begin{array}{l}\text{troubled}\\\text{anxious}\\\text{upset}\\\text{annoyed}\\\text{worried}\end{array}\right\}$, $\left\{\begin{array}{l}\text{nervous}\\\text{tense}\end{array}\right\}$ or $\left\{\begin{array}{l}\text{angry.}\\\text{mad.}\\\text{irritated.}\\\text{furious.}\end{array}\right\}$

3. Take me $\begin{Bmatrix} \text{as an example.} \\ \text{for example.} \end{Bmatrix}$ I used to have

insomnia.

4. $\begin{Bmatrix} \text{As} \\ \text{Being} \end{Bmatrix}$ a student, I $\begin{Bmatrix} \text{used to} \\ \text{would often} \end{Bmatrix}$ get so

nervous before $\begin{Bmatrix} \text{a test} \\ \text{an exam(ination)} \end{Bmatrix}$ that I

could not sleep.

5. Then, when I took the test, I felt $\begin{Bmatrix} \text{sleepy} \\ \text{drowsy} \\ \text{tired} \end{Bmatrix}$

and $\begin{Bmatrix} \text{did} \\ \text{performed} \end{Bmatrix} \begin{Bmatrix} \text{poorly.} \\ \text{badly.} \end{Bmatrix}$

6. But now, I have learned to relax as much as

$\begin{Bmatrix} \text{I can} \\ \text{possible} \end{Bmatrix}$ and I $\begin{Bmatrix} \text{make efforts} \\ \text{try} \end{Bmatrix}$ not to let

$\begin{Bmatrix} \text{anxiety} \\ \text{worry} \end{Bmatrix}$ influence my sleep.

【註】 insomnia〔ɪnˋsɑmnɪə〕n. 失眠
　　　 sleeplessness〔ˋsliplɪsnɪs〕n. 失眠
　　　 widespread〔ˋwaɪdˋsprɛd〕adj. 普遍的
　　　 prevalent〔ˋprɛvələnt〕adj. 普遍的
　　　 occur〔əˋkɝ〕v. 發生　　troubled〔ˋtrʌbḷd〕adj. 困擾的
　　　 anxious〔ˋæŋkʃəs〕adj. 焦慮的
　　　 upset〔ʌpˋsɛt〕adj. 心煩的
　　　 annoyed〔əˋnɔɪd〕adj. 心煩的
　　　 nervous〔ˋnɝvəs〕adj. 緊張的　　tense〔tɛns〕adj. 緊張的
　　　 mad〔mæd〕adj. 生氣的　　irritated〔ˋɪrəˌtetɪd〕adj. 發怒的
　　　 furious〔ˋfjʊrɪəs〕adj. 狂怒的　　**used to** 以前
　　　 drowsy〔ˋdraʊzɪ〕adj. 想睡的
　　　 perform〔pɚˋfɔrm〕v. 表現　　**make efforts** 努力
　　　 anxiety〔æŋˋzaɪətɪ〕n. 焦慮
　　　 influence〔ˋɪnfluəns〕v. 影響

PART 2 引導寫作 (60%)

　　Residents in many Taiwanese cities are required
to observe the "keep garbage off the ground" policy.
That is, they have to take out their garbage to the
garbage trucks at designated times, rather than leave
it in outdoor garbage bins. What do you think of this
policy? Do you agree or disagree with it?

　　台灣有很多城市要求居民遵守「垃圾不落地」的政策。
也就是，他們必須在指定的時間把垃圾拿出去丟到垃圾車
裡，而不是把垃圾放在戶外的垃圾箱。你對這項政策有什麼
想法？你同不同意這項政策？

【作文範例】

Keeping Garbage off the Ground

In my opinion, the "keep garbage off the ground" policy is necessary in Taiwan's big cities. If people were allowed to put out their garbage at any time of the day, it might go uncollected for a whole day. Given Taiwan's hot climate, this would result in a bad smell and an unclean environment. The garbage would also attract animals like dogs, cats and rats. They might knock over the garbage cans and create a big mess. *Needless to say*, few would be willing to clean it up.

Requiring residents to take their garbage to the trucks themselves also ensures that they separate recyclables from the rest of their trash. A public garbage bin would tempt people to throw in anything they wanted to get rid of whether or not it was the appropriate place. Some people might also place garbage in the bin without the appropriate blue bag. *In the end*, this would create more work for the garbage collectors and make the recycling policy less effective.

Although being required to meet the garbage trucks
at a specific time causes inconvenience to some, I believe
it is a small price to pay for a pleasant environment.

【註】 ***keep…off*** 不讓…接近

policy〔'pɑləsɪ〕*n.* 政策　　go〔go〕*v.* 變得

uncollected〔ˌʌnkə'lɛktɪd〕*adj.* 未收的

given〔'gɪvən〕*prep.* 如果有　　***result in*** 導致

smell〔smɛl〕*n.* 味道　　rat〔ræt〕*n.* 老鼠

knock over 打翻　　can〔kæn〕*n.* 桶

mess〔mɛs〕*n.* 亂七八糟　　***needless to say*** 不用說

willing〔'wɪlɪŋ〕*adj.* 願意的　　***clean up*** 清理乾淨

require〔rɪ'kwaɪr〕*v.* 要求

ensure〔ɪn'ʃʊr〕*v.* 確保

separate〔'sɛpəˌret〕*v.* 使分開

recyclable〔ri'saɪkləb!〕*n.* 可回收再製的東西

rest〔rɛst〕*n.* 剩餘　　bin〔bɪn〕*n.* 箱

tempt〔tɛmpt〕*v.* 誘使　　***get rid of*** 丟棄

appropriate〔ə'proprɪɪt〕*adj.* 適當的

place〔ples〕*v.* 放置

collector〔kə'lɛktɚ〕*n.* 收集者

recycling〔ri'saɪklɪŋ〕*adj.* 回收的

effective〔ɪ'fɛktɪv〕*adj.* 有效的

meet〔mit〕*v.* 迎接；與…相遇

specific〔spɪ'sɪfɪk〕*adj.* 特定的

price〔praɪs〕*n.* 代價

pleasant〔'plɛzn̩t〕*adj.* 令人愉快的；舒適的

口説能力測驗詳解

PART 1 回答問題

1. **To take the test, how did you get to this classroom?**
   爲了考這個試，你是怎麼到這間教室的？

【回答範例1】

I took a bus from my home to the MRT.

After I got off the MRT, I transferred to another bus.

After I got off, I walked to where the test would take place.

A funny thing happened on the way.

I got lost, and I asked a passerby if he knew the way.

He said he did, and he directed me to the classroom.

I told him that it was unnecessary to walk me all the way.

He just replied: "Oh, it's okay.

I'm the test monitor."

【中文翻譯】

我從我家搭公車到捷運站。

我下了捷運後,再轉乘另一班公車。

下車後,我走到舉行考試的地點。

在路上發生了一件有趣的事。

我迷路了,我問一位路人是否知道路。

他說他知道,然後指示我到教室的路。

我告訴他不必一路陪我走。

他就回答:「喔,沒關係。

我是監考員。」

**

take a test 參加考試　　*get off* 下 (車)

transfer 〔 træns'fɝ 〕 *v.* 轉乘

take place 舉行

funny 〔 'fʌnɪ 〕 *adj.* 好笑的;有趣的

get lost 迷路

passerby 〔 'pæsə'baɪ 〕 *n.* 過路人

direct 〔 də'rɛkt 〕 *v.* 給…指路

walk sb. 陪某人走　　*all the way* 一路上

monitor 〔 'mɑnətə 〕 *n.* 監視員

【回答範例2】

Getting to the classroom was a nightmare.

I was really nervous the night before,
　　so I didn't sleep well.

In fact, I woke up at least four times
　　during the night.

Of course, not having slept well made
　　me wake up late.

When I woke up, I was shocked to
　　see there was just half an hour left
　　before the test!

I hurried out of bed and ran straight
　　outside.

Needless to say, I took a cab.

The ride couldn't have been slower.

However, I made it to the classroom
　　on time, and that's what counts.

【中文翻譯】

來到這間教室是一場惡夢。

前一晚我真的很緊張，所以我沒睡好。

事實上，在夜裡我至少醒來四次。

當然，沒睡好使我睡過頭。

當我起床的時候，知道離考試只剩半小時，

讓我很震驚！

我趕緊從床上起來，然後直接跑出門。

不用說，我搭了計程車。

車子真是慢到不能再慢了。

不過，我準時到了教室，這才是重點。

** ───────────────

get to 到達

nightmare〔'naɪt,mɛr〕*n.* 惡夢

wake up 醒來　　***at least*** 至少

shocked〔ʃɑkt〕*adj.* 震驚的

see〔si〕*v.* 知道　　hurry〔'hɝɪ〕*v.* 匆忙

straight〔stret〕*adv.* 直接地

cab〔kæb〕*n.* 計程車　　ride〔raɪd〕*n.* 搭乘

on time 準時　　count〔kaʊnt〕*v.* 重要

2. **Have you ever made any special achievements during your school days? Give one example.**
   在學生時代，你曾經有過任何特殊的成就嗎？舉一個例子。

【回答範例 1】

I wasn't an outstanding student during my
   school days.

I was mediocre not only in my studies but also
   in athletics.

However, I was probably the most famous person
   in my high school for a special reason.

In high school, I liked a girl in the next class
   very much.

It was a secret crush, but soon everyone in my
   class found out.

They soon came up with a so-called
   "fail-proof plan."

During a school-wide meeting, I ran onto the stage
   and shouted out my affections for her.

It was a stunt to catch her attention, but she was
   actually quite embarrassed.

In the end, I didn't even get to talk to her, but I
   became the most famous person in school
   because of her.

【中文翻譯】

我在學生時代不是一位傑出的學生。

我不只學業普通，連運動也是。

不過，因為一個特殊的理由，我可能是我那所高中裡面最出名的人。

高中時，我非常喜歡隔壁班的一個女生。

這是暗戀，但很快地我班上的每個人都發現了。

他們馬上想出一個所謂的「防失敗計畫」。

在全校集會上，我跑到台上，然後大聲說出我對她的愛。

這是要引起她注意的行為，但她其實相當尷尬。

最後，我甚至沒能跟她說話，但是我因為她而成為學校最出名的人。

**　——————————

achievements〔ə'tʃivmənts〕*n. pl.* 成就

school days 學生時代

outstanding〔'aʊt'stændɪŋ〕*adj.* 傑出的

mediocre〔'midɪ,okə〕*adj.* 普通的

studies〔'stʌdɪz〕*n. pl.* 學業　　athletics〔æθ'lɛtɪks〕*n. pl.* 運動

crush〔krʌʃ〕*n.* 迷戀　　***come up with*** 提出；想出

so-called〔'so'kɔld〕*adj.* 所謂的

fail-proof〔'fel'pruf〕*adj.* 防失敗的

school-wide〔'skul'waɪd〕*adj.* 全校性的

meeting〔'mitɪŋ〕*n.* 集會　　stage〔stedʒ〕*n.* 講台

affection〔ə'fɛkʃən〕*n.* 愛慕

stunt〔stʌnt〕*n.* 引人注意的行動

catch〔kætʃ〕*v.* 吸引（注意）

【回答範例 2】

Dodge ball is without a doubt the number
　　one elementary school sport.

Like my fellow classmates and friends,
　　I was crazy about it.

We'd play after school until it was dark.

I was quite good at dodge ball, and I was
　　probably the best player in school.

Because I was so good, my teacher
　　decided to form a dodge ball team
　　with me as the captain.

I was thrilled, and of course I took up
　　the position.

As I look back now, I think my teacher
　　didn't really care that much about
　　forming a team.

He did it just to give me a sense of
　　accomplishment.

I thank him for that, because to this day,
　　it's still an achievement I treasure.

【中文翻譯】

躲避球無疑是國小運動中的第一名。

跟我的同學和朋友一樣，我也很喜歡躲避球。

我們放學後會玩到天黑。

我相當擅長打躲避球，而且我大概是學校裡面
打得最好的。

因為我很擅長，所以我的老師決定組一個躲避
球隊，由我當隊長。

我很興奮，而且我當然擔任了這個職位。

現在回想起來，我認為我的老師並不是真的那
麼在乎組一個球隊。

他這麼做只是想讓我有成就感。

我很感謝他這麼做，因為直到今天，這仍然是
我很珍惜的成就。

**　****

dodge ball 躲避球　　*without a doubt* 無疑地

fellow〔ˈfɛlo〕*adj.* 同輩的　　*be crazy about* 很熱愛

be good at 擅長　　form〔fɔrm〕*v.* 組成

captain〔ˈkæptən〕*n.* 隊長

thrilled〔θrɪld〕*adj.* 興奮的　　*take up* 開始做；承擔

look back 回顧；回想　　*care about* 關心；在乎

accomplishment〔əˈkɑmplɪʃmənt〕*n.* 成就

treasure〔ˈtrɛʒɚ〕*v.* 珍惜

3. **Are you a sports lover? Give an example of one or two sports that you like.**

你是個運動愛好者嗎？舉出一個或兩個你喜歡的運動。

【回答範例 1】

I'm a sports maniac.

I'm always ready to go on the field
and play.

If I had to choose my favorite sport,
it would definitely be soccer.

Soccer is the most popular sport in
the world.

It's a game of stamina, speed, and skill.

It's also a game of passion and
sportsmanship.

I love soccer because it's so exciting
and easy to play.

All you need is a ball, and you're
ready to go.

I play it and watch it whenever I have
a chance.

【中文翻譯】

我是個運動狂。

我總是準備好要上場打球。

如果我必須選出我最喜歡的運動，那一定是

足球。

足球是世界上最受歡迎的運動。

它是一場耐力、速度和技巧的比賽。

它也是一場充滿熱情和運動家精神的比賽。

我愛足球，因為踢足球很刺激也很簡單。

你只需要一顆球，你就可以開始踢了。

只要我一有機會，我就會踢足球和看足球

比賽。

** ————————————————

maniac〔'menɪˌæk 〕*n.* …迷；…狂

go on 登上　　field〔 fild 〕*n.* 球場

definitely〔'dɛfənɪtlɪ 〕*adv.* 一定

soccer〔'sɑkɚ 〕*n.* 足球

stamina〔'stæmənə 〕*n.* 耐力

passion〔'pæʃən 〕*n.* 熱情

sportsmanship〔'sportsmənˌʃɪp 〕*n.* 運動家精神

go〔 go 〕*v.* 開始行動

【回答範例2】

Most people think that sports need to be
    played on the field.

There needs to be physical contact
    and pouring sweat.

However, for skinny little guys like me,
    it's not that appealing.

That's why I fell in love with pool.

There's no sun, no sweat, and no big
    muscular man trying to run me down.

It's just me, my cue stick, and the
    pool table.

Outdoor sports require muscles and power,
    whereas pool requires brains and skills.

Calculating the strength with which to hit
    the ball is very challenging.

That's why it's my favorite sport.

【中文翻譯】

大部分的人認為必須在球場上才能運動。

必須有肢體接觸以及不斷地流汗。

然而，對於像我這種瘦小的人來說，那一點也
不吸引人。

這就是我愛上撞球的原因。

沒有陽光、沒有汗水，沒有高大強壯的男士在
努力追趕我。

只有我、我的球桿，和撞球台。

戶外運動需要肌肉和體力，然而撞球需要頭腦
和技巧。

計算用多少力量來撞球是非常有挑戰性的。

這就是為什麼它會是我最喜愛的運動。

**─────────────

physical〔'fɪzɪkl̩〕*adj.* 身體的

contact〔'kɑntækt〕*n.* 接觸　　pour〔por〕*v.* 不斷流出

sweat〔swɛt〕*n.* 汗　　skinny〔'skɪnɪ〕*adj.* 很瘦的

guy〔gaɪ〕*n.* 人；傢伙　　appealing〔ə'pilɪŋ〕*adj.* 吸引人的

fall in love with 愛上

pool〔pul〕*n.* 花式撞球；美式撞球（= *billiards*〔'bɪljɚdz〕）

muscular〔'mʌskjələ〕*adj.* 強壯的

run *sb.* ***down*** 追趕某人　　cue〔kju〕*n.*（撞球用的）球桿

stick〔stɪk〕*n.* 棍子；（撞球的）球桿

whereas〔hwɛr'æz〕*conj.* 然而

calculate〔'kælkjə,let〕*v.* 計算　　strength〔strɛŋθ〕*n.* 力量

challenging〔'tʃælɪndʒɪŋ〕*adj.* 有挑戰性的

4. **Do you have a habit of doing chores at home?**
   What chores do you do?

   你在家有做家事的習慣嗎？你會做哪些家事？

【回答範例1】

I do a lot of chores at home, because
　　both my parents have to work.

I usually split the work with my sister.

I see it as a way to relieve my parents of
　　their pressure after a long day at work.

During the weekdays, I'm in charge of
　　keeping the bathroom clean and tidy.

I also take out the trash every night.

During the weekends, I get to take a break.

I think it's a good idea for everyone in
　　the family to do chores.

It fosters independence.

When we grow up and move out, we will
　　know how to take care of ourselves.

【中文翻譯】

我在家會做很多家事，因為我的父母都要上班。

我通常是和姊姊分攤家事。

我認為它是在父母漫長的一天工作後，減輕他們
壓力的方法。

平日我都負責保持浴室乾淨及整齊。

我每天晚上也要倒垃圾。

週末我就能休息。

我覺得讓家裡的每個人都做家事是個好主意。

它能培養獨立。

當我們長大搬出去住時，我們就會知道要如何
照顧自己。

** ─────────────────────

habit〔'hæbɪt〕n. 習慣　　chores〔tʃɔrz〕n. pl. 雜事

split〔splɪt〕v. 分攤　　relieve〔rɪ'liv〕v. 減輕

relieve sb. of~　減輕某人的~

weekday〔'wik͵de〕n. 平日

in charge of 負責　　tidy〔'taɪdɪ〕adj. 整齊的

take a break 休息一下　　foster〔'fɔstɚ〕v. 培養

independence〔͵ɪndɪ'pɛndəns〕n. 獨立

take care of 照顧

【回答範例 2】

I don't do chores at all.

Don't get me wrong; I'm not the type
　of kid who hates helping out.

It's my mom who doesn't want me to
　do chores.

My parents put high emphasis on grades,
　so they wish for me to study whenever
　I can.

They think making me do chores is a
　waste of my time.

So they do all the chores, and expect
　me to study hard in return.

Sometimes, I'm jealous of kids who
　have to do chores.

But my friend jokingly told me that I
　have chores, too.

My chore is to study hard.

【中文翻譯】

我完全不做家事。

不要誤會我；我不是那種討厭幫忙的小孩。

是我媽媽不想讓我做家事。

我父母很重視成績，所以他們希望只要我能
唸書時就唸書。

他們認為叫我做家事是在浪費我的時間。

所以他們會做所有的家事，期待我努力用功
作為回報。

有時候，我會羨慕必須做家事的小孩。

但是我的朋友開玩笑地說，我也有家事。

我的家事就是努力用功。

** ────────────────

get sb. wrong 誤會某人

type〔taɪp〕*n.* 類型　　*help out* 幫忙

emphasis〔ˈɛmfəsɪs〕*n.* 強調；重視

put emphasis on 對…重視

grade〔gred〕*n.* 成績

wish for 希望；想要　　*in return* 作為回報

jealous〔ˈdʒɛləs〕*adj.* 嫉妒的；羨慕的

jokingly〔ˈdʒokɪŋlɪ〕*adv.* 開玩笑地

5. **If you could change anything about your room, what would you change?**

如果你可以改變你房間的任何東西，你會做什麼改變？

【回答範例 1 】

If I could change anything about my room,
    I'd start with the walls.

I like bright colors, so I'd change my
    wallpaper to bright blue.

I'd also put up posters of my favorite bands.

My bookshelf is also kind of old.

I want to buy a new one, and put it beside
    my bed.

I like to read before I sleep, so it'd be more
    convenient that way.

Last but not least, I'd like to get rid of
    the carpet.

It's kind of hard to clean carpet stains,
    so I want to change it to a wooden floor.

It would make the room cooler during
    summer, too.

【中文翻譯】

如果我可以改變我房間的任何東西，我會從
牆壁開始。
我喜歡明亮的顏色，所以我會把我的壁紙換
成蔚藍色。
我也會貼一些我最喜歡的樂團的海報。

我的書架也有一點舊。
我想買一個新的，然後將它放在我的床邊。
我喜歡在睡前閱讀，所以那樣會比較方便。

最後一項要點是，我想把地毯丟掉。
清除地毯的污漬有點困難，所以我想換成
木頭地板。
這樣也會使房間在夏天的時候比較涼爽。

** ————————————————————

wallpaper〔ˈwɔlˌpepɚ〕 *n.* 壁紙　　***bright blue*** 蔚藍
put up 張貼　　poster〔ˈpostɚ〕 *n.* 海報
bookshelf〔ˈbʊkˌʃɛlf〕 *n.* 書架　　***kind of*** 有一點
last but not least 最後但不是最不重要的；最後一項
　　要點是
get rid of 丟棄　　carpet〔ˈkɑrpɪt〕 *n.* 地毯
hard〔hɑrd〕 *adj.* 困難的　　stain〔sten〕 *n.* 污漬
wooden〔ˈwʊdn̩〕 *adj.* 木製的

【回答範例 2】

I would like my own bathroom attached
to my room.

Because there are a lot of people in my
family, the line for the bathroom can
get pretty long sometimes.

If I had a bathroom of my own, I'd be
able to use it whenever I wanted.

Secondly, I would get a larger wardrobe.

My collection of clothes has grown so
rapidly that I have to fold them and
place them wherever I can find space.

It would be much more convenient if
I had a bigger wardrobe.

Finally, I'd like a larger window.

The one I have is rather small, so my
room is kind of dark and gloomy.

I want a bright and sunny room,
where I can keep plants.

【中文翻譯】

我想在我的房間裝一個自己的廁所。
因為我家有很多人，有時排隊要上廁所的人
會很多。
如果我有自己的廁所，只要我想用的時候就能用。

其次，我要買一個大一點的衣櫃。
我的衣服累積得太快，以致於我必須把它們
摺起來，能在哪裡找到空間就放哪裡。
如果我有大一點的衣櫃就會方便多了。

最後，我想要大一點的窗戶。
我的窗戶相當小，所以我的房間有點昏暗。
我想要一個明亮而且陽光充足的房間，我可以把
植物放在那裡。

** ─────────────────

bathroom〔ˈbæθˌrum〕n. 浴室；廁所
attach〔əˈtætʃ〕v. 使附著；使附屬
be attached to 附屬於
wardrobe〔ˈwɔrdˌrob〕n. 衣櫃
collection〔kəˈlɛkʃən〕n. 收藏
grow〔gro〕v. 成長　　rapidly〔ˈræpɪdlɪ〕adv. 迅速地
fold〔fold〕v. 摺疊　　gloomy〔ˈglumɪ〕adj. 昏暗的
sunny〔ˈsʌnɪ〕adj. 陽光充足的
keep〔kip〕v. 放（= *put*）

6. **Your two best friends are having a fight. Convince them to make up.**

你的兩個最好的朋友在吵架。說服他們和好。

【回答範例】

John, I know you are mad at Eric for
   yelling at you.

But he did so because you were breaking
   the school rules.

He didn't want you to be punished.

Eric, I know you care about John.

He was doing something wrong,
  and you tried to correct him.

But next time you should tell him in a
   better way, because no one likes to
   be yelled at.

I believe we are all still friends.

You guys just flew into a temper.

Why don't you make up and talk to
   each other again?

【中文翻譯】

約翰，我知道你在氣艾瑞克對你大吼。

但是他這麼做，是因為你違反校規。

他不希望你被處罰。

艾瑞克，我知道你關心約翰。

他做錯事，而你想要糾正他。

但是下次你應該用比較好的方式告訴他，因為沒

有人喜歡被大吼。

我相信我們都還是朋友。

你們只是在發脾氣。

為什麼你們不和好，再和彼此說話？

** ────────────────

fight〔faɪt〕 *n.* 打架；爭吵

convince〔kən'vɪns〕 *v.* 說服

make up 和好　　mad〔mæd〕 *adj.* 生氣的

yell〔jɛl〕 *v.* 吼叫　　break〔brek〕 *v.* 違反

punish〔'pʌnɪʃ〕 *v.* 處罰　　***care about*** 關心

correct〔kə'rɛkt〕 *v.* 糾正　　***you guys*** 你們

fly into a temper 發脾氣

7. **Celebrities' scandals and rumors are favorites of gossip magazines. What do you think are their effects on the society?**
名人的醜聞和謠言是八卦雜誌的最愛。你認為它們對社會有什麼影響？

【回答範例】

> *Everybody* likes to see scandals.
> *Everybody* wants to know about the lives
> 　of celebrities.
> It's gotten to the point where celebrities have
> 　no private life.
>
> Of course, it might be fun for some to see people
> 　who they thought were so high above them fall.
> However, the frantic search for news and rumors
> 　has severely damaged the journalism industry.
> The human right of privacy has also been
> 　severely violated.
>
> Princess Diana's death is a perfect example
> 　of tabloid excess.
> Digging for exclusive news hurts not only the
> 　celebrities, but also the society.
> So I think we should not support this kind of
> 　behavior.

【中文翻譯】

大家都喜歡看醜聞。

大家都想知道名人的生活。

直截了當地說，就是名人沒有私生活。

當然，對某些人而言，看那些他們以為高高在上的

人跌落谷底很有趣。

然而，這種瘋狂尋找新聞和謠言的行為，已經嚴重

損壞了新聞業。

人們的隱私權也受到嚴重的侵犯。

戴安娜王妃的死就是小報做得太過火的典型例子。

挖掘獨家新聞傷害的不只有名人，也傷害到社會。

所以我認為我們不應該支持這種行為。

**　―――――――――――

celebrity〔səˈlɛbrətɪ〕n. 名人　　scandal〔ˈskændḷ〕n. 醜聞
rumor〔ˈrumə〕n. 謠言　　gossip〔ˈgɑsəp〕n. 花邊新聞
get to the point 提到要點；直截了當地說
private〔ˈpraɪvɪt〕adj. 私人的
fall〔fɔl〕v.（聲望）下跌；評價下降
frantic〔ˈfræntɪk〕adj. 瘋狂的　　severely〔səˈvɪrlɪ〕adv. 嚴重地
journalism〔ˈdʒɝnḷˌɪzəm〕n. 新聞界
industry〔ˈɪndəstrɪ〕n. 產業　　privacy〔ˈpraɪvəsɪ〕n. 隱私
violate〔ˈvaɪəˌlet〕v. 侵犯
tabloid〔ˈtæblɔɪd〕n.（以轟動性報導為特點的）小報
excess〔ɪkˈsɛs〕n. 過度；過分　　dig〔dɪg〕v. 挖掘
exclusive〔ɪkˈsklusɪv〕adj. 獨家的

8. **There are many kinds of music. What type of music do you listen to? Who's your favorite artist?**

音樂的種類有很多。你會聽什麼類型的音樂？誰是你最喜愛的藝術家？

【回答範例 1】

I listen to different types of music, but
    my favorite genre has to be hip hop.

There is a special energy to it.

It's an addictive type of music.

The beat is hard and fast.

Some lyrics are funny, and some
    are serious.

The music varies from slow ballads to
    upbeat dance tracks.

My favorite hip-hop artist is Eminem.

He is one of the best rappers in the world.

I like him because he writes good lyrics
    and has a soft and sensitive side
    underneath his tough looks.

【中文翻譯】

我會聽不同種類的音樂，但我最喜愛的類型是嘻哈。

它有一種獨特的力量。

它是會讓人上癮的音樂類型。

節奏強烈而且快速。

有些歌詞很有趣，而有些很嚴肅。

音樂從節奏緩慢的情歌到快樂的舞曲都有。

我最喜歡的嘻哈歌手是阿姆。

他是全世界最棒的饒舌歌手之一。

我喜歡他，因為他會寫很棒的歌詞，而且在他強壯

的外表下有溫柔敏感的一面。

** ————————

artist〔'ɑrtɪst〕n. 藝術家　　genre〔'ʒɑnrə〕n. 類型

hip hop〔'hɪp,hɑp〕n. 嘻哈【1980 年代源起於美國城市黑人青

　少年的一種文化，其特色為霹靂舞、牆上塗鴉和節奏強烈的音樂】

addictive〔ə'dɪktɪv〕adj. 使人上癮的

beat〔bit〕n. 拍子　　hard〔hɑrd〕adj. 激烈的

lyrics〔'lɪrɪks〕n. pl. 歌詞　　vary〔'vɛrɪ〕v. 改變；變化

ballad〔'bæləd〕n. 情歌　　upbeat〔'ʌp,bit〕adj. 快樂的

track〔træk〕n. 音軌；歌曲　　rapper〔'ræpɚ〕n. 饒舌歌手

soft〔sɔft〕adj. 溫柔的　　sensitive〔'sɛnsətɪv〕adj. 敏感的

underneath〔,ʌndɚ'niθ〕prep. 在…之下

tough〔tʌf〕adj. 強壯的

【回答範例 2】

　　Classical music has always been my favorite.

　　I've been taking violin and piano lessons
　　　　since 1st grade.

　　This has given me the skill to fully appreciate
　　　　a good song when I hear one.

　　My favorite composers include Mozart,
　　　　Beethoven, and Vivaldi.

　　Not only do I love listening to their works,
　　　　I like playing them, too.

　　It's quite a different experience to hear
　　　　classics played by your own hands.

　　Classical music, in my opinion, is indeed
　　　　"classical."

　　Simply put, it's music for the ages.

　　No one will ever forget amazing works
　　　　of art such as "Für Elise" and "The
　　　　Four Seasons."

【中文翻譯】

古典音樂一直是我的最愛。

我從一年級就開始上小提琴和鋼琴課。

這讓我能夠在聽到一首好曲子的時候，能充分地欣賞它。

我最喜愛的作曲家包括莫札特、貝多芬和韋瓦第。

我不只愛聽他們的作品，我也喜歡演奏。

聽你自己雙手所彈奏出的經典作品，是很不一樣的體驗。

古典音樂，依我看來，是眞正的「經典」。

簡言之，它是適合各個時代的音樂。

任何人都不會忘記這些驚人的藝術作品，例如「給愛麗絲」和「四季」。

** ——————————————————

classical〔ˋklæsɪkl̩〕 *adj.* 古典的；經典的

grade〔gred〕*n.* 年級　　skill〔skɪl〕*n.* 技能；本事

appreciate〔əˋpriʃɪͺet〕*v.* 欣賞

composer〔kəmˋpozɚ〕*n.* 作曲家

Mozart〔ˋmozɑrt〕*n.* 莫札特【1756-1791，奧地利作曲家】

Beethoven〔ˋbetovən〕*n.* 貝多芬【1770-1827，德國作曲家】

Vivaldi〔vɪˋvɑldɪ〕*n.* 韋瓦第【1675-1741，義大利小提

　　琴家、作曲家】　　classic〔ˋklæsɪk〕*n.* 經典作品

indeed〔ɪnˋdid〕*adv.* 眞正地　　***simply put*** 簡言之

age〔edʒ〕*n.* 時代　　***work of art*** 藝術品

PART 2 看圖敘述

1. **What is this place?** 這是什麼地方？

   This is a cybercafé or an Internet café. 這是一間網咖。

2. **What do you suppose the people in the picture are doing?** 你認為照片裡的人在做什麼？

   The people in the picture are playing online games. I can see that there are games on several of the screens and the people are wearing headsets.

   照片裡的人在玩線上遊戲。我可以看到遊戲出現在好幾台螢幕上，而且大家都戴著耳機。

** ——————————————————

cybercafé ('saɪbəkə'fe) *n.* 網咖

café (kə'fe) *n.* 咖啡店　　online ('ɑn,laɪn) *adj.* 線上的

screen (skrin) *n.* 螢幕　　headset ('hɛd,sɛt) *n.* 雙耳式耳機

3. **Have you ever been to such a place? If not, why not?**

你曾經去過這樣的地方嗎？如果沒有，爲什麼不去？

【回答範例 1】

Yes, I sometimes go to such places to play online games. It's a good way to relax after a hard day, and it's also a challenge to try to improve my score.

有，我有時會去這種地方玩線上遊戲。在辛苦的一天之後，這會是一個放鬆的好方法，而且這也是想要使自己分數進步的挑戰。

【回答範例 2】

No, I have never been to such a place. For one thing, I don't have to go to this kind of place because I have my own computer at home. I can do what I like at home. For another, I don't like to play online games. I am not interested in games at all.

不，我不曾去過這種地方。首先，我不需要去這種地方，因爲我在家有我自己的電腦。我在家可以做自己喜歡做的事。其次，我不喜歡玩線上遊戲。我對遊戲一點興趣也沒有。

**　——————————————————

challenge〔ˈtʃælɪndʒ〕 *n.* 挑戰
improve〔ɪmˈpruv〕 *v.* 改善　　score〔skor〕 *n.* 分數
for one thing 首先　　*for another* 其次

4. **If you still have time, please describe the picture in as much detail as you can.**

如果你還有時間，請儘可能描述照片中的細節。

This is a picture of an Internet café or Internet shop. The people in this place are playing games. They wear headsets because some of the games are quite loud, and they are sitting in comfortable chairs because they will probably be there for a long time. The Internet shop is big and very crowded. It looks as though every seat is taken. Interestingly, all of the customers are male.

這是一張網咖的照片。這個地方的人都在玩遊戲。他們戴著耳機，因為有些遊戲會很大聲，他們坐在舒服的椅子上，因為他們可能會在那裡待很久。這間網咖很大又很擁擠。看起來好像每個位子都有人坐了。有趣的是，所有的顧客都是男性。

** ─────────────────────

crowded〔'kraʊdɪd〕*adj.* 擁擠的　　male〔mel〕*adj.* 男性的

PART 3　申述題 ●──────────

Do you read newspapers every day? What section(s) do you like best and what section(s) aren't you interested in? Please explain.

你會每天看報紙嗎？你最喜歡哪一版？你對哪一版沒興趣？請說明。

【回答範例】

　　I try to read the newspaper every day, but there are some days when I just don't have time. I usually read the headlines first and, if a story sounds interesting, I will quickly read it. I also read the sports and entertainment sections. I like those parts of the paper best because they are interesting and not so serious. I also read the technology section, which appears once a week, because I like to keep up with the latest trends. I can't afford to buy the latest gadgets, but I like to talk about them with my friends.

　　I don't really like to read about politics but I will read the local news if there is something in it that relates to my life. Otherwise, I find it kind of boring. I also don't care for the business section because I am still a student. It doesn't have much to do with my life right now. But I think in the future I will be more interested in these sections.

【中文翻譯】

　　我會試著每天看報紙，但是有幾天我眞的沒有時間。我通常會先看標題，如果報導聽起來很有趣，我會快速地閱讀它。我也看體育版和娛樂版。我最喜歡報紙的這些部分，因爲它們很有趣，而且沒有那麼嚴肅。我也會看科技版，它每週會出現一次，因爲我想跟上最新的趨勢。我買不起最新的酷炫的小玩意，但是我喜歡和我的朋友討論它們。

　　我其實不喜歡看政治，但是我會看地方新聞，如果裡面有和我的生活相關的事的話。否則，我會覺得它有點無聊。我也不喜歡商業版，因爲我還是個學生。它和我現在的生活沒有太大的關係。但是我認爲未來我會對這些版比較有興趣。

** —————————————————

　　headline〔'hɛd,laɪn〕n. 標題

　　sports〔sports〕adj. 運動的

　　entertainment〔,ɛntɚ'tenmənt〕n. 娛樂

　　section〔'sɛkʃən〕n. (報紙、雜誌的)版

　　technology〔tɛk'nɑlədʒɪ〕n. 科技

　　keep up with 跟上

　　latest〔'letɪst〕adj. 最新的　　trend〔trɛnd〕n. 趨勢

　　gadget〔'gædʒɪt〕n. 設計精巧的小機械；酷炫的小玩意

　　politics〔'pɑlə,tɪks〕n. 政治

　　local〔'lokl̩〕adj. 當地的；地方的

　　relate to 和…有關　　***care for*** 喜歡

　　have to do with 和～有關

 全民英語能力分級檢定測驗
中高級寫作能力測驗答案紙

座位號碼：＿＿＿＿＿＿＿＿＿＿   試題別：＿＿＿＿＿＿＿

第一部份請由本頁第 1 行開始作答，請勿隔行書寫。第二部份請翻至第 2 頁作答。

_____

_____

_____

_____

_____

_____

_____

_____

_____

_____

_____

_____

_____

_____

_____

_____

_____

_____

_____

_____

55

60

65

70

寫作口說能力測驗 ⑦

寫作能力測驗

Part I: Chinese-English Translation (40%)

Translate the following Chinese passage into an English passage, and write your answer on the Writing Test Answer Sheet.

　　大自然是一本能教導我們有關生命本身重要課程的偉大的書。大自然賦予萬物生命；藉由它，我們學到了生命的珍貴。大自然也具有強大的毀滅力；藉由它，我們也學到了生命的殘酷。在此同時，我們還看到在這個世界上的每件事物，是如何相互依賴的。認識大自然是一種開拓心智的經驗。

Part II: Guided Writing (60%)

Write an essay of **150-180 words** in an appropriate style on the following topic. Write your answer on the Writing Test Answer Sheet.

　　You were an English major in college. You have two years of experience teaching junior high school English. Now you would like to apply to a language school for the position of an English teacher. Please write a letter of self-introduction to the head of personnel.

口説能力測驗

Please read the self-introduction sentence.

My seat number is （複試座位號碼）, and my registration number is （初試准考證號碼）.

Part I: Answering Questions

You will hear 8 questions. Each question will be spoken once. Please answer the question immediately after you hear it.

For questions 1 to 4, you will have 15 seconds to answer each question.

For questions 5 to 8, you will have 30 seconds to answer each question.

Part II: Picture Description

Look at the picture, think about the questions below for 30 seconds, and then record your answers for 1 ½ minutes.

1. What is this place?

2. What do the people in the picture do?

3. Have you ever been to such a place and done what the gentleman in the picture is doing?

4. If you still have time, please describe the picture in as much detail as you can.

Part III: Discussion

Think about your answer(s) to the question(s) below for 1 ½ minutes, and then record your answer(s) for 1 ½ minutes.

You may use your test paper to make notes and organize your ideas.

Describe one ordinary day of your life, whether you are a student or an office worker. Tell about what you normally do from morning to night and your interaction with people around you.

Please read the self-introduction sentence again.

My seat number is （複試座位號碼）, and my registration number is （初試准考證號碼）.

寫作口說能力測驗 ⑦ 詳解

寫作能力測驗詳解

PART 1 中譯英 (40%)

　　大自然是一本能教導我們有關生命本身重要課程的偉大的書。大自然賦予萬物生命；藉由它，我們學到了生命的珍貴。大自然也具有強大的毀滅力；藉由它，我們也學到了生命的殘酷。在此同時，我們還看到在這個世界上的每件事物，是如何相互依賴的。認識大自然是一種開拓心智的經驗。

1. Nature is a great book $\begin{Bmatrix} \text{that} \\ \text{which} \end{Bmatrix}$ teaches us

　　how unterpendent everything is.

important lessons about life itself.

2. Nature $\begin{Bmatrix} \text{gives everything life;} \\ \text{gives life to everything;} \\ \text{brings everything to life;} \\ \text{vitalizes everything;} \\ \text{animates everything;} \end{Bmatrix}$ $\begin{Bmatrix} \text{by means of} \\ \text{through} \end{Bmatrix}$

it, we $\begin{Bmatrix} \text{have learned} \\ \text{learn} \end{Bmatrix}$ the $\begin{Bmatrix} \text{preciousness} \\ \text{value} \end{Bmatrix}$ of life.

3. Nature also has $\left\{\begin{array}{l} \text{great,} \\ \text{strong,} \\ \text{violent,} \end{array}\right\}$ $\left\{\begin{array}{l} \text{destructive} \\ \text{devastating} \end{array}\right\}$

$\left\{\begin{array}{l} \text{power;} \\ \text{force;} \end{array}\right\}$ $\left\{\begin{array}{l} \text{by means of} \\ \text{through} \end{array}\right\}$ it, we $\left\{\begin{array}{l} \text{have also learned} \\ \text{also learn} \end{array}\right\}$

the $\left\{\begin{array}{l} \text{cruelty} \\ \text{ruthlessness} \\ \text{mercilessness} \end{array}\right\}$ of life.

4. $\left\{\begin{array}{l} \text{In the meantime} \\ \text{At the same time} \\ \text{Meanwhile} \end{array}\right\}$, we see

$\left\{\begin{array}{l} \text{how interdependent everything } \left\{\begin{array}{l} \text{in this world} \\ \text{on earth} \end{array}\right\} \text{ is.} \\ \\ \text{how everything in this world depends on } \left\{\begin{array}{l} \text{one another.} \\ \text{each other.} \\ \text{everything else.} \end{array}\right\} \end{array}\right.$

5. Knowing nature is a $\left\{\begin{array}{l} \text{mind-expanding} \\ \text{mind-broadening} \end{array}\right\}$ experience.

或 Knowing nature is an experience that $\left\{\begin{array}{l} \text{expands} \\ \text{broadens} \end{array}\right\}$

our mind.

【註】 vitalize〔'vaɪtḷ,aɪz〕v. 使有生命

　　　 animate〔'ænə,met〕v. 使有生命

　　　 by means of 藉由

　　　 preciousness〔'prɛʃəsnɪs〕n. 珍貴

　　　 destructive〔dɪ'strʌktɪv〕adj. 破壞性的；毀滅性的

　　　 devastating〔'dɛvəs,tetɪŋ〕adj. 破壞性的；毀滅性的

　　　 cruelty〔'kruəltɪ〕n. 殘酷

　　　 ruthlessness〔'ruθlɪsnɪs〕n. 冷酷

　　　 mercilessness〔'mɝsɪlɪsnɪs〕n. 殘酷

　　　 in the meantime 在這期間；同時

　　　 meanwhile〔'min,hwaɪl〕adv. 同時

　　　 interdependent〔,ɪntɚdɪ'pɛndənt〕adj. 互相依賴的

　　　 mind-expanding〔'maɪnd,ɪks'pændɪŋ〕adj. 開拓心智的

　　　 mind-broadening〔'maɪnd'brɔdṇɪŋ〕adj. 開拓心智的

　　　 expand〔ɪk'spænd〕v. 擴展

　　　 broaden〔'brɔdṇ〕v. 拓展

PART 2　引導寫作 (60%)

You were an English major in college. You have two years of experience teaching junior high school English. Now you would like to apply to a language school for the position of an English teacher. Please write a letter of self-introduction to the head of personnel.

　　你大學時是主修英文的學生。你有兩年教國中英文的經驗。現在你想應徵語言學校英文老師的職位。請寫一封自我介紹的信給人事部的主管。

【作文範例】

August 19, 2009

Dear Sir or Madam:

I am writing to you in response to your announcement of a vacancy at your language school. I am currently looking for a new teaching position and your company sounds ideal.

For the past two years, I have been employed as an English teacher at Ren Ai Junior High School. I have enjoyed working with the students and faculty there very much but I am ready for a new challenge. I would like to become more involved with curriculum development and teach a wider variety of students. I understand that the students at your school come from a variety of backgrounds and are learning English for many different purposes. I think it would be interesting to tailor courses for such diverse clients.

With a BA in English from National Taiwan University and two years of full-time work experience, I believe that I would be able to fulfill the responsibilities of a teacher at your school.

Thank for your interest in me and I look forward to hearing from you.

Faithfully yours,

Sandra Tsai

【註】 madam〔'mædəm〕n. 女士

in response to 作爲對…的回覆

announcement〔ə'naʊnsmənt〕n. 公告

vacancy〔'vekənsɪ〕n.（職位等的）空缺

currently〔'kɝntlɪ〕adv. 目前

position〔pə'zɪʃən〕n. 職位

ideal〔aɪ'diəl〕adj. 理想的

employ〔ɪm'plɔɪ〕v. 雇用

faculty〔'fækl̩tɪ〕n. 全體教職員

challenge〔'tʃælɪndʒ〕n. 挑戰

be involved in 參與

curriculum〔kə'rɪkjələm〕n. 課程

a wider variety of 更多各式各樣的

background〔'bæk͵graʊnd〕n. 背景

purpose〔'pɝpəs〕n. 目的

tailor〔'telɚ〕v. 調整

diverse〔də'vɝs , daɪ-〕adj. 各種的；各式各樣的

client〔'klaɪənt〕n. 客戶

BA 文學士（= *Bachelor of Arts*）

fulfill〔fʊl'fɪl〕v. 履行；完成

look forward to 期待

hear from 接到某人的來信；得到…的消息

Faithfully yours 敬上

口說能力測驗詳解

PART 1 回答問題

1. Do you read comics? What do you think about them?

你看漫畫嗎？你對它們有什麼看法？

【回答範例1】

Yes, I'm a comic lover.

I have hundreds of comic books.

I especially love Japanese comics, or manga.

Comics are easy-to-access books.

With pictures, it's easier to know what is
   going on.

Most people think they are for kids,
   but now more and more adults read them.

I love comics about courage and friendship.

They are the most popular type of "manga,"
   and they range from ones about ninjas to
   stories about pirates.

I get all pumped up reading them.

【中文翻譯】

是的，我是個漫畫愛好者。
我有好幾百本的漫畫。
我特別喜歡日本漫畫。

漫畫是容易懂的書。
有圖片，就比較容易了解發生了什麼事。
大部分的人認爲它們是給小孩看的，但是現在
越來越多的大人在看。

我喜歡關於勇氣和友誼的漫畫。
它們是最受歡迎的漫畫類型，漫畫情節從忍者
到海盜的故事都有。
我看漫畫時會感到很興奮。

** ─────────────────

comic〔ˋkɑmɪk〕n. 漫畫書（= comic book）
lover〔ˋlʌvɚ〕n. 愛好者
manga〔ˋmæŋgə〕n. 日本漫畫
access〔ˋæksɛs〕v. 接近；使用
easy-to-access adj. 容易了解的（= easy to understand）
go on 發生　　range〔rendʒ〕v.（範圍）包括
range from A ***to*** B 範圍從 A 到 B 都有
ninja〔ˋnɪndʒə〕n. 忍者
pirate〔ˋpaɪrət〕n. 海盜
pump〔pʌmp〕v. 使激動；使興奮
get all pumped up 變得很興奮

【回答範例 2】

I don't read comics, and I don't plan to.

I think I am past the age where I need pictures to tell me a story.

I prefer to read the text and use my own imagination.

I'm not saying the authors are not skilled.

In fact, I think it's great to be able to draw a story.

Yet most of the time they lack the skills real writers have.

The language ability of our children has gone down.

I think one reason is comics, because they don't need a good vocabulary and language skills to read them.

Kids will lose the ability to imagine on their own.

【中文翻譯】

我不看漫畫，而且我也不打算看。
我想我已經過了需要用圖片來告訴我故事的
年紀。
我比較喜歡閱讀文章並運用自己的想像力。

我不是說作者的功力不足。
事實上，我認為能夠畫出一個故事是很棒的。
但是他們往往都缺乏真正作家擁有的技巧。

我們孩子的語言能力已經下降。
我認為原因之一就是漫畫，因為他們不需要相
當多的字彙量和語言技能去閱讀它們。
小孩會失去自己想像的能力。

**　————————————————

　text〔tɛkst〕*n.* 本文；文章
　skilled〔skɪld〕*adj.* 熟練的；有技巧的
　most of the time 通常
　lack〔læk〕*v.* 缺乏
　good〔gʊd〕*adj.* 相當多的
　vocabulary〔voˈkæbjə͵lɛrɪ〕*n.* 字彙
　imagine〔ɪˈmædʒɪn〕*v.* 想像

2. What's your motto in life?

你人生的座右銘是什麼？

【回答範例1】

My motto is "Live every day like it's your last."

It doesn't mean you are going to die tomorrow.

It means that you should make the most of everything.

It's important to try hard and give it your best shot.

We don't want to look back and regret not doing something.

We want to be able to say: "I did my best and have no regrets."

This motto also means you should try new things, while you have the chance.

Try to appreciate life as if you could only live till the end of the day.

It'll make life much more pleasant.

【中文翻譯】

我的座右銘是「把每一天當作是你生命中的最後一天來過。」

這不表示你明天就要死了。

它的意思是你應該充分利用一切事物。

努力嘗試和盡你最大的努力是很重要的。

我們不希望回顧過去時，後悔沒做過某件事。

我們希望能夠說：「我盡力了，而且沒有遺憾。」

這句座右銘也表示當你有機會時，你應該嘗試新事物。

試著重視生命，好像你只能活到今天結束。

它會讓生活更加愉快。

**　——————————

motto〔'mato〕n. 座右銘

make the most of 充分利用

shot〔ʃɑt〕n. 嘗試

give it one's best shot 盡力

look back 回憶　　regret〔rɪ'grɛt〕v. n. 後悔

have no regrets 沒有遺憾

appreciate〔ə'priʃɪ,et〕v. 欣賞；重視

pleasant〔'plɛznt〕adj. 令人愉快的

【回答範例2】

My motto is "As you sow, so shall
   you reap."

I was not born with a silver spoon in
   my mouth.

Nor am I gifted in many things.

However, I make great efforts.

I take pains with whatever I do.

I believe that success is not possible
   without effort.

I know that I have no one to rely on
   but myself.

As long as I work hard enough,
   I will achieve my goal.

This belief motivates me to keep
   trying and never give up.

【中文翻譯】

我的座右銘是「種瓜得瓜，種豆得豆。」
我不是生在富有的家庭。
我也沒有很多才能。

然而，我很努力。
我盡力做任何我要做的事。
我相信不努力就不可能成功。

我知道我除了自己之外，沒有別人可以依靠。
只要我夠努力，我將會達到我的目標。
這個信念激勵我繼續努力，而且絕不放棄。

** _____

sow〔so〕v. 播種　　reap〔rip〕v. 收穫
As you sow, so shall you reap.【諺】種瓜得瓜，
　種豆得豆。　　spoon〔spun〕n. 湯匙
be born with a silver spoon in one's mouth 含著銀
　湯匙出生；生在富有的家庭
gifted〔'gɪftɪd〕adj. 有才能的
make great efforts 非常努力
take pains 努力；盡力
rely〔rɪ'laɪ〕v. 依靠 < on >
achieve〔ə'tʃiv〕v. 達到　　belief〔bə'lif〕n. 信念
motivate〔'motə,vet〕v. 激勵　　*give up* 放棄

3. **Who do you think best represents the Chinese culture? Explain why.**

你認爲誰是中國文化最佳的代表人物？請說明理由。

【回答範例 1】

Confucius would be the first choice.

No one has ever affected a culture as much as he has.

He defined many traditional values that Chinese people live by to this day.

Confucius taught the Chinese people respect, compassion, and courtesy.

He also told us about the power of knowledge.

There is a book of dialogues collected by his students and their students.

Confucius affected the Chinese culture greatly, and so did his students and followers.

He also influenced many foreign philosophers.

All in all, without him, we would have a completely different culture and history.

【中文翻譯】

孔子是第一人選。
沒有人曾經像他一樣深深影響一個文化。
他界定了許多傳統的價值觀，直到現在還是中國
人的生活準則。

孔子教導中國人尊敬、同情，和禮貌。
他也告訴我們知識的力量。
有一本對話的書，是由他的學生及其學生的學生
收集而成。

孔子對中國文化影響很大，而他的學生和信徒也
是如此。
他也影響了許多外國哲學家。
總之，如果沒有他，我們會有完全不同的文化和歷史。

**　——————————

represent〔ˏrɛprɪˋzɛnt〕v. 代表；作為…的代表人物
Confucius〔kənˋfjuʃəs〕n. 孔子【551-479 B.C.，中國的
　思想家，儒家的始祖】
define〔dɪˋfaɪn〕v. 下定義；界定
values〔ˋvæljuz〕n. pl. 價值觀
compassion〔kəmˋpæʃən〕n. 同情
courtesy〔ˋkɝtəsɪ〕n. 禮貌　　affect〔əˋfɛkt〕v. 影響
follower〔ˋfaloɚ〕n. 信徒；弟子
influence〔ˋɪnfluəns〕v. 影響　　foreign〔ˋfɔrɪn〕adj. 外國的
philosopher〔fəˋlasəfɚ〕n. 哲學家　***all in all*** 總之
completely〔kəmˋplitlɪ〕adv. 完全地

【回答範例 2】

Who united the entire Chinese continent?

Who defeated the Muslim world?

Whose army rode all the way to Europe?

The answer, if you don't know,
 is Genghis Khan.

He was the founder and ruler of the
 Mongol empire.

It was the largest empire ever.

He was a genius at military strategy,
 and used smart battlefield tactics to
 beat his enemy.

He shocked the Westerners, and is well
 known throughout the world.

He is the most famous Chinese figure,
 and certainly deserves to represent
 the Chinese culture.

【中文翻譯】

誰統一了整個中國大陸？
誰打敗了回教世界？
誰的軍隊騎馬遠征歐洲？

如果你不知道，答案就是成吉思汗。
他是蒙古帝國的創立者和統治者。
那是史上最大的帝國。

他是一個軍事戰略天才，會運用高明的戰場戰術
打敗他的敵人。
他使西方人感到震驚，而且聞名全世界。
他是最有名的中國人物，當然應該就是中國文化
的代表人物。

** ————————————

unite〔juˊnaɪt〕v. 使統一　　entire〔ɪnˊtaɪr〕adj. 整個的
continent〔ˊkɑntənənt〕n. 大陸　　defeat〔dɪˊfit〕v. 打敗
Muslim〔ˊmʌzləm〕adj. 回教的　　*all the way* 老遠地
Genghis Khan〔ˊdʒɛŋ‧gɪzˊkɑn , ˊgɛŋ-〕n. 成吉思汗【1162-1227，
　征服亞洲之大部分及歐洲東部之蒙古帝國始祖，即元太祖】
founder〔ˊfaʊndɚ〕n. 創立者　　ruler〔ˊrulɚ〕n. 統治者
Mongol〔ˊmɑŋgəl〕adj. 蒙古人的　　empire〔ˊɛmpaɪr〕n. 帝國
ever〔ˊɛvɚ〕adv. 有史以來　　genius〔ˊdʒinjəs〕n. 天才
military〔ˊmɪlə,tɛrɪ〕adj. 軍事的
strategy〔ˊstrætədʒɪ〕n. 策略；戰略
battlefield〔ˊbætḷ,fild〕n. 戰場　　tactics〔ˊtæktɪks〕n. pl. 戰術
shock〔ʃɑk〕v. 使震驚　　*well known* 有名的（= *well-known*）
figure〔ˊfɪgjɚ〕n. 人物　　certainly〔ˊsɝtṇlɪ〕adv. 當然
deserve〔dɪˊzɝv〕v. 應得

4. **Have you ever had a crush on somebody? Did you tell him or her in the end?**

你曾經非常喜歡過別人嗎？你最後有告訴他（她）嗎？

【回答範例】

I once had a crush on the girl who sat next
　　to me in cram school.

At first, all I knew was her name and school.

Once she asked me a question, and then we
　　started to chat from time to time.

She had good grades, so I used this as an
　　opportunity to ask her questions.

She always gave me real good answers,
　　although I was never really listening.

She had me looking forward to cram school.

However, I was not bold enough to tell her
　　how I felt.

I just hid my feelings for her deep down in
　　my heart.

I was afraid of being turned down or even
　　laughed at.

【中文翻譯】

我曾經非常喜歡一個女生，在補習班她坐我隔壁。

一開始，我只知道她的名字和學校。

她曾經問我一個問題，之後我們就開始常常聊天。

她的成績很好，所以我把這當作機會去問她問題。

她總是給我很好的答案，雖然我從來沒有真的
在聽。

她讓我期待去補習班。

然而，我沒有足夠的勇氣跟她說我的感覺。

我只好把我對她的感情藏在內心深處。

我怕被拒絕或甚至被嘲笑。

** ——————————————————

have a crush on sb. 迷戀某人；非常喜歡某人

cram school 補習班

from time to time 時常

grade〔gred〕*n.* 成績

look forward to 期待

bold〔bold〕*adj.* 大膽的；勇敢的

turn down 拒絕　　***laugh at*** 嘲笑

5. **Superhero comics and movies have been very popular lately. If you could have a superhuman ability, what would it be and why?**

超級英雄的漫畫和電影最近非常受歡迎。如果你可以擁有一種超能力，它會是什麼能力？為什麼？

【回答範例1】

The best superhuman ability would definitely be flying.

Flying is the equivalent of total freedom.

There is no need to worry about being late or being stuck in traffic.

You have the best view, and there's always enough space.

It takes only a couple of minutes to get from one place to another.

You could even travel abroad free!

However, I think flying will soon be a regular human ability.

Scientists will make machines that allow us to hover around freely.

By then, I will have started thinking about space travel.

【中文翻譯】

最棒的超能力一定是飛行。

飛行就相當於完全的自由。

不需要擔心遲到或塞在車陣中。

你能有最好的視野，而且永遠都有足夠的空間。

從一個地方到另一個地方只要花幾分鐘的時間。

你甚至可以免費到國外旅遊！

然而，我認為飛行不久將變成人類的一般能力。

科學家會製造出使我們能自由到處翱翔的機器。

到那時候，我將會開始想去太空旅行。

** ——————

superhero〔'supɚ͵hɪro〕*n.* 超級英雄

lately〔'letlɪ〕*adv.* 最近

superhuman〔͵supɚ'hjumən〕*adj.* 超人的；神奇的

definitely〔'dɛfənɪtlɪ〕*adv.* 一定

equivalent〔ɪ'kwɪvələnt〕*n.* 相等物

stick〔stɪk〕*v.* 使卡住；使動彈不得

view〔vju〕*n.* 視野　　abroad〔ə'brɔd〕*adv.* 到國外

free〔fri〕*adv.* 免費地

regular〔'rɛgjələ〕*adj.* 一般的

hover〔'hʌvɚ〕*v.* 盤旋；翱翔　　*space travel* 太空旅行

【回答範例 2】

Superman can fly and shoot lasers from
　　his eyes and has super strength.

Spiderman can shoot webs and swing
　　and crawl around.

But I don't want to be like them.

If I could choose a superhuman ability,
　　I would choose mind control.

With it, I would be able to have my way
　　all the time.

I would never pay a cent, never do
　　homework, and never have to listen to
　　my parents anymore.

It might sound evil, but I would use it
　　for good, too.

It would be real easy for me to catch
　　criminals.

I would just control their minds and they
　　would turn themselves in.

【中文翻譯】

超人可以飛行、從眼睛發出雷射，以及擁有特大的力量。
蜘蛛人可以射出蜘蛛網、盪來盪去和到處爬行。
但我不想跟他們一樣。

如果我可以選擇一種超能力，我會選心靈控制。
有了它，我就能夠一直隨心所欲。
我絕不會付任何一分錢、不做作業，而且不必再聽父母的話。

這聽起來或許很壞，但我也會將它用在好的方面。
對我來說，抓犯人會變得非常容易。
我只要控制他們的心靈，讓他們去自首就行了。

** ———————————————————

shoot〔ʃut〕v. 發射；射出　　laser〔'lezɚ〕n. 雷射
super〔'supɚ〕adj. 超級的；特大的
strength〔strɛŋθ〕n. 力量
web〔wɛb〕n. 蜘蛛網　　swing〔swɪŋ〕v. 搖盪
crawl〔krɔl〕v. 爬行
have one's way 隨心所欲
evil〔'ivḷ〕adj. 邪惡的；壞的
criminal〔'krɪmɛnḷ〕n. 犯人
turn oneself in 自首

6. **Brands such as LV, Prada, and Gucci are the favorites of celebrities and the rich. What are your views on brand name worship?**

像 LV、Prada 和 Gucci 這樣的品牌是名人和富人的最愛。
你對崇拜名牌有什麼看法？

【回答範例】

Some people buy brand names simply because they
   are guaranteed products that are of good quality.

However, some people buy brand names because
   they feel it is vital to their social status.

Those people are the so-called brand name
   worshippers.

These people have an obsession with buying
   these expensive brands.

They will do anything they can to get these
   products, even when they don't have the money.

It's an obsession that affects their normal life.

If you have the money to afford these luxuries,
   go ahead and do so if you like.

However, if you only make a modest amount
   of money, save it.

There are other things that are worth far more.

【中文翻譯】

有些人買名牌，只是因為它們保證是品質良好的產品。
然而，有些人買名牌，是因為他們覺得這樣對他們的社
會地位是非常重要的。
那些人就是所謂的名牌崇拜者。

這些人對於買這些昂貴的品牌很著迷。
即使當他們沒錢的時候，為了得到這些產品，要他們做
什麼都行。
對名牌的著迷會影響他們正常的生活。

如果你有錢買得起這些奢侈品，你喜歡的話就去買吧。
然而，如果你賺的錢不多，就存起來吧。
還有其他更有價值的事物。

** ————————————

celebrity〔səˋlɛbrətɪ〕*n.* 名人　　view〔vju〕*n.* 看法
brand〔brænd〕*n.* 名牌　　***brand name*** 名牌產品
worship〔ˋwɝʃəp〕*n.* 崇拜
guaranteed〔͵gærənˋtid〕*adj.* 保證的
vital〔ˋvaɪtḷ〕*adj.* 非常重要的　　status〔ˋstetəs〕*n.* 地位
so-called〔ˋsoˋkɔld〕*adj.* 所謂的
worshipper〔ˋwɝʃəpɚ〕*n.* 崇拜者
obsession〔əbˋsɛʃən〕*n.* 著迷
afford〔əˋfɔrd〕*v.* 買得起
luxury〔ˋlʌkʃərɪ〕*n.* 奢侈品　　***go ahead*** 開始；繼續
modest〔ˋmɑdɪst〕*adj.* 不太多的

7. **In an emergency, you took some money from your mom's wallet without asking. How should you explain it to her when she comes home?**

在緊急的情況下，你沒有問就從你媽媽的皮夾拿了一些錢。當她回家時，你該如何跟她解釋？

【回答範例】

Mom, I have to tell you something.

I took some money from your wallet.

Before you get angry, let me explain.

I went shopping with my friends yesterday, and I saw a jacket on sale.

I wanted it really bad, but I didn't have enough money.

If I waited till I got my allowance, the sale would be over.

So I "borrowed" some money from you.

Please forgive me, because to me it was an emergency.

I'll pay you back, with interest!

【中文翻譯】

媽，我必須告訴妳一件事。

我從妳的皮夾拿了一些錢。

在妳生氣之前，讓我解釋一下。

我昨天跟我朋友去購物，然後我看到一件夾克
在特賣。

我真的很想要，但是我沒有足夠的錢。

如果等我拿到零用錢，特賣就會結束。

所以我跟妳「借」了一些錢。

請原諒我，因為對我而言這是緊急情況。

我會還給妳，加上利息！

** ─────────────────────

emergency〔ɪˈmɝdʒənsɪ〕 *n.* 緊急情況

wallet〔ˈwɑlɪt〕 *n.* 皮夾

on sale 特價；拍賣　　bad〔bæd〕 *adv.* 很

allowance〔əˈlaʊəns〕 *n.* 零用錢

forgive〔fɚˈgɪv〕 *v.* 原諒

interest〔ˈɪntrɪst〕 *n.* 利息

8. **Give a few examples of things that foreigners may have difficulty coping with when coming to Taiwan.**
   舉幾個關於外國人來台灣時可能會難以應付的事的例子。

【回答範例】

First of all, the weather would pose
  a problem.

Many foreigners come from countries at
  high latitudes.

They are not used to the hot and especially
  humid weather.

Second, some foreigners aren't
  accustomed to the traffic here, either.

There are way too many scooters on
  the road.

Many riders weave their way through
  the traffic.

That's why a lot of foreigners I know
  don't like scooters.

They are so dangerous.

And the roads aren't as wide as in other
  countries.

Third, the languages of Mandarin and
　　Taiwanese may confuse them.

In some areas, people use Taiwanese
　　more than Mandarin.

Foreigners may not be able to understand
　　or may be puzzled by the stress or accent.

Besides, Chinese characters are especially
　　difficult for foreigners.

Each of them is a unique picture.

Foreigners find it hard to memorize or even
　　write them.

Last, foreigners also find some Chinese
　　food very weird.

Chinese people love to eat animal entrails,
　　which horrifies some foreigners.

And the famous stinky tofu scares away
　　many foreigners, too.

【中文翻譯】

首先，天氣會引起一個問題。
許多外國人來自高緯度的國家。
他們不習慣炎熱且特別潮濕的天氣。

其次，有些外國人也不習慣這裡的交通。
馬路上有太多摩托車。
許多騎士在車陣中穿梭而過。

這就是為什麼許多我認識的外國人不喜歡
摩托車。
它們太危險了。
而且道路不像其他國家的道路那樣寬闊。

＊＊ ————————————————

cope with　應付；處理
pose〔poz〕*v.* 引起
latitude〔ˈlætəˌtjud〕*n.* 緯度
be used to　習慣於
humid〔ˈhjumɪd〕*adj.* 潮濕的
be accustomed to　習慣於
way too many　太多
scooter〔ˈskutɚ〕*n.* 摩托車
weave〔wiv〕*v.* 穿梭而行；編織

第三，國語和台語可能會使他們感到困惑。

在某些地區，人們使用台語多過國語。

外國人可能沒辦法了解，或者對抑揚頓挫或腔調
感到困惑。

此外，中國字對外國人來說特別困難。

每一個字都是獨特的圖畫。

外國人覺得很難記，或甚至將它們寫出來。

最後，外國人也覺得有些中國食物很怪異。

中國人喜歡吃動物的內臟，這使一些外國人感到
恐怖。

有名的臭豆腐也嚇跑許多外國人。

＊＊————————————————

Mandarin〔ˈmændərɪn〕n. 國語

Taiwanese〔ˌtaɪwɑˈniz〕n. 台灣話

confuse〔kənˈfjuz〕v. 使困惑

puzzle〔ˈpʌzl̩〕v. 使困惑　　stress〔strɛs〕n. 重音

accent〔ˈæksɛnt〕n. 腔調

character〔ˈkærɪktə〕n.（中國）字

find〔faɪnd〕v. 覺得

memorize〔ˈmɛməˌraɪz〕v. 背誦；記憶

weird〔wɪrd〕adj. 怪異的

entrails〔ˈɛntrelz〕n. pl. 內臟

horrify〔ˈhɔrəˌfaɪ〕v. 使恐怖

stinky tofu 臭豆腐　　*scare away* 嚇跑

PART 2　看圖敘述

1. **What is this place?**　這是什麼地方？

   This is the check-in counter at an airport.

   這是機場辦理登機手續的櫃台。

2. **What do the people in the picture do?**

   照片裡的人從事什麼行業？

   The man is a traveler.　It looks as though he may be
   traveling on business.　The woman works for an airline.
   She will check his ticket and give him a boarding pass.

   這位男士是旅客。看起來好像他是要去出差。這位女士是航
   空公司的員工。她要檢查他的機票，然後給他登機證。

   **————————————————————

   check-in〔ˋtʃɛkˏɪn〕 *n.* 登機手續；住宿登記手續
   counter〔ˋkaʊntɚ〕 *n.* 櫃台　　　***on business*** 因公
   travel on business 出差　　airline〔ˋɛrˏlaɪn〕 *n.* 航空公司
   check〔tʃɛk〕 *v.* 檢查；託運　　***boarding pass*** 登機證

3. **Have you ever been to such a place and done as the gentleman in the picture is doing?**

你曾經去這樣的地方做過和照片裡的男士一樣的事嗎？

Yes, I have traveled by plane to Hong Kong. When I went to the airport, I also had to check a large suitcase and get my boarding pass.

是的，我曾經搭飛機到香港旅行。當我去到機場時，我也必須將大的手提箱託運，然後取得登機證。

4. **If you still have time, please describe the picture in as much detail as you can.**

如果你還有時間，請儘可能描述照片中的細節。

This is a picture of a large and modern airport. The man, who is wearing a business suit, is placing his suitcase on the scale. The woman will check his ticket, find a seat for him on the plane and issue a boarding pass. I can also see another woman in the background. She is not wearing a uniform, so she is probably a traveler, too.

這是一張大型且現代化的機場的照片。這位穿著西裝的男士，將手提箱放在磅秤上。這位女士會檢查他的機票、找個飛機上的座位給他，然後發給他登機證。我也可以在背景中看到另外一位女士。她沒有穿制服，所以她也可能是個旅客。

** ───────────────

suitcase〔'sut,kes〕*n.* 手提箱　　***business suit*** 西裝

place〔ples〕*v.* 放置　　scale〔skel〕*n.* 磅秤

issue〔'ɪʃu〕*v.* 發給　　uniform〔'junə,fɔrm〕*n.* 制服

PART 3　申述題

Describe one ordinary day of your life, whether you are a student or an office worker. Tell about what you normally do from morning to night and your interaction with people around you.

描述你生活中平常的一天，不論你是學生或公司職員。說說你從早到晚通常都做些什麼，以及你與周圍的人的互動。

【回答範例 1】

    I arrive at my office before nine o'clock most of the time. Sometimes I am late because of traffic. The office gets very busy by ten o'clock and at times I feel like the phone is attached to my ear! For lunch, I usually go to a nearby restaurant with my co-workers, but if we are very busy, we will get takeout and eat at our desks. I am lucky because my boss rarely asks me to work overtime, and I usually leave around five o'clock. Sometimes I meet a friend for dinner in town, and sometimes I go home to eat with my family. In the evening, I like to go shopping or see a movie, but if I am tired, I will just stay in and watch TV.

【中文翻譯】

    我通常都在九點以前到達公司。有時我會因為交通的關係而遲到。公司到十點的時候就會變得非常忙碌，有時我覺得電話好像就黏在我的耳朵上！我通常會和同事到附近的餐廳吃午餐，但如果我們很忙，我們就會買外帶的食物，然後在自己的辦公桌吃。我很幸運，因為我的老闆很少叫我加班，我通常在五點鐘左右離開公司。有時我會和朋友在市區內碰面吃晚餐，有時我會回家和家人吃飯。晚上我喜歡去購物或看電影，但是如果我很累，我就會留在家裡看電視。

** ————————————

at times 有時　　***be attached to*** 黏在
nearby〔'nɪr,baɪ〕*adj.* 附近的
co-worker〔ko'wɜkə〕*n.* 同事　　get〔gɛt〕*v.* 買
takeout〔'tek,aʊt〕*n.* 外帶的食物
rarely〔'rɛrlɪ〕*adv.* 很少　　***work overtime*** 加班
in town 在城裡；在市區　　***stay in*** 在家；不出門

【回答範例 2】

　　I am a student, so I get up early every morning. I usually leave the house before anyone else in my family has even woken up! After putting on my uniform, I grab my books and head downstairs to the bus stop. It takes me about 20 minutes to get to my school. It is important that I arrive on time because we often have a test in the first class.

　　After sitting through classes all morning, I eat lunch with my good friends. We like to gossip, so we often chat for the whole hour rather than sleep. In the afternoon I have more classes, and sometimes a PE class. I enjoy that because it is a nice break from the books and it also gives me a chance to exercise. In the evening, I often have dinner with my friends before going to a cram school. If I have no class in the evening, I will go home to eat with my family. Usually I have homework or assignments to do and tests to prepare for. After my work is all done, I like to relax by watching television or surfing the Internet for a while before I go to sleep.

【中文翻譯】

　　我是個學生，所以我每天早上都很早起床。我通常在我們家其他人甚至還沒醒來之前就出門了！穿上制服之後，我就會抓著我的書，下樓去公車站。我要花大約二十分鐘才到學校。準時到校是很重要的，因為我們通常第一堂課就有考試。

　　在上完一整個早上的課之後，我會和我的好朋友一起吃午餐。我們喜歡閒聊，所以我們通常聊一整個小時而不睡覺。下午我有更多的課，而且有時會有一堂體育課。我喜歡這樣，因為那是不用看書的快樂休息時間，而且這也讓我有機會運動。晚上去補習班之前，我常會和朋友吃晚餐。如果我晚上沒課，我會回家和家人吃飯。通常我會有功課或作業要做，有考試要準備。在我所有的作業都完成後，我喜歡在睡前看電視或上網放鬆一下。

** ─────────────────────────────

put on 穿上　　grab〔græb〕v. 緊抓
head〔hɛd〕v.（朝…）前進
downstairs〔ˋdaʊnˋstɛrz〕adv. 到樓下　　***bus stop*** 公車站
sit through 耐著性子聽完（或看完）
gossip〔ˋgɑsəp〕v. 閒聊　　chat〔tʃæt〕v. 聊天
rather than 而不是　　PE〔ˋpiˋi〕n. 體育（＝ *physical education*）
break〔brek〕n. 休息時間
assignment〔əˋsaɪnmənt〕n. 作業　　***surf the Internet*** 上網

GEPT 全民英語能力分級檢定測驗
中高級寫作能力測驗答案紙

座位號碼：＿＿＿＿＿＿＿＿＿＿＿＿＿　　　試題別：＿＿＿＿＿＿＿＿

第一部份請由本頁第 1 行開始作答，請勿隔行書寫。第二部份請翻至第 2 頁作答。

_____

_____

_____

_____

_____

_____

_____

_____

_____

_____

_____

_____

_____

_____

_____

_____

_____

_____

_____

_____

_____

寫作口説能力測驗 ⑧

寫作能力測驗

Part I: Chinese-English Translation (40%)

Translate the following Chinese passage into an English passage, and write your answer on the Writing Test Answer Sheet.

親愛的約翰和珍妮：

我和傑克將在下星期六下午三點鐘，在我們家，為我們的女兒蘇珊，舉行她十八歲的生日派對。如果你們能帶著你們的兒子彼得光臨寒舍，我們將倍感榮幸。我也邀請了蘇珊的一些好朋友一起來。蘇珊的一位朋友海倫，應我們的要求將在派對上獻唱，還有另一位朋友傑夫會以鋼琴伴奏。而如果彼得也願意將他的小提琴帶來表演一曲，那就太好了。相信我們必能賓主盡歡。我們殷切期待你們的回覆。

羅絲　敬上

Part II: Guided Writing (60%)

Write an essay of **150-180 words** in an appropriate style on the following topic. Write your answer on the Writing Test Answer Sheet.

Where do you usually shop for what you need? Do you shop at a department store or a night market, at a traditional market or a supermarket, and what do you buy in these locations? Please describe your shopping habits.

口說能力測驗

Please read the self-introduction sentence.

My seat number is (複試座位號碼), and my registration number is (初試准考證號碼).

Part I: Answering Questions

You will hear 8 questions. Each question will be spoken once. Please answer the question immediately after you hear it.

For questions 1 to 4, you will have 15 seconds to answer each question.

For questions 5 to 8, you will have 30 seconds to answer each question.

Part II: Picture Description

Look at the picture, think about the questions below for 30 seconds, and then record your answers for 1 ½ minutes.

1. What is this place?

2. What are these people doing?

3. Have you ever watched such a performance or have you ever taken part in such an activity?

4. What do you think of this kind of activity?

5. If you still have time, please describe the picture in as much detail as you can.

Part III: Discussion

Think about your answer(s) to the question(s) below for 1 ½ minutes, and then record your answer(s) for 1 ½ minutes.
You may use your test paper to make notes and organize your ideas.

Many department stores hold anniversary sales or year-end sales and, during these periods, they are always crowded with shoppers. Do you like to shop during these periods? Or do you like to shop during usual times? Please explain.

Please read the self-introduction sentence again.

My seat number is （複試座位號碼）, and my registration number is （初試准考證號碼）.

寫作口說能力測驗 ⑧ 詳解

寫作能力測驗詳解

PART 1 中譯英 (40%)

親愛的約翰和珍妮：

　　我和傑克將在下星期六下午三點鐘，在我們家，為我們的女兒蘇珊，舉行她十八歲的生日派對。如果你們能帶著你們的兒子彼得光臨寒舍，我們將倍感榮幸。我也邀請了蘇珊的一些好朋友一起來。蘇珊的一位朋友海倫，應我們的要求將在派對上獻唱，還有另一位朋友傑夫會以鋼琴伴奏。而如果彼得也願意將他的小提琴帶來表演一曲，那就太好了。相信我們必能賓主盡歡。我們殷切期待你們的回覆。

羅絲　敬上

Dear John and Jenny,

Jack and I $\left\{\begin{array}{l}\text{are going to}\\\text{will}\end{array}\right\}$ $\left\{\begin{array}{l}\text{hold}\\\text{have}\\\text{throw}\\\text{give}\end{array}\right\}$ a birthday

party for our daughter Susan for her 18th birthday at

our house at 3 p.m. next Saturday. We $\left\{\begin{array}{l}\text{would}\\\text{will}\end{array}\right\}$

$\left\{\begin{array}{l}\text{be}\\\text{feel}\end{array}\right\}$ $\left\{\begin{array}{l}\text{greatly}\\\text{highly}\end{array}\right\}$ honored if you $\left\{\begin{array}{l}\text{could}\\\text{can}\end{array}\right\}$ come (to our humble house) with your son Peter. I also

invited $\begin{Bmatrix} \text{some good friends of Susan's} \\ \text{some of Susan's good friends} \end{Bmatrix}$ (to come).

One of Susan's friends, Helen, will sing at the party

$\begin{Bmatrix} \text{at our request} \\ \text{as we requested} \end{Bmatrix}$ and another friend, Jeff, will

accompany her $\begin{Bmatrix} \text{on} \\ \text{at} \end{Bmatrix}$ the piano. If Peter agrees to

bring his violin along and perform a piece of music,

that $\begin{Bmatrix} \text{would} \\ \text{will} \end{Bmatrix}$ be $\begin{Bmatrix} \text{great.} \\ \text{wonderful.} \end{Bmatrix}$ I $\begin{Bmatrix} \text{believe} \\ \text{am convinced} \\ \text{am sure} \end{Bmatrix}$

that all of us will have $\begin{Bmatrix} \text{a great time.} \\ \text{great fun.} \end{Bmatrix}$ We eagerly

$\begin{Bmatrix} \text{look forward to} \\ \text{await} \end{Bmatrix}$ your $\begin{Bmatrix} \text{answer.} \\ \text{reply.} \end{Bmatrix}$

$\begin{Bmatrix} \text{Sincerely} \\ \text{Truly} \end{Bmatrix}$ yours,

Rose

【註】 hold〔hold〕v. 舉行　　throw〔θro〕v. 舉行

greatly〔'gretlɪ〕adv. 非常

highly〔'haɪlɪ〕adv. 非常

honored〔'ɑnəd〕adj. 感到光榮的

humble〔'hʌmbḷ〕adj. 簡陋的

request〔rɪ'kwɛst〕n. v. 要求

at one's request 應某人的要求

accompany〔ə'kʌmpənɪ〕v. 為…伴奏

piece〔pis〕n. 首

convinced〔kən'vɪnst〕adj. 確信的

eagerly〔'igəlɪ〕adv. 渴望地；熱切地

look forward to 期望

await〔ə'wet〕v. 等待；期待

sincerely〔sɪn'sɪrlɪ〕adv. 真誠地

Sincerely yours 敬上

truly〔'trulɪ〕adv. 真誠地　　*Truly yours* 敬上

PART 2 引導寫作 (60%)

Where do you usually shop for what you need? Do you shop at a department store or a night market, at a traditional market or a supermarket, and what do you buy in these locations? Please describe your shopping habits.

你通常是在哪裡買你要的東西？你會在百貨公司、夜市、傳統市場，還是超級市場買？你在這些地方買些什麼？請描述你的購物習慣。

【作文範例 1】

My Shopping Habits

When I need to buy something—whether it's clothing, food or something for my house—I usually head for a traditional market. *The main reason I go to these markets is that* the goods are much cheaper there than in modern department stores and supermarkets, but that is not the only reason. I also enjoy the atmosphere.

A traditional market tends to be noisier and messier than a modern store, but, *in my opinion*, that just makes it lively and interesting. I like to look around at the small stalls. They sell such a variety of goods that I can always find what I need as well as a few things I did not expect. More modern stores rarely surprise me with what they sell. I also feel that the food there is fresher because the vendors buy it straight from the farmers.

The vendors themselves are another reason why I like traditional markets. They are the owners of their own businesses, not just hired workers, so they really care about their customers. They will recognize regular shoppers and make them feel truly welcome. It's fun to stop and chat with them *as well as* with the neighbors I often meet there. *To sum up*, I prefer traditional markets *not just for* their lower prices, *but for* the way they make me feel part of the community.

【註】 ***head for*** 前往　　traditional〔trəˋdɪʃənḷ〕*adj.* 傳統的
goods〔gʊdz〕*n. pl.* 商品
atmosphere〔ˋætməsˌfɪr〕*n.* 氣氛　　***tend to V.*** 傾向於～
messy〔ˋmɛsɪ〕*adj.* 髒亂的　　lively〔ˋlaɪvlɪ〕*adj.* 熱鬧的
stall〔stɔl〕*n.* 攤位　　***a variety of*** 各式各樣的
as well as 以及　　rarely〔ˋrɛrlɪ〕*adv.* 很少
fresh〔frɛʃ〕*adj.* 新鮮的　　vendor〔ˋvɛndɚ〕*n.* 小販
straight〔stret〕*adv.* 直接地
recognize〔ˋrɛkəgˌnaɪz〕*v.* 認得
regular〔ˋrɛgjəlɚ〕*adj.* 定期的；固定的
shopper〔ˋʃɑpɚ〕*n.* 顧客　　***to sum up*** 總之
community〔kəˋmjunətɪ〕*n.* 社區

【作文範例 2】

My Shopping Habits

　　My favorite place to shop is a large, modern department store. I can find everything I need there from household appliances and furniture to clothes and groceries. It is truly a one-stop shopping experience, which is a convenience I highly value. I don't want to waste my time going from shop to shop or even across town looking for a special item.

　　Although some people complain that the goods in department stores are high-priced, I don't mind paying more for quality and convenience. ***Besides***, I can often find some good bargains during the storewide sales. It's also a wonderful place to browse and see all of the latest fashions, even those I can't afford.

Furthermore, I enjoy the atmosphere. It is air-conditioned, clean and brightly lit. All of these factors make a department store a pleasant place to spend some time. I often meet my friends there for a shopping spree, a meal or just a coffee. It's a great place to catch up on each other's lives or just sit and people-watch.

All things considered, a department store is a wonderful place to spend an afternoon, whether or not I really need to buy something. Shopping in one is convenient, comfortable and fun, and that is why it is my favorite place to shop.

【註】household〔'haʊs,hold〕*adj.* 家庭的
appliance〔ə'plaɪəns〕*n.* 器具;電器製品
furniture〔'fɜnɪtʃə〕*n.* 家具
grocery〔'grosərɪ〕*n.* 食品雜貨
one-stop〔'wʌnstɑp〕*adj.*（指商店）能提供各種商品,
　　一趟就能買齊的 *one-stop shopping* 一次購足
value〔'vælju〕*v.* 重視　　across〔ə'krɔs〕*prep.* 橫越
item〔'aɪtəm〕*n.* 物品　　complain〔kəm'plen〕*v.* 抱怨
high-priced〔'haɪ'praɪst〕*adj.* 高價的

bargain〔'bɑrgɪn〕*n.* 特價品
storewide〔'stor'waɪd〕*adj.* 全店的
a storewide sale 全面大減價　　browse〔braʊz〕*v.* 瀏覽
latest fashions 最新流行式樣　　afford〔ə'fɔrd〕*v.* 買得起
air-conditioned〔'ɛrkən,dɪʃənd〕*adj.* 有冷氣的
brightly lit 燈光明亮的（＝*brightly-lit*）
pleasant〔'plɛznt〕*adj.* 令人愉快的　　spree〔spri〕*n.* 狂歡
catch up on 得到關於…的消息
all things considered 從各方面考慮起來

口說能力測驗詳解

PART 1　回答問題

1. **Do you prefer Western food or Chinese food? Why?** 你比較喜歡西式食物還是中式食物？為什麼？

【回答範例 1 】

　　I love Western food.

　　Steak, burgers, sandwiches, or spaghetti.

　　You name it—I love it.

　　Western food is convenient.

　　You can get a tasty burger and milkshake

　　　at a drive thru.

　　You can buy a sandwich or hot dog from

　　　a street vendor.

　　One reason I like Western food is because

　　　of its use of cheese and sauces like ketchup.

　　I love the smell of cheese, and the taste

　　　of different sauces.

　　Western food is everywhere, so you'd better

　　　get used to it.

【中文翻譯】

我喜歡西式食物。

牛排、漢堡、三明治，或義大利麵。

你說得出來的——我都喜歡。

西式食物很方便。

你可以在得來速買到好吃的漢堡和奶昔。

你可以向街上的小販買三明治或熱狗。

我喜歡西式食物的一個理由，是因為它有用起

司和像蕃茄醬那樣的醬汁。

我喜歡起司的氣味，和不同醬汁的味道。

西式食物無所不在，所以你最好要習慣它。

** ——————————————————

steak〔stek〕n. 牛排

spaghetti〔spə'gɛtɪ〕n. 義大利麵

name〔nem〕v. 舉出

tasty〔'testɪ〕adj. 好吃的

milkshake〔'milk,ʃek〕n. 奶昔

drive thru 得來速　　vendor〔'vɛndɚ〕n. 小販

sauce〔sɔs〕n. 醬汁；調味醬

ketchup〔'kɛtʃəp〕n. 蕃茄醬

get used to 習慣

【回答範例 2 】

I like traditional Chinese food more than
　　Western food.

Chinese food is an art.

The color, the display, and the taste are
　　all top-notch.

Chinese food is also about being together,
　　a concept that runs through our entire
　　culture.

Rather than each person eating from his
　　own plate, Chinese food is for all
　　to share.

That's a big reason why Chinese restaurants
　　always seem to be quite lively.

My favorite dish is Gong-Pau Chicken.

It is a dish of chicken stir-fried with
　　different spices.

It is spicy, and I always eat a lot of rice
　　when I eat it.

【中文翻譯】

我喜歡傳統的中式食物勝過西式食物。
中式食物是一種藝術。
顏色、擺盤,和味道都是一流的。

中式食物也和團圓有關,這是一個普遍存在於
我們整個文化裡的概念。
中式食物是大家一起分享,而不是每個人吃自
己盤子裡的食物。
這就是中國餐廳總是看起來很熱鬧的一大原因。

我最喜歡的菜餚是宮保雞丁。
這是一道將雞肉和各種香料一起炒的菜餚。
它很辣,當我吃這道菜時,我總是要吃很多飯。

**─────────────────────────

traditional〔trəˋdɪʃən!〕adj. 傳統的
display〔dɪˋsple〕n. 陳列   notch〔natʃ〕n. 等;級
top-notch〔ˋtapˋnatʃ〕adj. 第一流的(= topnotch)
concept〔ˋkansɛpt〕n. 概念
run through 普遍存在於
entire〔ɪnˋtaɪr〕adj. 整個的   **rather than** 不…而~
lively〔ˋlaɪvlɪ〕adj. 熱鬧的   dish〔dɪʃ〕n. 菜餚
stir-fry〔ˋstɝˏfraɪ〕v. 快炒;炒(菜)
spice〔spaɪs〕n. 香料   spicy〔ˋspaɪsɪ〕adj. 辛辣的
rice〔raɪs〕n. 米飯

2. **Do you bargain when you go shopping? How do you do it?**

你購物時會討價還價嗎？你都怎麼做？

【回答範例】

I always bargain when I buy things at the
　　night market.

Sometimes I even bargain for gifts at the
　　department store.

If you can get more for less, why not do it?

Some people don't bargain because they
　　feel embarrassed.

But the truth is, most vendors set the
　　prices higher than they should be.

You're just wasting your money if you
　　don't make them take a few bucks off.

The trick is that you have to make them
　　think you don't really need the product.

That way, if you turn away, they will try
　　to make you stay.

That's your chance to cut down the price.

【中文翻譯】

我在夜市買東西時總是會討價還價。

有時我甚至會爲了贈品在百貨公司討價還價。

如果你可以用較少的錢買到較多東西，爲什麼
不做呢？

有些人不討價還價，因爲他們會覺得不好意思。

但事實是，大部分的小販都把價格定得比它們
該有的價格還高。

如果你不讓他們少幾塊錢，你就是在浪費自己
的錢。

秘訣是，你必須讓他們覺得你沒有眞的很需要
這個產品。

如此一來，如果你轉頭要走，他們會試著把你
留下。

這就是你殺價的機會了。

**

bargain〔ˋbɑrgɪn〕v. 討價還價

night market 夜市　　gift〔gɪft〕n. 贈品

vendor〔ˋvɛndɚ〕n. 小販

set〔sɛt〕v. 定（價）　　***take off*** 減去

buck〔bʌk〕n. 一美元　　trick〔trɪk〕n. 秘訣；詭計

turn away 走開；離開　　***cut down*** 削減

3. **What's the best present you've ever received?**
   What was the occasion?
   你曾經收過最好的禮物是什麼？是什麼時候收到的？

【回答範例】

As a kid, video games meant the world to me.

So on one Christmas, my parents bought me
　a PlayStation.

I was thrilled and so excited I couldn't sleep
　the first time I played it.

But the best present was one I got when I
　graduated from college.

My parents bought me a car.

To thank them, I took them out to dinner that
　night in my new car.

A present is a way of showing you care about
　someone.

It doesn't matter how much the present costs.

It's the thought that counts.

【中文翻譯】

小時候，電玩遊戲對我來說就是全世界。
所以在某個聖誕節，我的父母買了 PS 給我。
我很興奮，而且我第一次玩 PS 時，興奮到
無法入睡。

但是我最好的禮物，是在我大學畢業時收
到的。
我的父母買了一輛車給我。
為了感謝他們，那天晚上我用新車帶他們
出去吃晚餐。

禮物是一種表示你關心別人的方式。
禮物值多少錢並不重要。
重要的是心意。

** ————————————————

occasion〔əˈkeʒən〕 *n.* 場合；時候
video game 電玩遊戲
PlayStation 簡稱 PS，1994 年推出的電視遊樂器。
thrill〔θrɪl〕 *v.* 使興奮
graduate〔ˈgrædʒʊˌet〕 *v.* 畢業
care about 關心
thought〔θɔt〕 *n.* 思想；想法；意圖
count〔kaʊnt〕 *v.* 有重要性

4. **Which country would you like to travel to? Why?**

你想去哪個國家旅行？為什麼？

【回答範例 1】

If I had the chance, I would like to go to China.

It's the land of our ancestors, the ancient kings
　　and dragons.

It's a land of culture and history, home of the
　　greatest civilization on earth.

China is a big country, so it has diverse
　　environments.

There are canyons and mountains that launch
　　into the sky.

There are deserts, as well as rivers that run
　　deep into the sea.

Ancient Chinese capitals can be seen in
　　their old forms.

Artificial and natural wonders such as the Great
　　Wall and the Yellow River are there, too.

All in all, China is a place worth traveling to,
　　no matter which part of it you go to.

【中文翻譯】

如果我有機會的話，我想去中國。

它是我們的祖先、古代帝王和龍的國家。

它是擁有文化和歷史的國家，是世界上最偉大的文明的發源地。

中國是個廣大的國家，所以它有多種的自然環境。

有峽谷和高聳入天的山脈。

有沙漠，也有流入深海的河流。

可以看到中國古都從前的樣子。

也有人造奇觀和自然奇觀，像是萬里長城和黃河。

總之，無論你要去中國的哪個地區，中國是一個值得去旅行的地方。

**　——————————

land〔lænd〕*n.* 國家　　ancestor〔'ænsɛstə〕*n.* 祖先
ancient〔'enʃənt〕*adj.* 古代的
dragon〔'drægən〕*n.* 龍　　home〔hom〕*n.* 發源地
civilization〔,sɪvḷə'zeʃən〕*n.* 文明
diverse〔də'vɜs , daɪ-〕*adj.* 多種的
canyon〔'kænjən〕*n.* 峽谷　　launch〔lɔntʃ〕*v.* 發射
launch into the sky 高聳入天 (= *rise up into the sky*)
desert〔'dɛzət〕*n.* 沙漠　　***as well as*** 以及
capital〔'kæpətḷ〕*n.* 首都　　form〔fɔrm〕*n.* 樣子
artificial〔,ɑrtə'fɪʃəl〕*adj.* 人造的　　wonder〔'wʌndə〕*n.* 奇景
the Great Wall 萬里長城　　***all in all*** 總之

【回答範例 2】

I would love to go to the U.S.

It is the most powerful country in the world, so it has a lot of big cities.

However, it also has historical sights and natural wonders.

I would love to visit big and modern cities like New York and L.A.

I want to see how the people there live their everyday lives and how they handle living in such a big city.

Of course, I want to go shopping there, too.

National parks such as Yellowstone and Yosemite have great scenery to offer.

The Grand Canyon is one of the most exciting and breathtaking places to visit.

There's so much more I could say about going to the U.S.!

【中文翻譯】

我想去美國。

它是世界上最強的國家，所以它有許多大城市。

然而，它也有名勝古蹟和自然奇觀。

我想去遊覽現代化的大城市，像紐約和洛杉磯。

我想看那裡的人每天如何生活，以及他們如何應付

住在像這樣的大都市裡的生活。

當然，我也想去那裡購物。

像黃石和優勝美地這樣的國家公園，都有很棒的

風景。

大峽谷是最刺激且最令人驚嘆的遊覽地點之一。

關於去美國的事，我有很多可以說！

** ─────────────

sight〔saɪt〕*n.* 景點　　*historical sight* 名勝古蹟

L.A. 洛杉磯（= *Los Angeles*）　　handle〔ˈhændḷ〕*v.* 應付

Yellowstone National Park 黃石國家公園【起自美國

懷俄明州西北部至愛達荷、蒙大拿兩州的一部分，有間歇

泉、瀑布、湖、大峽谷等】

Yosemite〔joˈsɛmətɪ〕*National Park* 優勝美地國家公園

【位於美國加利福尼亞州中東部，以峽谷、瀑布、巨木林聞名】

have…to offer 有；提供　　scenery〔ˈsinərɪ〕*n.* 風景

Grand Canyon 大峽谷【指美國亞利桑那州西北部科羅拉

多河的大峽谷，為國家公園的一部分】

breathtaking〔ˈbrɛθˌtekɪŋ〕*adj.* 令人驚嘆的

5. **TV series such as CSI, Lost, and Desperate Housewives have become must-sees. Is there any TV show that you wouldn't miss? Please explain.**

像 CSI 犯罪現場、Lost 檔案和慾望師奶這樣的電視影集，已經成為必看的節目。有任何一個節目是你不會錯過的嗎？請說明。

【回答範例 1】

Reality shows have become a staple on TV
　　nowadays.
The idea of seeing people duke it out for a prize
　　in front of millions of people is really unique.
Who ever thought of it is a genius.

My current favorite reality show is one
　　about supermodels.
The host and judge of the show is
　　world-famous supermodel Tyra Banks.
I have not missed a single episode since the
　　first season.

Why do I love reality shows?
Not only do I get to watch people trying hard
　　to win a prize, I also get to see vicious
　　backstabbing and competition.
These shows really bring a new meaning to
　　the expression "Life is a cabaret."

【中文翻譯】

現在實境節目已經成為電視上的主要節目。

看大家在數百萬人面前為了獎品而拼輸贏，這個構思真的很獨特。

想到這個主意的人是個天才。

我目前最喜愛的實境節目是關於超級名模的節目。

節目主持人兼評審是世界著名的超級名模泰拉・班克斯。

從第一季開始，我連一集都沒錯過。

為什麼我愛實境節目？

我不只能看到大家盡力去贏得獎品，我也能看到惡毒的中傷和競爭。

這些實境節目真的為「人生如戲」這個說法帶來一個新的意義。

** ―――――――――――――――――――――――

series〔ˋsɪrɪz〕n. 影集

CSI 犯罪現場調查（= *Crime Scene Investigation*）

desperate〔ˋdɛspərɪt〕adj. 不顧一切的

Desperate Housewives 慾望師奶【美國影集】

must-see〔ˋmʌstˋsi〕n. 必看之物　　*reality show* 實境節目

staple〔ˋstepḷ〕n. 主要產品；主要內容　　duke〔djuk〕v. 搏鬥

duke it out 打出個輸贏　　unique〔juˋnik〕adj. 獨特的

current〔ˋkɝənt〕adj. 目前的

supermodel〔ˋsupɚ͵madḷ〕n. 超級名模　　host〔host〕n. 主持人

judge〔dʒʌdʒ〕n. 評審　　episode〔ˋɛpə͵sod〕n.（連續劇的）一集

vicious〔ˋvɪʃəs〕adj. 惡毒的

backstabbing〔ˋbæk͵stæbɪŋ〕n. 以卑鄙的手段陷害

expression〔ɪkˋsprɛʃən〕n. 說法

cabaret〔͵kæbəˋre〕n. 歌舞秀　　*Life is a cabaret.* 人生如戲。

【回答範例 2 】

CSI is my favorite TV series.

I try to watch it every time it's on.

Even if I miss it, I still have the chance
    to watch the reruns.

I love stories about law enforcement.

Watching the crime lab investigating
    all the cases is extremely exciting.

The dialogues and characters are really
    interesting.

I also learn a lot from this TV show.

Be as careful and thorough as possible
    in doing things.

Never jump to conclusions without
    enough evidence.

【中文翻譯】

CSI 犯罪現場是我最喜愛的電視影集。

每次它播映時，我都會設法收看。

即使我錯過，我還有看重播的機會。

我喜歡關於執法的故事。

看犯罪研究室調查所有的案件是非常刺激的。

對話和人物真的都很有趣。

我也從這個電視節目學到很多。

做事要儘量小心仔細。

沒有足夠的證據絕不貿然下結論。

** —————————————————

on〔ɑn〕adv. 上演中

rerun〔'ri,rʌn〕n. 重播

enforcement〔ɪn'forsmənt〕n. 執行

lab〔læb〕n. 實驗室；研究室

investigate〔ɪn'vɛstə,get〕v. 調查

extremely〔ɪk'strimlɪ〕adv. 非常

dialogue〔'daɪə,lɔg〕n. 對話

character〔'kærɪktɚ〕n. 人物；角色

thorough〔'θɝo〕adj. 徹底的；仔細周到的

jump to conclusions 遽下結論

evidence〔'ɛvədəns〕n. 證據

6. **Which traditional Chinese holiday is your favorite?**
   Please explain why.

   哪個中國傳統節日是你最喜愛的？請說明理由。

【回答範例 1】

Traditional Chinese holidays are all
　　so meaningful.
They all represent a part of the Chinese
　　culture.
My favorite has to be the Chinese New Year.

We all know that everyone comes home,
　　and kids get red envelopes.
We gamble for fun, and play with firecrackers.
However, that is not the best part.

I love Chinese New Year because of the
　　atmosphere it brings.
People become more polite and forgiving,
　　and we greet each other, even strangers.
It's the time of year when we all become
　　considerate.

【中文翻譯】

中國傳統節日都很有意義。

它們全代表中國文化的一部分。

我最喜愛的一定是農曆新年。

我們都知道，每個人會回家鄉，而且小孩會拿
到紅包。

我們賭博是爲了好玩，還會放鞭炮。

然而，這不是最棒的部分。

我愛農曆新年是因爲它帶來的氣氛。

大家變得較有禮貌和寬容，我們會問候彼此，
甚至是陌生人。

這是一年裡面我們全都會變得體貼的時候。

** ───────

represent〔ˌrɛprɪˈzɛnt〕v. 代表

red envelope 紅包

gamble〔ˈgæmbḷ〕v. 賭博　　**for fun** 爲了好玩

firecrackers〔ˈfaɪrˌkrækəz〕n. pl. 鞭炮

atmosphere〔ˈætməsˌfɪr〕n. 氣氛

forgiving〔fəˈgɪvɪŋ〕adj. 寬容的

greet〔grit〕v. 問候

stranger〔ˈstrendʒə〕n. 陌生人

considerate〔kənˈsɪdərɪt〕adj. 體貼的

【回答範例 2】

I really love Mid-Autumn Festival.

I think it is the Chinese Christmas.

Westerners have a white Christmas while
　　we have the bright full moon.

Moon Festival is also a time for reunion.

All the family members getting together
　　make the home full and complete,
　　just like the moon.

Families enjoy moon cakes and pomelos
　　together in the pure moonlight.

Besides, this is also a festival full of
　　romantic atmosphere.

I cannot help giving a sigh thinking
　　of the legend of Chang-O behind
　　the festival.

What's more interesting is that it has
　　become a holiday for barbecue, too.

【中文翻譯】

我真的很喜歡中秋節。
我認爲它是中國的聖誕節。
西方人有下雪的聖誕節，而我們有明亮的滿月。

中秋節也是團聚的時刻。
全家人都聚在一起，月圓人團圓。
全家人一起在皎潔的月光下品嚐月餅和柚子。

此外，這也是個充滿浪漫氣氛的節日。
想到這個節日背後嫦娥的傳說，我就忍不住發
出一聲嘆息。
更有趣的是，中秋節也成爲烤肉的節日。

** ————————————————

Mid-Autumn Festival 中秋節
white〔hwaɪt〕*adj.* 降雪的；積雪的
while〔hwaɪl〕*conj.* 然而　***full moon*** 滿月
Moon Festival 中秋節　reunion〔riˈjunjən〕*n.* 團聚
full and complete 毫無欠缺【在此指全家人「全員到齊」】
moon cake 月餅　pomelo〔ˈpaməlo〕*n.* 柚子
pure〔pjur〕*adj.* 潔淨的　***cannot help + V-ing*** 忍不住~
sigh〔saɪ〕*n.* 嘆息　legend〔ˈlɛdʒənd〕*n.* 傳說
barbecue〔ˈbarbɪˌkju〕*n.* 烤肉

7. **What was the best trip you've ever taken? Who was it with? Where did you go?**

    你曾經去過最棒的旅行是怎樣的？和誰一起去？你去了哪裡？

【回答範例 1】

I once went to the U.S. during summer
  vacation.

I went with my parents and relatives,
  ten people in all.

We rented a van, and toured the entire
  west coast on our own.

We saw the Grand Canyon and Yellowstone
  National Park.

We went to Las Vegas and had a lot of
  fun there.

We went to Four Corners, the only place
  where four states meet.

The entire trip took about ten days.

We came back tired yet satisfied and happy.

It was a trip to remember.

【中文翻譯】

我曾經在暑假期間去美國。

我跟父母和親戚一起去，總共十個人。

我們租了一輛廂型車，然後自己遊覽整個西

海岸。

我們參觀大峽谷和黃石國家公園。

我們去拉斯維加斯，並在那裡玩得很愉快。

我們去四州界，唯一有四個州交會的地方。

整個旅程花了大約十天。

我們疲累地回國，但是很滿足和快樂。

這是個難忘的旅行。

** ———————————————

relative〔ˈrɛlətɪv〕n. 親戚　　***in all*** 總計

van〔væn〕n. 廂型車

tour〔tʊr〕v. 漫遊；遊歷

Las Vegas〔lɑsˈvegəs〕n. 拉斯維加斯

　　【美國內華達州東南部的城市】

Four Corners 四州界【美國西南方四個州的

　　交會處，四州分別是猶他州、科羅拉多州、

　　新墨西哥州和亞利桑那州】

state〔stet〕n. 州

meet〔mit〕v. 會合；接觸

【回答範例 2】

I just can't forget my high school
　graduation trip.

We went to Alishan and Kenting.

It was a three-day, two-night trip.

Traveling with friends is always a blast.

We had fun everywhere, not just at the
　places we traveled to.

In fact, I think we had more fun on the
　bus and in the hotel.

It was the last big thing we did together
　before we graduated.

It's a special memory for all of us.

Now I just can't wait for my college
　graduation trip!

【中文翻譯】

我實在忘不了我的高中畢業旅行。

我們去阿里山和墾丁。

那是一個三天兩夜的旅行。

和朋友一起旅行總是很歡樂。

我們到處都玩得很開心，不只有在我們去旅
行的地方。

事實上，我想我們在巴士車上和旅館裡玩得
比較快樂。

這是我們畢業前一起做的最後一件大事。

對我們所有人而言，這是個特別的回憶。

現在我等不及要去我的大學畢業旅行了！

** ————————————————————————

graduation trip 畢業旅行
blast〔blæst〕*n.* 歡樂
memory〔'mɛmərɪ〕*n.* 回憶

8. **In recent years, online computer games have become more and more popular. Many young children as well as adults have become addicted. What do you think about this?** 近年來，線上電腦遊戲變得越來越受歡迎。許多年幼的小孩和大人都很入迷。你對此事有什麼看法？

【回答範例】

With the Internet boom, it's only reasonable that people
　　start looking for entertainment and friends on the Net.
Internet games provide both of these.
Not only can you play games online, you can also
　　interact with live players instead of just the computer.

However, as with all these forms of entertainment
　　and fun, people can get lost and become addicted
　　to games.
This is even worse when it's an online game, because
　　it is a fake world.
When people are addicted to this fake world, they often
　　forget about the real world.

I think it's great that people from all over the world
　　can get together and have fun.
But losing yourself in a virtual game is ridiculous.
Online games need to be controlled, or else they will
　　affect the next generation deeply.

【中文翻譯】

隨著網路的興起，大家開始在網路上尋找娛樂和朋友
是一件很合理的事。
網路遊戲兩者皆備。
你不只可以在線上玩遊戲，你也可以和活生生的玩家
互動，而不是只和電腦互動。

然而，因爲有這些種類的娛樂消遣，大家可能會迷失
並沉迷於遊戲中。
當它是線上遊戲時就更糟了，因爲它的世界是假的。
當大家沉迷於這個虛假的世界時，他們常會忘記眞實
的世界。

我認爲來自世界各地的人，可以聚在一起並玩得快樂
是件好事。
但迷失在虛擬遊戲中是很荒謬的。
線上遊戲需要被管制，否則它們會深深影響下一代。

** ─────────────────

addicted〔ə'dɪktɪd〕adj. 上癮的；入迷的
boom〔bum〕n. 繁榮；興起
reasonable〔'riznəbḷ〕adj. 合理的
entertainment〔,ɛntɚ'tenmənt〕n. 娛樂
Net〔nɛt〕n. 網路（= Internet）
interact〔,ɪntɚ'ækt〕v. 互動　　live〔laɪv〕adj. 活的
get lost 迷失　　fake〔fek〕adj. 假的
lose〔luz〕v. 使沉迷；使專注於　　virtual〔'vɝtʃuəl〕adj. 虛擬的
ridiculous〔rɪ'dɪkjələs〕adj. 可笑的；荒謬的
affect〔ə'fɛkt〕v. 影響　　generation〔,dʒɛnə'reʃən〕n. 世代

PART 2 看圖敘述

1. **What is this place?** 這是什麼地方？

   This is a gymnasium. It is probably at a high school or university.

   這是一個體育館。它可能是在一所高中或大學裡。

2. **What are these people doing?** 這些人在做什麼？

   The girls are cheerleaders and they are leading a cheer.

   這群女生是啦啦隊隊員，她們在帶動歡呼。

** ———————————————

　　gymnasium〔dʒɪmˈnezɪəm〕*n.* 體育館（= *gym*）
　　cheerleader〔ˈtʃɪrˌlidɚ〕*n.* 啦啦隊隊員
　　cheer〔tʃɪr〕*n. v.* 歡呼

3. **Have you ever watched such a performance or have you ever taken part in such an activity?**

你曾經看過這樣的表演或曾經參加這樣的活動嗎？

I have seen cheerleaders perform before basketball games.　They chant loudly and sometimes perform a dance or some gymnastics.

我曾經看過啦啦隊在籃球比賽前表演。他們會大聲呼喊，有時會表演舞蹈或一些體操。

4. **What do you think of this kind of activity?**

你對這種活動有什麼想法？

I think cheerleading is fun to watch.　It also gets the crowd excited and encourages them to cheer loudly for their team, so it is important to the game.

我認爲看啦啦隊表演很有趣。它也能讓群衆感到興奮，並激勵他們爲自己支持的隊伍大聲歡呼，所以它對比賽是很重要的。

5. **If you still have time, please describe the picture in as much detail as you can.**

如果你還有時間，請儘可能描述照片中的細節。

** ——————————

chant〔tʃænt〕v. 反覆地說
gymnastics〔dʒɪm'næstɪks〕n. 體操
cheerleading〔'tʃɪrˌlidɪŋ〕n. 當啦啦隊
crowd〔kraud〕n. 群衆

The cheerleaders are performing on the gym floor.
They are wearing T-shirts and shorts. They are in
the middle of a cheer and they are holding
pom-poms in the air. It is a very large gym and
there are many people in the stands waiting for the
game to begin.

啦啦隊在體育館的地板上表演。他們穿 T 恤和短褲。
他們正在歡呼，而且他們將彩球拿在空中。這是一個
很大的體育館，有很多人在看台上等比賽開始。

**　─────────────────────────

　　floor〔flor〕*n.* 地板；場地　　shorts〔ʃɔrts〕*n. pl.* 短褲
　　in the middle of　在…中途；在…當中
　　pom-pom〔'pam,pam〕*n.* (啦啦隊手持的) 彩球
　　in the air　在空中　　stand〔stænd〕*n.* 看台；觀眾席

PART 3　申 述 題

Many department stores hold anniversary sales or
year-end sales and, during these periods, they are
always crowded with shoppers. Do you like to shop
during these periods? Or do you like to shop during
usual times? Please explain.

許多百貨公司舉辦週年慶特賣或年終特賣，在這些期間，
它們總是擠滿了顧客。你喜歡在這些期間購物嗎？還是你
喜歡在平時購物？請說明。

【回答範例 1】

Oh, I love to go to sales at the department stores because I can always find some good bargains. Sometimes the goods are reduced by as much as ninety percent! I usually look for clothes and other things I need, but I also like to browse. Some deals are so good that I can't pass them up even if I don't really need the item. Some people don't like the crowds that are attracted by these sales, but I actually enjoy them. So many people make the atmosphere more exciting. *Besides*, it gives me a good chance to people-watch. I only wish that stores had these kinds of sales more often.

【中文翻譯】

喔，我喜歡去百貨公司的特賣會，因為我總是可以找到一些不錯的特價品。有時商品甚至會降到一折！我通常是找衣服和其他我需要的東西，但我也喜歡隨便看看。有些東西便宜得讓我無法忽視，即使我不是真的需要那個東西。有些人不喜歡被這些特賣會吸引來的人群，但我真的很喜歡他們。這麼多的人會讓氣氛更刺激。此外，它給我一個不錯的機會去觀察人。我只希望商店能更常舉辦這樣的特賣會。

** ─────────────

bargain〔'bɑrgɪn〕 n. 便宜貨；特價品
goods〔gʊdz〕 n. pl. 商品　　reduce〔rɪ'djus〕 v. 降低
browse〔braʊz〕 v. 瀏覽；隨意觀看商品
deal〔dil〕 n. 交易　　**pass up** 忽視
item〔'aɪtəm〕 n. 物品；項目

【回答範例 2】

　　I don't care much for the sales at the department stores because the stores will usually become so unbearably crowded. Though the prices of goods in general are reduced, so is the quality of service. Sometimes you have to wait quite a long time to pay. *Besides*, influenced by the lower prices, we tend to become unreasonable. We may purchase a lot of stuff that we don't really need or buy some discounted clothes in such a rush that we don't bother to try them on, only to find they don't fit well. Shopping at sales often makes me feel full of regret afterwards; therefore, I prefer shopping during usual times in a more leisurely and reasonable manner.

【中文翻譯】

　　我不太喜歡百貨公司的特賣會，因為店內通常會擁擠得令人無法忍受。雖然商品的價格大致上都有降低，但服務品質也跟著下降。有時你必須等相當久才能結帳。此外，受到低價的影響，我們會容易變得不理性。我們可能會買很多我們其實不需要的東西，或是在這麼匆忙的狀況下，買一些打折的衣服，以致於懶得試穿，結果卻發現衣服不是很合身。在特賣會購物常常使我事後充滿後悔；因此，我比較喜歡更悠閒且更理智地在平時購物。

**

care for 喜歡

unbearably〔ʌnˈbɛrəblɪ〕*adv.* 令人無法忍受地

crowded〔ˈkraʊdɪd〕*adj.* 擁擠的

in general 大致上　　influence〔ˈɪnfluəns〕*v.* 影響

tend to V. 易於～；傾向於～

unreasonable〔ʌnˈriznəbḷ〕*adj.* 非理性的

purchase〔ˈpɝtʃəs〕*v.* 購買　　stuff〔stʌf〕*n.* 東西

discounted〔dɪsˈkaʊntɪd〕*adj.* 打折的　　*in a rush* 匆忙地

bother〔ˈbaðɚ〕*v.* 費事　　*try on* 試穿

only to V. 結果卻～　　*fit well* 很合身

regret〔rɪˈgrɛt〕*n.* 後悔

afterwards〔ˈæftɚwɚdz〕*adv.* 之後

leisurely〔ˈliʒɚlɪ〕*adj.* 悠閒的

reasonable〔ˈriznəbḷ〕*adj.* 有理智的

manner〔ˈmænɚ〕*n.* 方式；樣子

全民英語能力分級檢定測驗
中高級寫作能力測驗答案紙

座位號碼：_____   試題別：_____

第一部份請由本頁第 1 行開始作答，請勿隔行書寫。第二部份請翻至第 2 頁作答。

_____

_____

_____

_____

_____

_____

_____

_____

_____

_____

_____

_____

_____

_____

_____

_____

_____

_____

_____

55

60

65

70

寫作口說能力測驗 ⑨

寫作能力測驗

Part I: Chinese-English Translation (40%)

Translate the following Chinese passage into an English passage, and write your answer on the Writing Test Answer Sheet.

謙虛是我們中國人重視的美德之一。然而，依我之見，謙虛是一把兩面的劍。一方面，謙虛的人知道人外有人，天外有天，因此他會更加勤奮、努力工作。另一方面，若因過度謙虛而一直貶低自己，反而會使自己缺乏自信心，而妨礙一個人勇往直前。我們應該要在兩個極端之中尋求中庸之道。

Part II: Guided Writing (60%)

Write an essay of **150-180 words** in an appropriate style on the following topic. Write your answer on the Writing Test Answer Sheet.

With the popularity of MP3s and iPods, now you can see many people listening to whatever they like while doing everything from studying to walking to taking public transportation. Do you yourself have such a habit and what do you think of this habit? Please explain.

口說能力測驗

Please read the self-introduction sentence.

My seat number is （複試座位號碼）, and my

registration number is （初試准考證號碼）.

Part I: Answering Questions

You will hear 8 questions. Each question will be
spoken once. Please answer the question immediately
after you hear it.

For questions 1 to 4, you will have 15 seconds to
answer each question.

For questions 5 to 8, you will have 30 seconds to
answer each question.

Part II: Picture Description

Look at the picture, think about the questions below for 30 seconds, and then record your answers for 1 ½ minutes.

1. Who are the people in the picture? What makes you think so?

2. What is this occasion?

3. Have you ever been to such an occasion?

4. If you still have time, please describe the picture in as much detail as you can.

Part III: Discussion

Think about your answer(s) to the question(s) below for 1 ½ minutes, and then record your answer(s) for 1 ½ minutes.
You may use your test paper to make notes and organize your ideas.

Many foreigners come to Taiwan and find nightlife in Taiwan, especially in big cities like Taipei and Kaohsiung, really fascinating. What do you think of this?

Please read the self-introduction sentence again.

My seat number is （複試座位號碼）, and my registration number is （初試准考證號碼）.

寫作口說能力測驗 ⑨ 詳解

寫作能力測驗詳解

PART 1 中譯英 (40%)

　　謙虛是我們中國人重視的美德之一。然而，依我之見，謙虛是一把兩面的劍。一方面，謙虛的人知道人外有人，天外有天，因此他會更加勤奮、努力工作。另一方面，若因過度謙虛而一直貶低自己，反而會使自己缺乏自信心，而妨礙一個人勇往直前。我們應該要在兩個極端之中尋求中庸之道。

1. $\begin{Bmatrix} \text{Modesty} \\ \text{Humility} \end{Bmatrix}$ is one of the $\begin{Bmatrix} \text{virtues} \\ \text{good qualities} \\ \text{good traits} \end{Bmatrix}$ that

   Chinese (people) $\begin{Bmatrix} \text{value.} \\ \text{emphasize.} \\ \text{respect.} \\ \text{esteem.} \end{Bmatrix}$

2. $\begin{Bmatrix} \text{However} \\ \text{Nevertheless} \end{Bmatrix}$, in my opinion, $\begin{Bmatrix} \text{modesty} \\ \text{humility} \end{Bmatrix}$ is

   a $\begin{Bmatrix} \text{two-edged} \\ \text{double-edged} \\ \text{double-bladed} \end{Bmatrix}$ sword.

3. On (the) one hand, a $\begin{Bmatrix} \text{modest} \\ \text{humble} \end{Bmatrix}$ person knows

(that) there is always someone better than him;

$\begin{Bmatrix} \text{thus} \\ \text{therefore} \\ \text{hence} \\ \text{consequently} \\ \text{as a result} \\ \text{as a consequence} \end{Bmatrix}$, he will be more $\begin{Bmatrix} \text{diligent} \\ \text{industrious} \end{Bmatrix}$

and work harder.

4. On the other hand, being $\begin{Bmatrix} \text{too} \\ \text{overly} \\ \text{excessively} \end{Bmatrix} \begin{Bmatrix} \text{humble} \\ \text{modest} \end{Bmatrix}$

and $\begin{Bmatrix} \begin{Bmatrix} \text{always} \\ \text{constantly} \end{Bmatrix} \begin{Bmatrix} \text{lowering} \\ \text{belittling} \\ \text{degrading} \\ \text{debasing} \end{Bmatrix} \text{himself} \\ \text{lowering himself all the time} \end{Bmatrix}$

will make him lack self-confidence and $\begin{Bmatrix} \text{prevent} \\ \text{hinder} \\ \text{obstruct} \\ \text{deter} \end{Bmatrix}$

him from $\begin{Bmatrix} \text{moving forward} \\ \text{advancing} \end{Bmatrix} \begin{Bmatrix} \text{bravely.} \\ \text{courageously.} \end{Bmatrix}$

5. We should $\left\{\begin{array}{l}\text{seek}\\\text{search for}\\\text{try to find}\end{array}\right\}$ a $\left\{\begin{array}{l}\text{happy medium}\\\text{middle course}\\\text{middle way}\\\text{middle ground}\\\text{golden mean}\end{array}\right\}$

between the two $\left\{\begin{array}{l}\text{extremes.}\\\text{extremities.}\end{array}\right\}$

【註】 modesty〔'mɑdəstɪ〕 n. 謙虛

humility〔hju'mɪlətɪ〕 n. 謙虛　　virtue〔'vɝtʃu〕 n. 美德

quality〔'kwɑlətɪ〕 n. 特質　　trait〔tret〕 n. 特點

value〔'vælju〕 v. 重視

emphasize〔'ɛmfə,saɪz〕 v. 強調；注重

respect〔rɪ'spɛkt〕 v. 尊敬；重視

esteem〔ə'stim〕 v. 重視

nevertheless〔,nɛvəðə'lɛs〕 adv. 然而

two-edged〔'tu'ɛdʒd〕 adj. 雙刃的

double-edged〔'dʌbḷ'ɛdʒd〕 adj. 雙刃的

double-bladed〔'dʌbḷ'bledɪd〕 adj. 雙刃的

modest〔'mɑdɪst〕 adj. 謙虛的

humble〔'hʌmbḷ〕 adj. 謙虛的

hence〔hɛns〕 adv. 因此

consequently〔'kɑnsə,kwɛntlɪ〕 adv. 因此

as a result 結果；因此　　*as a consequence* 結果；因此

diligent〔'dɪlədʒənt〕 adj. 勤勉的

industrious〔ɪn'dʌstrɪəs〕 adj. 勤勉的

overly〔'ovəlɪ〕 adv. 過度地

excessively〔ɪk'sɛsɪvlɪ〕 adv. 過度地

constantly〔'kɑnstəntlɪ〕*adv.* 不斷地

belittle〔bɪ'lɪtl̩〕*v.* 輕視

degrade〔dɪ'gred〕*v.* 降低…的人格

debase〔dɪ'bes〕*v.* 貶低…的人格

self-confidence〔,sɛlf'kɑnfədəns〕*n.* 自信

prevent〔prɪ'vɛnt〕*v.* 預防;妨礙

hinder〔'hɪndɚ〕*v.* 妨礙　　obstruct〔əb'strʌkt〕*v.* 妨礙

deter〔dɪ'tɝ〕*v.* 妨礙

courageously〔kə'redʒəslɪ〕*adv.* 勇敢地

medium〔'midɪəm〕*n.* 中間;中庸

happy medium 中庸之道　　course〔kors〕*n.* 路線

ground〔graʊnd〕*n.* 立場　　mean〔min〕*n.* 中間;中庸

golden mean 中庸之道　　extreme〔ɪk'strim〕*n.* 極端

extremity〔ɪk'strɛmətɪ〕*n.* 極度;極端

PART 2 引導寫作 (60%)

　　With the popularity of MP3s and iPods, now you can see many people listening to whatever they like while doing everything from studying to walking to taking public transportation. Do you yourself have such a habit and what do you think of this habit? Please explain.

　　隨著 MP3 和 iPod 的普及,現在你可以看到許多人無論做什麼事,從讀書到走路到搭大眾運輸工具,都在聽他們喜歡的東西。你自己有這樣的習慣嗎?你對這個習慣有什麼想法?請說明。

【作文範例 1】

Mobile Music

    I often listen to my iPod, and I don't think that it is a bad habit. Listening to music helps me pass the time during long bus rides or any time that I have to wait for something. This keeps me from becoming impatient and irritable. *Also*, it can screen out any annoying noises such as car horns or shouting children. *Better yet*, I can use the music to change or enhance my mood. *For instance*, if I am feeling blue, I will take a walk outside and listen to some upbeat songs. I soon find myself walking quickly in step with the music and even singing quietly along. *On the other hand*, if I am upset or angry over something, I will play calm, relaxing music.

    People often criticize me for using my iPod when I study, but I don't find the music distracting. *In fact*, certain types of music help me to remember things. *Then*, when I want to recall the facts, I think of the song and they come back to me more easily.

Music is a big part of my life, and having convenient access to it through my iPod is wonderful. It entertains me, calms me or invigorates me as needed. ***Therefore***, I am unlikely to give up this delightful habit any time soon.

【註】 mobile〔'mobḷ〕adj. 可移動的

impatient〔ɪm'peʃənt〕adj. 不耐煩的

irritable〔'ɪrətəbḷ〕adj. 易怒的

screen〔skrin〕v. 隔絕

annoying〔ə'nɔɪɪŋ〕adj. 煩人的

horn〔hɔrn〕n. 喇叭　***better yet*** 更好的是

enhance〔ɪn'hæns〕v. 提高

mood〔mud〕n. 心情　***for instance*** 例如

blue〔blu〕adj. 憂鬱的　upbeat〔'ʌp,bit〕adj. 快樂的

in step with 和…步調一致　along〔ə'lɔŋ〕adv. 一起

on the other hand 另一方面

upset〔ʌp'sɛt〕adj. 不高興的

calm〔kɑm〕adj. 平靜的　v. 使平靜

criticize〔'krɪtə,saɪz〕v. 批評；指責

distracting〔dɪ'stræktɪŋ〕adj. 使人分心的

recall〔rɪ'kɔl〕v. 回想

come back to sb. 重現於某人的記憶中

access〔'æksɛs〕n. 接近；使用 <to>

entertain〔,ɛntə'ten〕v. 娛樂；使快樂

invigorate〔ɪn'vɪgə,ret〕v. 鼓舞

as needed 無論我需要什麼 (= *whichever one I need*)

delightful〔dɪ'laɪtfəl〕adj. 令人愉快的

any time soon 很快；在不久的將來 (= *in the near future*)

【作文範例 2】

The Disadvantages of Mobile Music

IPods and other personal music devices have become very popular. It seems that wherever you look, you see people with earphones. Although it is fine to listen to music now and then, I personally think that this craze has gotten out of control. Listening to music all the time is a bad habit because it may be dangerous or impolite.

We most often see people listening to MP3 players when they are on the bus or MRT. There is nothing wrong with that *as long as* they don't let it cut them off from the world completely. *For example*, some people turn up the volume so high that they cannot hear anything around them. This is very dangerous since they may not hear an approaching car or an emergency announcement, *not to mention the fact that* their hearing will be severely damaged.

Listening to music distracts people from what is going on around them. That is why I don't approve of people listening to music while studying or working. How can they concentrate and do a good job? *Even worse*, some people carry on conversations with others while still listening to their music players. That sends the message that the person they are talking to is not worth their full attention.

In short, while music is an important part of life, it is not more important than other people. We should enjoy it at appropriate times, not all the time.

【註】 disadvantage〔͵dɪsəd'væntɪdʒ〕*n.* 缺點
　　 device〔dɪ'vaɪs〕*n.* 裝置
　　 earphones〔'ɪr͵fonz〕*n. pl.* 耳機　　*now and then* 偶爾
　　 personally〔'pɜsn̩lɪ〕*adv.* 就我個人而言
　　 craze〔krez〕*n.* 狂熱；熱中　　*out of control* 失去控制
　　 impolite〔͵ɪmpə'laɪt〕*adj.* 無禮的
　　as long as 只要　　*cut off* 斷絕

　　 completely〔kəm'plitlɪ〕*adv.* 完全地
　　turn up 開大聲；調高　　volume〔'vɑljəm〕*n.* 音量
　　 approaching〔ə'protʃɪŋ〕*adj.* 接近的
　　 emergency〔ɪ'mɝdʒənsɪ〕*adj.* 緊急的
　　 announcement〔ə'naʊnsmənt〕*n.* 宣布；聲明
　　not to mention 更不用說　　hearing〔'hɪrɪŋ〕*n.* 聽力

　　 severely〔sə'vɪrlɪ〕*adv.* 嚴重地
　　 distract〔dɪ'strækt〕*v.* 使分心；轉移（注意力）
　　 approve〔ə'pruv〕*v.* 贊成＜*of*＞
　　 concentrate〔'kɑnsn̩͵tret〕*v.* 集中；專心
　　even worse 更糟的是　　*carry on* 繼續；進行
　　in short 簡言之　　while〔hwaɪl〕*conj.* 雖然
　　 appropriate〔ə'proprɪɪt〕*adj.* 適當的

口說能力測驗詳解

PART 1　回答問題

1. **What's your favorite movie and why?**
   你最喜愛的電影是哪部？爲什麼？

【回答範例1】

My favorite movie of all time is "Forrest Gump."

It is a touching and motivating movie.

I have seen it many times, yet whenever I see
　　it on TV I still watch it till the end.

The main character, Forrest, is mentally
　　challenged.

He has a devoted mother who gives all her love
　　to him.

The most important thing in his life is the
　　woman he loves, who gives birth to his child.

This movie covers almost half a century
　　of American history.

It is told through the eyes of an ordinary yet
　　extraordinary man.

If you haven't seen it, I strongly suggest you do.

【中文翻譯】

我最喜愛的電影是「阿甘正傳」。
它是一部感人且激勵人心的電影。
我看了很多遍,但是我每次看到電視播出時,
還是會看到最後。

主角福雷斯特有智能障礙。
他有個愛他的母親,給他所有的愛。
他一生中最重要的就是他所愛的女人,她為他
生了一個小孩。

這部電影涵蓋了幾乎半個世紀的美國歷史。
它是透過一個普通但卻不平凡的人的觀點來敘述。
如果你沒看過,我強烈建議你去看。

** ─────────────────

of all time 有史以來
Forrest Gump 阿甘正傳【電影名】
touching〔ˈtʌtʃɪŋ〕*adj.* 感人的
motivating〔ˈmotəˌvetɪŋ〕*adj.* 激勵人心的
character〔ˈkærɪktɚ〕*n.* 人物;角色
mentally〔ˈmɛntḷɪ〕*adv.* 心理上;智力上
challenged〔ˈtʃælɪndʒd〕*adj.* 有障礙的
devoted〔dɪˈvotɪd〕*adj.* 摯愛的
give birth to 生(孩子)
through the eyes of *sb.* 透過某人的觀點來看
ordinary〔ˈɔrdṇˌɛrɪ〕*adj.* 普通的;平凡的
extraordinary〔ɪkˈstrɔrdṇˌɛrɪ〕*adj.* 特別的;非凡的

【回答範例 2】

My favorite movie is not just one,
　　but three movies.

It is "The Lord of the Ring" trilogy.

It is based on an all-time classic by
　　J.R.R. Tolkien.

The movies are an epic, just like the
　　novel itself.

The fantasy story about hobbits, elves,
　　and dwarves fighting alongside humans
　　to destroy the ring is captivating.

The cast is great, and the battle scenes
　　are the best ever.

I read the novel first, and I must say quite
　　a lot is taken out in the films, but I
　　understand.

The original story was just too big to
　　make into a movie.

However, that doesn't take away from the
　　best trilogy and fantasy movies ever made.

【中文翻譯】

我最喜愛的電影不只一部，而是三部。

它是「魔戒」三部曲。

它是根據 J.R.R.托爾金空前的文學名著拍成的。

這些電影是史詩般的作品，就像小說本身一樣。

這個關於哈比人、精靈和矮人，為了摧毀魔戒而與人類並肩作戰的奇幻故事令人著迷。

演員陣容龐大，而且戰鬥場景是有史以來最好的。

我先讀過小說，我必須說，有許多部分在電影中被拿掉了，但我能明白。

原本的故事太長，無法全部拍進電影裡。

然而，這樣還是無損於它是有史以來最好的奇幻三部曲電影的事實。

** ————————————————————

***not* A *but* B** 不是 A 而是 B

The Lord of the Ring 魔戒【電影名】

trilogy〔'trɪlədʒɪ〕 *n.* 三部曲　　***be based on*** 以…為根據

all-time〔'ɔl,taɪm〕 *adj.* 空前的　　classic〔'klæsɪk〕 *n.* 文學名著

epic〔'ɛpɪk〕 *n.* 史詩；史詩般的小說（或戲劇、電影等）

fantasy〔'fæntəsɪ〕 *n.* 幻想

hobbit〔'hɑbət〕 *n.* 哈比人【英國作家托爾金筆下創造的生性善良
　平和的穴居矮人】　　elf〔ɛlf〕 *n.* 精靈

dwarf〔dwɔrf〕 *n.* 侏儒　　alongside〔ə'clɔŋ'saɪd〕 *prep.* 和…一起

destroy〔dɪ'strɔɪ〕 *v.* 破壞；摧毀

captivating〔'kæptə,vetɪŋ〕 *adj.* 令人著迷的

cast〔kæst〕 *n.* 演員陣容；卡司　　battle〔'bætḷ〕 *n.* 戰爭；戰鬥

scene〔sin〕 *n.* 場景　　***take out*** 去除

original〔ə'rɪdʒənḷ〕 *adj.* 原本的　　***take away from*** 有損於；減損

2. **Have you ever been jealous of somebody? What was the reason?**　你曾經嫉妒過別人嗎？理由是什麼？

【回答範例】

As a kid, I was jealous of my younger brother.

Everyone in the family loved him because
　　he was really cute.

I felt ignored and sometimes took it out on
　　my brother.

Also, I used to be real jealous of my
　　classmate, Joe.

He always got No. 1 on all the tests,
　　and I was No. 2.

I was jealous of him because he got all
　　the attention from the teachers.

Nowadays I'm hardly ever jealous of
　　other people.

I believe that doing what you are supposed
　　to do is more important than being jealous
　　of what others have.

If you work hard, you can get whatever you
　　want, so there's no point in being jealous.

【中文翻譯】

小時候，我嫉妒我弟弟。

家中的每個人都愛他，因為他真的很可愛。

我感到被忽視，有時我會把氣出在我弟弟身上。

我以前也很嫉妒我的同學喬。

他總是所有的考試都拿第一名，而我是第二名。

我嫉妒他，因為他受到所有老師的注意。

現在，我很少嫉妒別人。

我相信做你該做的事，會比嫉妒別人所擁有的

更重要。

如果你努力工作，你可以得到任何你想要的東

西，所以沒有嫉妒的必要。

** ———————————————————————

jealous〔'dʒɛləs〕adj. 嫉妒的 < of >

ignore〔ɪg'nor〕v. 忽視

take out 發洩   **used to V.** 以前～

real〔'riəl〕adv. 真正地；非常

hardly ever 很少

be supposed to 應該

point〔pɔɪnt〕n. 必要

3. **Managing our temper is very important. How do you calm down after getting angry?**

管理我們的情緒非常重要。你生氣後是如何冷靜下來的？

【回答範例】

There are many ways to calm down.

Some count to ten, while others read or take
   a nap.

I choose to sit in front of my computer
   and surf the Web, listen to music,
   or play computer games.

Surfing the Internet is a good way to
   distract myself from anger.

I visit one website, link to another, and soon
   I totally forget what I was thinking about.

Playing video games has the same effect,
   because I focus on the game instead
   of my emotions.

I choose to listen to real loud music when
   I am angry.

Why do I do this?

Because I think I can vent my anger with
   the noise.

【中文翻譯】

冷靜下來的方法有很多。

有些人會數到十，而有些人會閱讀或小睡一下。

我選擇坐在我的電腦前面，然後上網、聽音樂，或玩電腦遊戲。

上網是一個使我自己不生氣的好方法。

我會去一個網站，再連到另一個網站，我很快就會完全忘記我剛剛在想的事。

玩電玩遊戲也有同樣的效果，因為我能專注在遊戲上，而不是我的情緒。

當我生氣時，我選擇聽很大聲的音樂。

為什麼我要這麼做？

因為我認為我可以用噪音來發洩憤怒。

** ——————————————

manage〔ˈmænɪdʒ〕v. 管理

temper〔ˈtɛmpɚ〕n. 情緒；脾氣

calm down 冷靜下來　　count〔kaʊnt〕v. 數

while〔hwaɪl〕*conj.* 然而　　***take a nap*** 小睡片刻

surf the Web 上網（= *surf the Internet*）

distract〔dɪˈstrækt〕v. 使分心；轉移

website〔ˈwɛbˌsaɪt〕n. 網站

link〔lɪŋk〕v. 連結　　***video game*** 電玩遊戲

focus on 專注於　　***instead of*** 而不是

emotion〔ɪˈmoʃən〕n. 情緒　　vent〔vɛnt〕v. 發洩

4. **What's your favorite season and why?**

你最喜愛的季節是哪一個？爲什麼？

【回答範例 1】

Spring makes me feel warm and happy.

Although sometimes it rains a lot during
spring in Taiwan, overall it is a pleasant
season.

And of course, the best holiday, the Chinese
New Year, is in spring.

Spring is a time when flowers bloom.

Nature definitely becomes lively.

The grass looks greener, and the air feels
fresher.

Spring makes me feel good because it is
the beginning of a new cycle.

Just like nature, we are reborn after a
whole year.

I feel like working harder in spring than
all the other seasons, because that feeling
motivates me.

【中文翻譯】

春天讓我覺得溫暖和快樂。

雖然台灣在春天有時會經常下雨，但是整體來
說，它是個令人愉快的季節。

當然，最棒的節日農曆新年，就是在春天。

春天是花朵盛開的時期。

大自然一定會變得生氣蓬勃。

草地看起來更加翠綠，而空氣也令人覺得更加清新。

春天讓我覺得很棒，因為它是一個新的循環的開始。

就像大自然一樣，我們也在一整年過後重生。

我在春天會想要比其他季節更努力，因為這種
感覺會激勵我。

** ──────────────

a lot 常常　　overall〔͵ovɚˈɔl〕*adv.* 就整體來說

pleasant〔ˈplɛznt〕*adj.* 令人愉快的

bloom〔blum〕*v.* 開花；盛開

definitely〔ˈdɛfənɪtlɪ〕*adv.* 一定

lively〔ˈlaɪvlɪ〕*adj.* 生氣蓬勃的

grass〔græs〕*n.* 草　　feel〔fil〕*v.* 使人感覺

fresh〔frɛʃ〕*adj.* 新鮮的　　cycle〔ˈsaɪkḷ〕*n.* 循環

reborn〔riˈbɔrn〕*adj.* 重生的

feel like* + *V-ing 想要～

motivate〔ˈmotəͺvet〕*v.* 激勵

【回答範例 2】

My favorite season, without a doubt,
　is summer.
It's the season of sun and good weather.
It's the season of outdoor fun.

To a student, summer means vacation
　time.
It's a time to go swimming, play sports,
　and hang around all day with friends.
Of course, there is the bothersome
　summer homework.

All in all, summer is a time of sweat,
　sunburns, and tans.
It's a time to relax and have fun.
After summer, we go back to school
　recharged.

【中文翻譯】

無疑地，我最喜愛的季節是夏天。

它是有陽光和好天氣的季節。

它是到戶外玩的季節。

對學生來說，夏天表示假期。

它是游泳、運動，以及整天和朋友閒蕩的
季節。

當然，會有討厭的暑假作業。

總之，夏天是流汗、曬傷和曬黑的季節。

它是放鬆和玩樂的季節。

夏天過後，我們會充滿活力地回到學校。

** ────────────

without a doubt 無疑地（ = *without doubt*）

hang around 閒蕩

bothersome〔ˋbɑðəsəm〕 *adj.* 討厭的

all in all 總之　　sweat〔swɛt〕 *n.* 汗；流汗

sunburn〔ˋsʌn͵bɝn〕 *n.* 曬傷

tan〔tæn〕 *n.* 皮膚經日曬而成的褐色

recharge〔riˋtʃɑrdʒ〕 *v.* 給…再充電

【回答範例 3】

I love the cool breeze in autumn.

It is not too hot and not too cold.

With summer gone, there is no more
　　heat to make me irritable.

Autumn is the season for harvest.

I like seeing the red and golden color
　　that covers the landscape.

It's always a pleasure to take an easy
　　walk after dinner in the fall.

Autumn also means the end of summer
　　vacation.

It's time to return to school and see
　　classmates and teachers again.

To me, autumn is a return to life, because
　　it is the beginning of a new semester.

【中文翻譯】

我喜歡秋天涼爽的微風。

天氣不會太熱也不會太冷。

在夏天過後,沒有會讓我煩躁的暑氣。

秋天是收成的季節。

我喜歡看到紅色和金黃色覆蓋著景色。

在秋天吃完晚餐後,悠閒地散步總是很快樂。

秋天也表示暑假的結束。

是返校並再次看見同學與老師的時候。

對我來說,秋天是回歸生活,因為這是一個新學期的開始。

**

breeze〔briz〕*n.* 微風

gone〔gɔn〕*adj.* 離去的;過去的

irritable〔'ɪrətəbḷ〕*adj.* 易怒的;煩躁的

harvest〔'hɑrvɪst〕*n.* 收成;收穫

landscape〔'lændskep〕*n.* 風景;景色

pleasure〔'plɛʒɚ〕*n.* 樂趣

take a walk 散步   easy〔'izɪ〕*adj.* 悠閒的

return〔rɪ'tɝn〕*v.* 返回   *n.* 回歸

semester〔sə'mɛstɚ〕*n.* 學期

【回答範例 4】

Winter is my favorite season.

It is a pity that we don't have snow
　　in Taiwan.

If there were snow, it would be
　　even better.

I don't mind the cold in winter.

Actually, winter in Taiwan is not as
　　cold as in some other countries.

Even if there is a cold wave, I can
　　always bundle myself up and keep
　　myself warm.

All in all, I'm a "cool" person.

I don't like the hustle and bustle in
　　hot weather.

I prefer the more laid-back, holiday-filled
　　winter.

【中文翻譯】

冬天是我最喜愛的季節。

可惜我們台灣沒下雪。

如果有下雪，就更好了。

我不在乎冬天的寒冷。

事實上，台灣的冬天不像其他某些國家那樣冷。

即使有寒流，我也可以一直把自己裹起來保持
溫暖。

總之，我是一個很「酷」的人。

我不喜歡天氣炎熱時的熙攘喧鬧。

我比較喜歡較悠閒和充滿假期的冬天。

** ───────────

pity〔'pɪtɪ〕 *n.* 可惜的事

actually〔'æktʃʊəlɪ〕 *adv.* 事實上

cold wave 寒流

bundle〔'bʌndḷ〕 *v.* 使穿著暖和衣服

bundle *oneself* ***up*** 把自己裹暖

hustle〔'hʌsḷ〕 *n.* 推擠；急忙

bustle〔'bʌsḷ〕 *n.* 忙亂；喧擾

hustle and bustle 擠來擠去；忙亂

laid-back〔'led͵bæk〕 *adj.* 悠閒的

5. **Do you collect things? What do you collect and why?**
   If you don't, what would you like to collect?

   你有收集東西嗎？你收集什麼東西？為什麼？如果沒有的
   話，你想要收集什麼？

【回答範例 1】

I'm a keen comic collector.

I have more than five hundred comic books.

I preserve each of them carefully on a shelf
   especially for comics.

It has cost me a lot, but I think it's worth it.

I have some comics in mint condition that
   should be worth a lot now.

But of course, I treasure them too much
   to sell them.

If I had the money and time, I would like to
   add action figures to my collection.

They are quite expensive and take up a lot
   of space, but I'd like to try.

Having a collection of things is always
   worth it.

【中文翻譯】

我是個熱愛收藏漫畫的人。

我有超過五百本的漫畫。

我每一本漫畫都小心地保存在專門放漫畫的架子上。

它花了我很多錢,但我認為很值得。

我有一些全新的漫畫,現在應該很值錢。

但當然,我太珍惜它們了,不會賣掉它們。

如果我有錢和時間,我想把公仔加到我的收藏中。

它們相當昂貴,而且很佔空間,但我想試試看。

收集東西總是值得的。

＊＊ ───────────────────

keen〔kin〕*adj.* 熱中的

comic〔'kɑmɪk〕*n.* 漫畫書 (= *comic book*)

collector〔kə'lɛktɚ〕*n.* 收藏者

preserve〔prɪ'zɝv〕*v.* 保存　　shelf〔ʃɛlf〕*n.* 架子

mint〔mɪnt〕*adj.* 嶄新的;無污損的

treasure〔'trɛʒɚ〕*v.* 珍惜　　***add* A *to* B** 把 A 加到 B

figure〔'fɪgjɚ〕*n.* 人物

action figure 公仔【手臂及腿部可以移動的玩偶,

　通常形似某故事中的英雄】

collection〔kə'lɛkʃən〕*n.* 收集;收藏品

take up 佔用　　space〔spes〕*n.* 空間

【回答範例 2 】

I have been collecting stamps since I
was little.

It was my father who introduced me to
this hobby.

I have already filled several albums.

At first, most of my stamps were used,
coming from the mail my family got.

However, with the popularity of e-mail,
letters are getting rarer.

In the past few years, part of my collection
has come from my family and friends.

They will try to bring me some from
wherever they travel.

I also make some exchanges with e-pals
on the Internet.

Stamp collecting helps me make more
friends and teaches me to appreciate
the beauty of culture.

【中文翻譯】

我從小就開始集郵。

是我爸爸讓我認識這個嗜好。

我已經集滿好幾本集郵冊。

一開始，我大部分的郵票都是用過的，來自我
家人收到的信件。

然而，隨著電子郵件的普及，信件越來越少。

在過去幾年，我一部分的收藏來自我的家人和
朋友。

他們會設法從他們去旅遊的任何地方帶一些給我。

我也會在網路上和網友交換。

集郵幫我交到更多朋友，並教導我欣賞文化之美。

** ——————————————————

stamp〔 stæmp 〕*n.* 郵票

introduce〔ˏɪntrə'djus 〕*v.* 介紹；使初次經驗

hobby〔'hɑbɪ 〕*n.* 嗜好

album〔'ælbəm 〕*n.*（黏貼或蒐集相片、郵票等的）簿冊

mail〔 mel 〕*n.* 信件

popularity〔ˏpɑpjə'lærətɪ 〕*n.* 普及

rare〔 rɛr 〕*adj.* 稀少的　　exchange〔 ɪks'tʃendʒ 〕*n.* 交換

e-pal〔'iˏpæl 〕*n.* 網友

appreciate〔 ə'priʃɪˏet 〕*v.* 欣賞

6. **A little girl has gotten lost in the department store and is crying. Help to calm her down.**

   一個小女孩在百貨公司迷路而且在哭。幫忙使她平靜下來。

【回答範例】

Hey, don't cry.

I'll help you look for your mom or dad.

But I can't help you if you don't stop
  crying, okay?

Good girl, here's a tissue.

Do you know your mom's name?

Where did you last see her?

I'll bring you to the information desk.

The ladies there will make an
  announcement.

They will help you find your parents,
  okay?

【中文翻譯】

嘿，不要哭。

我會幫妳找到妳的媽媽或爸爸。

但如果妳不停止哭泣，我就沒辦法幫妳了，

好嗎？

好孩子，面紙給妳。

妳知道妳媽媽叫什麼名字嗎？

妳最後在哪裡看到她？

我會帶妳去服務台。

那裡的小姐會廣播通知。

她們會幫妳找到妳的父母，好嗎？

** ——————————————————

get lost 迷路

calm sb. down 使某人平靜下來

tissue〔ˈtɪʃu〕 *n.* 面紙

last〔læst〕 *adv.* 最後；上次

information desk 服務台

announcement〔əˈnaʊnsmənt〕 *n.* 宣布；通知

7. **You're the coach of a basketball team and your team is down by 20 points at halftime. Give your team a pep talk to revitalize them.**

    你是一個籃球隊的教練，你的隊伍在中場休息時已經輸了二十分。跟你的隊伍講一些鼓勵性的話，使他們恢復活力。

【回答範例】

Guys, I have to admit, we're in a deep hole.

But when a brave man is at a disadvantage,
    he fights back.

We are brave, aren't we?

When you are on the court, *you* give it your all.

When you are on the court, *you* fight till the
    last moment.

When you are on the court, *you* strive to be
    the best and win.

So let's go out and let them know we're not
    going down that easily.

We are warriors, with one goal, and that is
    to win.

Come on, team!

【中文翻譯】

各位，我必須承認，我們陷入很大的困境。

但是勇敢的人處於不利的情況下，他會反擊。

我們很勇敢，不是嗎？

當你們在球場上，你們要盡全力。

當你們在球場上，你們要奮鬥到最後一刻。

當你們在球場上，你們要努力成為最棒的球員

然後獲勝。

所以，我們上場讓他們知道我們不會那麼容易

被打敗。

我們是戰士，只有一個目標，就是獲勝。

走吧，團隊！

** ————————————————

down〔daʊn〕*adv.* 輸掉　　point〔pɔɪnt〕*n.* 分

halftime〔'hæf,taɪm〕*n.* 中場休息

pep〔pɛp〕*n.* 活力；精力　　***pep talk*** 鼓勵性的話

revitalize〔ri'vaɪtḷ,aɪz〕*v.* 使恢復元氣；再給予…活力

hole〔hol〕*n.* 困境　　brave〔brev〕*adj.* 勇敢的

disadvantage〔,dɪsəd'væntɪdʒ〕*n.* 不利的情況

fight back 反擊　　court〔kort〕*n.* 球場

give it *one's* ***all*** 盡全力　　strive〔straɪv〕*v.* 努力

go down 被打敗　　warrior〔'wɔrɪɚ〕*n.* 戰士

8. **"Blogs" have become the biggest thing on the Web in the past couple of years. Do you keep a blog? Why or why not?**

在過去幾年，「部落格」已經成為網路上最重要的東西。

你有經營部落格嗎？為什麼有或為什麼沒有？

【回答範例 1】

I keep a blog, just like the rest of my friends.

It's a great way to share what you think with people all over the Web.

It's just like a diary, but one you choose to share with others.

I usually update my blog every one or two days.

I write about my day, my thoughts on current events, and sometimes put jokes or videos on it.

It has become a part of my everyday routine to check on my blog.

Keeping a blog also gives me a sense of achievement.

When people reply to what you write or give comments, it's encouraging.

It's a great way to feel that you are appreciated for showing who you are.

【中文翻譯】

我有經營一個部落格，就像我其他的朋友一樣。

這是一個與全部網友分享想法的好方法。

它就像個日記，但它是你選擇與別人分享的日記。

我通常每一到兩天會更新我的部落格。

我寫關於我的一天、我對時事的看法，有時會放

笑話和影片在上面。

檢查我的部落格已經變成我每天例行公事的一

部分。

經營部落格也給我成就感。

當大家對你寫的東西作出回應或給予評論時，是

會振奮人心的。

這是一個讓你感覺到你因為表現自己而受到欣賞

的好方法。

** ——————————————

blog〔blɑg〕 n. 部落格　　 ***the Web*** 網路 (= *the Internet*)

diary〔'daɪərɪ〕 n. 日記　　 update〔ʌp'det〕 v. 更新

current events 時事　　 video〔'vɪdɪ͵o〕 n. 影片

routine〔ru'tin〕 n. 例行公事　　 ***check on*** 檢查；查看

achievement〔ə'tʃivmənt〕 n. 成就

comment〔'kɑmɛnt〕 n. 評論

encouraging〔ɪn'kɝɪdʒɪŋ〕 adj. 鼓勵的；振奮人心的

appreciate〔ə'priʃɪ͵et〕 v. 欣賞

【回答範例2】

I don't have a blog.

For one thing, I am not so good at computers.

I don't know how to keep a blog.

Second, I am too busy to keep a blog.

If you have a blog, you have to post stuff on
　 it frequently and update it.

That will take a lot of time.

Some people say a blog is like a diary.

But in my mind, a diary is very personal.

I won't share it with other people.

【中文翻譯】

我沒有部落格。

首先，我不是很擅長使用電腦。

我不知道如何經營部落格。

其次，我太忙了，無法經營部落格。

如果你有個部落格，你必須經常貼東西上去，並更新它。

這會花很多時間。

有些人說部落格像日記。

但我認為，日記是很私人的。

我不會和別人分享它。

** ─────────────

for one thing 首先　　***be good at*** 擅長；精通

post〔post〕*v.* 貼　　stuff〔stʌf〕*n.* 東西

frequently〔ˈfrikwəntlɪ〕*adv.* 常常　　personal〔ˈpɜsn̩l〕*adj.* 私人的

PART 2　看圖敘述

1. **Who are the people in the picture? What makes you think so?**

   照片裡的人是誰？是什麼讓你這麼想的？

   I think the children in the picture are the winners of a contest because they are holding prizes. The man behind them may be a judge or their teacher.

   我想照片裡的小孩是一項比賽的優勝者，因為他們拿著獎品。他們後面的男士可能是評審或他們的老師。

   ** ────────────

   contest〔'kɑntɛst〕n. 比賽
   judge〔dʒʌdʒ〕n. 評審

2. **What is this occasion?** 這是什麼場合？
This is an award ceremony.
這是一個頒獎典禮。

3. **Have you ever been to such an occasion?**
你曾經去過這樣的場合嗎？

Yes. My younger brother once won a calligraphy
competition and we all attended the ceremony.
It was great to see him up on the stage.
有。我的弟弟曾經在書法比賽中獲勝，然後我們全都
去參加典禮。看到他上台是很棒的。

4. **If you still have time, please describe the picture
in as much detail as you can.**
如果你還有時間，請儘可能描述照片中的細節。

The children are standing on a stage. The stage
is decorated with very large banners, one of
which is a picture of Confucius. They have
just won an award and they are posing for
pictures. They each hold a box in their hands
and are standing in a straight line. A man is
standing behind them. I think he is presenting
the winners to the audience.

這些小孩正站在台上。台上用很大的旗幟來裝飾,其中有
一個是孔子的圖片。他們剛贏得一個獎項,而且他們正在
擺姿勢要照相。他們每個人手中都拿著一個盒子,並站成
一直線。有一位男士站在他們後面。我想他是在為觀眾介
紹優勝者。

**

occasion〔ə'keʒən〕n. 場合　　award〔ə'wɔrd〕n. 獎
ceremony〔'sɛrə,monɪ〕n. 典禮
calligraphy〔kə'lɪgrəfɪ〕n. 書法
competition〔,kɑmpə'tɪʃən〕n. 比賽
attend〔ə'tɛnd〕v. 參加　　decorate〔'dɛkə,ret〕v. 裝飾
banner〔'bænɚ〕n. 旗幟
Confucius〔kən'fjuʃəs〕n. 孔子
pose〔poz〕v. 擺姿勢　　straight〔stret〕adj. 直的
in a straight line　成一直線
present〔prɪ'zɛnt〕v. 介紹
audience〔'ɔdɪəns〕n. 觀眾

PART 3　申述題

Many foreigners come to Taiwan and find nightlife
in Taiwan, especially in big cities like Taipei and
Kaohsiung, really fascinating.　What do you think
of this?

許多外國人來到台灣,覺得台灣的夜生活,尤其是在像台北
和高雄那樣的大都市,真的很迷人。你對此有什麼看法?

【回答範例】

　　I think many foreigners find the nightlife here interesting because it is different from what they have experienced at home. In cities in Taiwan you can see a lot of people out at night. They enjoy eating out, having a drink together, even window-shopping. Night markets are also a unique part of city life here. When foreigners visit a night market they are often amazed by the variety of goods and food for sale. *Needless to say*, they are lively and crowded places. There are also more formal performances of traditional music, dance and theater. And, in addition to all that, Taiwan's cities, just like big cities the world over, have a fair number of clubs for visitors to go and explore. There they can often find a unique mix of east and west and easily strike up conversations and make friends with local young people.

【中文翻譯】

　　我認為許多外國人會覺得這裡的夜生活很有趣，是因為和他們在家鄉體驗到的不同。在台灣的都市，你可以看到很多人在晚上外出。他們喜歡外食、一起喝一杯，甚至逛街瀏覽櫥窗。夜市也是這裡的都市生活很獨特的部分。當外國人去夜市時，他們經常會對所販售的各式各樣商品和食物感到驚訝。不用說，那些都是熱鬧而且擁擠的地方。那裡也有比較多傳統音樂、舞蹈和戲劇的正式表演。而且，除了這些之外，台灣的都市就像世界各地的大城市一樣，有相當多俱樂部供觀光客去逛一逛。他們在那裡常會發現獨特的東西方文化的融合，而且很容易和當地年輕人交談和交朋友。

**　　*　*

nightlife〔'naɪt,laɪf〕*n.* 夜生活
fascinating〔'fæsn̩,etɪŋ〕*adj.* 迷人的　　***at home*** 在家鄉
window-shop〔'wɪndo,ʃɑp〕*v.* 逛街瀏覽櫥窗
unique〔ju'nik〕*adj.* 獨特的；特有的
amaze〔ə'mez〕*v.* 使驚訝　　variety〔və'raɪətɪ〕*n.* 多樣性
goods〔gʊdz〕*n. pl.* 商品　　***needless to say*** 不用說
lively〔'laɪvlɪ〕*adj.* 熱鬧的　　crowded〔'kraʊdɪd〕*adj.* 擁擠的
formal〔'fɔrml̩〕*adj.* 正式的

performance〔pɚ'fɔrməns〕*n.* 表演
traditional〔trə'dɪʃənl̩〕*adj.* 傳統的　　theater〔'θiətɚ〕*n.* 戲劇
the world over 世界各地　　fair〔fɛr〕*adj.* 相當的；頗多的
a fair number of 很多的
explore〔ɪk'splor〕*v.* 探險；實地察看　　mix〔mɪks〕*n.* 混合
a mix of east and west 東西方文化的混合（＝ *a mixture of
　eastern culture and western culture*）　　***strike up*** 開始
strike up a conversation with sb. 開始與某人交談
local〔'lokl̩〕*adj.* 當地的

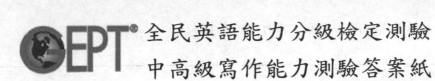

座位號碼：_____　　　　試題別：_____

第一部份請由本頁第1行開始作答，請勿隔行書寫。第二部份請翻至第2頁作答。

_____

_____

_____

_____

_____

_____

_____

_____

_____

_____

_____

_____

_____

_____

_____

_____

_____

_____

_____

_____

_____

_____

5

10

15

20

25

55

60

65

70

寫作口說能力測驗 ⑩

寫作能力測驗

Part I: Chinese-English Translation (40%)

Translate the following Chinese passage into an English passage, and write your answer on the Writing Test Answer Sheet.

　　對我而言，讀書不只是一種樂趣，也是一種需要。當我想要充實自我、拓展視野時，閱讀是我獲取知識的最佳方法。當我感到無聊時，讀書可以幫助我快樂地度過時光。在各類書籍中，我最喜歡小說，因為小說最貼近我們的生活。以小說裡的人物做為借鏡，我可以學習到許多寶貴的教訓。

Part II: Guided Writing (60%)

Write an essay of **150-180 words** in an appropriate style on the following topic. Write your answer on the Writing Test Answer Sheet.

　　Fitness centers, spas, and yoga practice are very popular in Taiwan these days. Many people go to these places for a workout or relaxation. What do you think of these places? Have you ever been to one of these places? Please describe your experience.

口說能力測驗

Please read the self-introduction sentence.

My seat number is ＿（複試座位號碼）＿, and my registration number is ＿（初試准考證號碼）＿.

Part I: Answering Questions

You will hear 8 questions. Each question will be spoken once. Please answer the question immediately after you hear it.

For questions 1 to 4, you will have 15 seconds to answer each question.

For questions 5 to 8, you will have 30 seconds to answer each question.

Part II: Picture Description

Look at the picture, think about the questions below for 30 seconds, and then record your answers for 1 ½ minutes.

1. What is this place?

2. What do you think this occasion is?

3. Who do you think these people are?

4. Have you ever taken part in such an activity?

5. If you still have time, please describe the picture in as much detail as you can.

Part III: Discussion

Think about your answer(s) to the question(s) below for 1 ½ minutes, and then record your answer(s) for 1 ½ minutes.

You may use your test paper to make notes and organize your ideas.

Some people don't think women can make good drivers and many people agree that women usually lack a sense of direction. Do you agree or disagree with these assumptions?

Please read the self-introduction sentence again.

My seat number is ＿（複試座位號碼）＿, and my registration number is ＿（初試准考證號碼）＿.

寫作口說能力測驗 ⑩ 詳解

寫作能力測驗詳解

PART 1 中譯英 (40%)

　　對我而言，讀書不只是一種樂趣，也是一種需要。當我想要充實自我、拓展視野時，閱讀是我獲取知識的最佳方法。當我感到無聊時，讀書可以幫助我快樂地度過時光。在各類書籍中，我最喜歡小說，因為小說最貼近我們的生活。以小說裡的人物做為借鏡，我可以學習到許多寶貴的教訓。

1. $\left\{ \begin{array}{l} \text{For me} \\ \text{As far as I am concerned} \end{array} \right\}$, reading is

　　not $\left\{ \begin{array}{l} \text{just} \\ \text{only} \\ \text{merely} \end{array} \right\}$ $\left\{ \begin{array}{l} \text{a pleasure} \\ \text{a delight} \\ \text{a pastime} \\ \text{an enjoyment} \\ \text{an amusement} \end{array} \right\}$ but (also) a

$\left\{ \begin{array}{l} \text{necessity.} \\ \text{need.} \\ \text{requirement.} \end{array} \right\}$

2. When I want to {educate / improve} myself and {broaden / expand / widen}

my horizons, reading {is / provides} the

{best / perfect / greatest} way (for me) to {gain / acquire / obtain} knowledge.

3. When I feel bored, reading helps me (to) {pass / spend}

the time {enjoyably. / happily. / cheerfully. / joyfully.}

4. {Of / Among} {all the various kinds / all kinds / (such) a (wide) variety} of books,

{novels are my favorites / I like novels {best / most}}, because novels are

the {closest / most relevant} to our lives.

5. (By) Using the characters in novels as a mirror, I can learn

$$
\left\{ \begin{array}{l} \text{many} \\ \text{a lot of} \\ \text{lots of} \\ \text{plenty of} \end{array} \right\}
\left\{ \begin{array}{l} \text{precious} \\ \text{treasured} \\ \text{valuable} \end{array} \right\} \text{lessons.}
$$

【註】*as far as…be concerned* 就…而言

merely〔'mɪrlɪ〕*adv.* 只　　pleasure〔'plɛʒɚ〕*n.* 樂趣

delight〔dɪ'laɪt〕*n.* 高興；樂趣

pastime〔'pæs,taɪm〕*n.* 消遣；娛樂

enjoyment〔ɪn'dʒɔɪmənt〕*n.* 樂趣

amusement〔ə'mjuzmənt〕*n.* 樂趣；娛樂

necessity〔nə'sɛsətɪ〕*n.* 需要

requirement〔rɪ'kwaɪrmənt〕*n.* 需要

broaden〔'brɔdn̩〕*v.* 拓展　　expand〔ɪk'spænd〕*v.* 擴展

widen〔'waɪdn̩〕*v.* 使變寬；拓展

horizons〔hə'raɪznz〕*n. pl.* 視野；知識範圍；眼界

gain〔gen〕*v.* 獲得　　acquire〔ə'kwaɪr〕*v.* 獲得

obtain〔əb'ten〕*v.* 獲得

enjoyably〔ɪn'dʒɔɪəblɪ〕*adv.* 快樂地

cheerfully〔'tʃɪrfəlɪ〕*adv.* 快樂地

joyfully〔'dʒɔɪfəlɪ〕*adv.* 快樂地

various〔'vɛrɪəs〕*adj.* 各種不同的　　*a variety of* 各式各樣的

relevant〔'rɛləvənt〕*adj.* 相關的

character〔'kærɪktɚ〕*n.* 人物

mirror〔'mɪrɚ〕*n.* 鏡子；真實的寫照

precious〔'prɛʃəs〕*adj.* 珍貴的

treasured〔'trɛʒɚd〕*adj.* 受珍視的

valuable〔'væljʊbl̩〕*adj.* 有價值的；珍貴的

lesson〔'lɛsn̩〕*n.* 教訓

PART 2 引導寫作 (60%)

Fitness centers, spas, and yoga practice are very popular in Taiwan these days. Many people go to these places for a workout or relaxation. What do you think of these places? Have you ever been to one of these places? Please describe your experience.

健身中心、水療俱樂部，和瑜伽練習最近在台灣很受歡迎。許多人到這些地方運動或放鬆。你對這些地方有什麼看法？你曾經去過這些地方嗎？請描述你的經驗。

【作文範例】

The Importance of Fitness

The appearance of fitness centers, spas, and yoga classes in Taiwan is very constructive, *in my opinion*. They provide people with more opportunities to stay in good shape and take care of their health. Their presence also makes the less active among us more aware of the importance of exercise and a positive self-image.

In my own experience, some fitness classes provide a chance for relaxing and socializing. I once took a yoga class at the local YMCA and I enjoyed it very much. The gentle exercise was an excellent way to unwind and relax my mind. Rather than tire me out, the class left me energized, confident and ready to face new challenges. *In addition*, I made several friends in the class. We always chatted cheerfully before and after our lessons.

Perhaps the most valuable thing that spas and fitness classes provide is the time to focus on ourselves. Not everyone enjoys rigorous exercise, but everyone can benefit from devoting some time and energy to themselves. Whether we indulge in a facial and massage or an aerobics class, it is important for us to take care of our mind and body.

【註】 fitness〔'fɪtnɪs〕*n.* 健康

spa〔spɑ〕*n.* 水療俱樂部　　yoga〔'jogə〕*n.* 瑜伽

constructive〔kən'strʌktɪv〕*adj.* 有建設性的；有助益的

in shape 健康的　　presence〔'prɛzn̩s〕*n.* 存在

active〔'æktɪv〕*adj.* 積極的

aware〔ə'wɛr〕*adj.* 知道的

positive〔'pɑzətɪv〕*adj.* 積極的；正面的

self-image〔'sɛlf'ɪmɪdʒ〕*n.* 自我形象

socialize〔'soʃə,laɪz〕*v.* 交際

YMCA 基督教青年會 (＝ *Young Men's Christian Association*)

gentle〔'dʒɛntl̩〕*adj.* 溫和的

unwind〔ʌn'waɪnd〕*v.* 解開；使放鬆

rather than 不…而～　　***tire sb. out*** 使某人筋疲力盡

leave〔liv〕*v.* 使處於 (某種狀態)

energized〔'ɛnɚ,dʒaɪzd〕*adj.* 精力充沛的

chat〔tʃæt〕*v.* 聊天　　rigorous〔'rɪgərəs〕*adj.* 嚴格的

benefit〔'bɛnəfɪt〕*v.* 獲益　　devote〔dɪ'vot〕*v.* 貢獻

indulge〔ɪn'dʌldʒ〕*v.* 沉迷；讓自己享受一下

facial〔'feʃəl〕*n.* 做臉　　massage〔mə'sɑʒ〕*n.* 按摩

aerobics〔,eə'robɪks〕*n.* 有氧運動

口説能力測驗詳解

1. **Under what situations do you panic?**

   你在什麼情況下會驚慌？

【回答範例】

> I'm quite confident of my abilities.
>
> But whenever I'm asked to speak in
>   front of a lot of people, I panic
>   and get nervous.
>
> As a result, I stutter and can't get my
>   point across.
>
>
> I also panic when I have to take a test.
>
> This happens to everybody, but I think
>   my case is exceptionally bad.
>
> I often sweat, my hands shake, and I
>   have to go to the bathroom.

Besides, I am used to doing things in an
　　organized way.

If things get out of my control, I easily
　　freak out.

I hate getting caught off guard.

I think I get nervous under these
　　situations because I want to have
　　everything done perfectly.

If I mess things up, I'm afraid I would
　　leave a bad mark on my record
　　or I would be worried about how
　　other people look at me.

I have no idea how to get over it.

【中文翻譯】

我對自己的能力相當有信心。
但每當我被要求在很多人面前說話時，我就會
驚慌而且緊張。
結果，我就會口吃，無法講清楚自己的想法。

當我必須參加考試時，我也會驚慌。

這會發生在每個人身上，但是我認為我的情況特別嚴重。

我常流汗、手會發抖，而且必須去上廁所。

此外，我習慣做事要有計畫。

如果事情不受我的控制，我會很容易抓狂。

我討厭措手不及。

我認為在這些情況下我會緊張，因為我想把每件事都做得很完美。

如果我把事情搞砸，我怕我會在我的記錄上留下污點，或者我會擔心別人會如何看我。

我不知道要如何克服它。

** ────────────────

panic〔ˈpænɪk〕v. 驚慌　　***as a result*** 結果

stutter〔ˈstʌtɚ〕v. 口吃

get across 使人了解；講清楚自己的意思

point〔pɔɪnt〕n. 論點；想法

exceptionally〔ɪkˈsɛpʃənlɪ〕adv. 特別地

sweat〔swɛt〕v. 流汗

bathroom〔ˈbæθˌrum〕n. 廁所

organized〔ˈɔrgənˌaɪzd〕adj. 有組織的；有計畫的

freak out 抓狂

catch *sb.* ***off guard*** 使某人措手不及

mess up 把…搞砸　　***bad mark*** 污點

have no idea 不知道　　***get over*** 克服

2. **What's your favorite course and why?**

你最喜愛的課程是什麼？為什麼？

【回答範例 1】

My favorite course has always been math.

People either hate it or love it.

I happen to like it very much.

I love the feeling of accomplishment
　　after solving a really difficult problem.

The process of figuring out the steps
　　and methods to use is good exercise
　　for the brain.

It keeps my mind thinking all the time.

I think the best way to gain interest in
　　a curriculum is not to look at it as
　　schoolwork.

That's how I look at math.

I see it as a way to an intellectual life.

【中文翻譯】

我最喜歡的科目一直是數學。

大家不是討厭它就是喜歡它。

我正好非常喜歡它。

我喜歡解完一道真的很難的題目之後的成就感。

想出要使用的步驟和方法，這個過程是一個很好的腦部運動。

它讓我的腦子經常不斷地思考。

我認為要對課程感興趣的最好方法，就是不要將它視為學校的作業。

我就是這樣看數學的。

我把它視為通往知性生活的道路。

** ─────────────────────

course〔kors〕 *n.* 課程   ***happen to V.*** 恰好～

accomplishment〔əˋkɑmplɪʃmənt〕*n.* 成就

solve〔salv〕*v.* 解決

process〔ˋprɑsɛs〕*n.* 過程

figure out 算出；想出   gain〔gen〕*v.* 獲得

curriculum〔kəˋrɪkjələm〕*n.* 課程

see A ***as*** B 把 A 視為 B

intellectual〔͵ɪntḷˋɛktʃʊəl〕*adj.* 智力的；知性的

【回答範例 2】

My favorite subject is Chinese.

It is often considered a boring
　　and difficult subject.

Yet it is the basis of our entire
　　knowledge and culture.

I think one of the reasons I like Chinese
　　is because I like to read.

Studying Chinese expands my view on
　　literature.

I also get to know more about the
　　thoughts of the authors and the
　　backgrounds of their works.

Besides, studying Chinese is an
　　advantage now.

Chinese is quickly becoming the most
　　important language in the world.

With good Chinese and English skills,
　　I have a good chance to build the
　　future I want.

【中文翻譯】

我最喜歡的科目是國文。

它常常被視為無聊且困難的科目。

然而，它是我們全部知識及文化的基礎。

我想我喜歡國文的原因之一，是因為我喜歡閱讀。

研讀國文能擴大我的文學視野。

我也能知道更多關於作者的思想，和他們作品

的背景。

此外，現在學中文是一種優勢。

中文很快就會成為世界上最重要的語言。

擁有優秀的中英文技能，我就會有很好的機會

去創造我想要的未來。

** ————————————————————

consider〔kən'sɪdɚ〕v. 認為

basis〔'besɪs〕n. 基礎

entire〔ɪn'taɪr〕adj. 全部的

expand〔ɪk'spænd〕v. 擴大

view〔vju〕n. 視野；看法

literature〔'lɪtərətʃɚ〕n. 文學　**get to** 得以

background〔'bæk,graʊnd〕n. 背景

work〔wɝk〕n. 作品

advantage〔əd'væntɪdʒ〕n. 優點；優勢

3. **Do you believe in love at first sight? Why or why not?**

你相信一見鍾情嗎？爲什麼相信或爲什麼不相信？

【回答範例1】

I believe in love at first sight.

Why? Because I believe that some people
　　are indeed made for each other.

When you see the one, you will know it,
　　so why wait?

It's not unusual to like a person a lot
　　without knowing them well.

Maybe it's the way they speak, act,
　　or look that just catches your attention.

No one can be sure why, but sometimes
　　it just works that way.

All in all, love is a strange thing.

You simply can't explain it in a logical
　　way.

When it does happen, it's a beautiful thing.

【中文翻譯】

我相信一見鍾情。
為什麼？因為我相信有些人真的是天生一對。
當你看到那個人，你就會知道，所以為什麼
要等？

沒有很熟就很喜歡一個人，這是很常見的事。
或許是他們說話的方式、動作，或長相，剛
好引起你的注意。
沒有人能確定這是為什麼，但有時事情就是
這樣。

總之，愛情是一個奇妙的東西。
你就是無法用合乎邏輯的方式解釋它。
當它真的發生時，它會是一件很美好的事。

**　———————————————

believe in 相信有
love at first sight 一見鍾情
indeed〔ɪnˋdid〕*adv.* 真正地
be made for each other 天生一對
unusual〔ʌnˋjuʒʊəl〕*adj.* 罕見的
catch〔kætʃ〕*v.* 引起（注意）
work〔wɝk〕*v.* 運作　　***all in all*** 總之
simply〔ˋsɪmplɪ〕*adv.* 絕對地；簡直
logical〔ˋlɑdʒɪkḷ〕*adj.* 合乎邏輯的

【回答範例 2】

I have never believed in such a thing.

*How can you fall in love with someone
　you* don't know?

*How can you fall in love with someone
　you* have just seen or met?

A relationship is built on trust and
　understanding.

You have to know and accept the other
　person first.

It doesn't work the other way round.

Love at first sight is something people
　use as a pickup line.

It just happens in movies, rarely in
　real life.

A steady and real process is the only
　way to a successful relationship.

【中文翻譯】

我從不相信這種事。

你怎麼會愛上一個你不認識的人？

你怎麼會愛上一個你才剛看見或認識的人？

一段感情是以信任和了解做基礎。

你必須先認識並接受另一個人。

倒過來則行不通。

一見鍾情是大家用來當作一句邂逅的台詞。

它只發生在電影裡，很少發生在現實生活中。

一個穩定和真實的過程，是通往成功的感情的

唯一道路。

** ──────────────

fall in love with 愛上

relationship〔rɪ'leʃən,ʃɪp〕 *n.* 關係；感情關係

the other way round 倒過來

pickup〔'pɪk,ʌp〕 *n.* 邂逅

line〔laɪn〕 *n.* 台詞

rarely〔'rɛrlɪ〕 *adv.* 很少

steady〔'stɛdɪ〕 *adj.* 穩定的

process〔'prɑsɛs〕 *n.* 過程

successful〔sək'sɛsfəl〕 *adj.* 成功的；結果圓滿的

4. **If you could have a pet, what animal would it be?**

如果你可以養一隻寵物，牠會是什麼動物？

【回答範例 1】

If I could have a pet, I'd definitely get
　　an iguana.
It might sound crazy, but I love reptiles.
I've wanted to get one for a long time.

Iguanas are majestic animals; they are like
　　the lion of the reptile world.
So it's no surprise that iguanas are usually
　　kept alone.
I think I, too, am a proud person, so I
　　like this characteristic in a pet.

They are hard to keep as pets, because
　　of their diet and scary looks.
You need to pay much attention to their
　　environment to keep them happy and
　　healthy.
But I think that's what makes them so
　　irresistible—you need to put a lot of
　　effort into keeping them.

【中文翻譯】

如果我可以養一隻寵物，我一定會買綠鬣蜥。
這聽起來可能很瘋狂，但是我喜歡爬蟲類動物。
我想買一隻已經想很久了。

綠鬣蜥是一種有威嚴的動物；牠們就像爬蟲動物界
的獅子。
所以綠鬣蜥通常會被單獨飼養，這一點也不令人意外。
我想我也是一個高傲的人，所以我喜歡寵物有這個
特性。

因為牠們的飲食和可怕的外表，所以很難被當成寵
物來養。
你必須非常注意牠們的環境，才能讓牠們保持快樂
和健康。
但我想這就是讓牠們這麼令人無法抗拒的原因——
你必須投入很多心力去養牠們。

**

definitely〔ˋdɛfənɪtlɪ〕adv. 一定
iguana〔ɪˋgwɑnə〕n. 綠鬣蜥
reptile〔ˋrɛptḷ, ˋrɛptaɪl〕n. 爬蟲類動物
majestic〔məˋdʒɛstɪk〕adj. 有威嚴的
keep〔kip〕v. 飼養
characteristic〔͵kærɪktəˋrɪstɪk〕n. 特性
diet〔ˋdaɪət〕n. 飲食   scary〔ˋskɛrɪ〕adj. 可怕的
looks〔lʊks〕n. pl. 外表
irresistible〔͵ɪrɪˋzɪstəbḷ〕adj. 令人無法抗拒的

【回答範例 2】

I would love to have a dog.

A collie would be the best.

I have wanted one since I saw Lassie.

Dogs are humans' most faithful
 companions.

They have an almost human nature
 to them.

They develop a bond with their
 owners.

Of course a dog needs to be washed,
 fed, and walked.

It's hard work to keep a dog, but it's
 worth it.

I would do my best to keep mine in
 top condition!

【中文翻譯】

我會想要養一隻狗。

柯利牧羊犬會是最佳選擇。

自從我看過「靈犬萊西」以後，我就一直想要一隻狗。

狗是人類最忠實的朋友。

牠們幾乎有和人類一樣的特性。

牠們會和主人培養關係。

當然需要幫狗洗澡、餵食，並陪牠散步。

養狗很辛苦，但這是值得的。

我會盡力讓我的狗保持在最佳狀態！

** ─────────────────

collie〔ˈkɑlɪ〕n. 柯利牧羊犬【原產蘇格蘭】

faithful〔ˈfeθfəl〕adj. 忠實的

companion〔kəmˈpænjən〕n. 同伴；朋友

human〔ˈhjumən〕adj. 人類的

nature〔ˈnetʃɚ〕n. 特質；特性

bond〔bɑnd〕n. 聯繫；關係

walk〔wɔk〕v. 遛（狗）

worth〔wɝθ〕adj. 值得…的

top〔tɑp〕adj. 最優良的

5. **Do you know how to dance? Which styles do you dance? If not, which styles are you interested in learning?**

你知道怎麼跳舞嗎？你會跳哪種類型的舞？如果不會，哪種類型的舞你會有興趣學呢？

【回答範例 1】

I started learning ballet when I was five.

The younger you are when you start,
　　the better.

At a young age, the body is more flexible
　　and easier to train.

I trained under a famous teacher until I
　　was fifteen.

Then I moved to a different city, so I stopped
　　taking classes.

I recently started taking classes again,
　　although I'm not back in top condition yet.

Dancing is a way for me to relax and exercise.

I have also looked into other dance classes.

But I would like to regain my ballet skills first.

【中文翻譯】

我五歲的時候，就開始學芭蕾舞。

你越早開始學越好。

在小時候，身體比較柔軟，而且比較容易
訓練。

我接受一位名師的訓練，直到我十五歲。

之後我搬到另一個城市，所以我就停止上
課了。

我最近又開始上課，雖然我還沒回復到最佳
狀態。

對我來說，跳舞是一種放鬆和運動的方法。

我也研究過其他舞蹈課程。

但是我想要先恢復我的芭蕾舞技能。

** ─────────────

ballet〔ˈbæˈle〕*n.* 芭蕾舞
flexible〔ˈflɛksəbḷ〕*adj.* 有彈性的
train〔tren〕*v.* 訓練；受訓練
look into 調查；研究
regain〔rɪˈgen〕*v.* 恢復

【回答範例 2】

Ever since I saw a breakdancing competition
　　on TV, I have fallen in love with it.

It's exciting and energetic.

It requires hard practice and extensive
　　training because it is a real physical dance.

There are many different and acrobatic
　　moves in breakdancing.

They are a mix of smooth body movement
　　and strength.

Seeing a pro breakdance is a real treat.

Some people think street dances such as
　　breakdancing are for bad kids.

That is not true at all, for breakdancing has
　　become one of the most popular dances
　　among young people.

I am not a great dancer, but I will work hard
　　to become one.

【中文翻譯】

自從我在電視上看到霹靂舞比賽後，我就愛上它了。
它很刺激而且充滿活力。
它需要辛苦的練習和大量的訓練，因為它是真正的
身體舞蹈。

霹靂舞有各式各樣的動作和特技動作。
它們是柔軟的肢體動作和力量的結合。
看行家跳霹靂舞是真正的樂事。

有些人認為街舞，像是霹靂舞，是給不良少年跳的。
這一點也不正確，因為在青少年之間，霹靂舞已經
成為最受歡迎的舞蹈之一。
我不是很會跳舞，但是我會努力成為很棒的舞者。

** ─────────────

breakdancing〔'brek͵dænsɪŋ〕 *n.* 霹靂舞
【一種起源於 1970 年代中期的特技舞藝】
competition〔͵kɑmpə'tɪʃən〕 *n.* 比賽
energetic〔͵ɛnɚ'dʒɛtɪk〕 *adj.* 充滿活力的
extensive〔ɪk'stɛnsɪv〕 *adj.* 大量的
physical〔'fɪzɪkl̩〕 *adj.* 身體的
acrobatic〔͵ækrə'bætɪk〕 *adj.* 特技的
move〔muv〕 *n.* 動作　　mix〔mɪks〕 *n.* 混合
smooth〔smuð〕 *adj.* （動作）流暢的；優美的
strength〔strɛŋθ〕 *n.* 力量　　pro〔pro〕 *adj.* 專業的
breakdance〔'brekdæns〕 *n.* 霹靂舞
treat〔trit〕 *n.* 樂事

6. **If you could choose to be a hero or a villain in a play, which would you be? Why?**

如果你可以選擇成為戲裡的英雄或壞人，你會成為哪一個？
為什麼？

【回答範例 1 】

I would definitely choose to be a villain.

I don't like heroes who do everything for "justice."

I think villains are just people who do things
everyone wants to do without making excuses
for them.

I want to be like my favorite villain, Darth Vader.

He started out as a good guy, but soon his thirst
for power overcame him.

Then just before he died, he realized the good in
himself and saved his son.

In the past couple of years, villains have become
more and more accepted.

Sometimes, characters usually seen as a "villain"
become the heroes.

For example, Jack Sparrow in the Pirates of the
Caribbean is a pirate but also the wacky hero.

【中文翻譯】

我一定會選擇成為壞人。

我不喜歡那種一切都是為了「正義」的英雄。

我認為壞人只是會去做人人都想做的事，而不會替自己找藉口的人。

我想要像我最喜愛的反派角色，黑武士。

他一開始是個好人，但是不久他對權力的渴望征服了他。

然後就在他死前，他認清自己善良的一面，然後救了自己的兒子。

在過去幾年，反派角色變得越來越能被大家接受。

有時候，被視為「壞人」的角色，通常會成為英雄。

例如，「神鬼奇航」的傑克‧史派羅是一個海盜，但也是個古怪的英雄。

＊＊ ───────────────

villain〔ˋvɪlən〕n. 壞人；反派角色

play〔ple〕n. 戲劇　　justice〔ˋdʒʌstɪs〕n. 正義

make an excuse for sb. 為某人找藉口；替某人辯解

Darth Vader 黑武士【電影「星際大戰」中的角色】

start out 開始　　thirst〔θɝst〕n. 渴望

overcome〔ˌovɚˋkʌm〕v. 征服　　good〔gud〕n. 善良

accepted〔əkˋsɛptɪd〕adj. 為大眾所接受的

pirate〔ˋpaɪrət〕n. 海盜

Caribbean〔ˌkærəˋbjən, kəˋrɪbɪən〕n. 加勒比海

Pirates of the Caribbean 神鬼奇航【電影名】

wacky〔ˋwækɪ〕adj. 古怪的

【回答範例2】

There is no need to think about it.

I would definitely be a hero.

A hero is the answer to evil, and defends
　　what is right.

I consider myself a person who is
　　righteous and brave.

I cannot stand other people getting
　　what they want in an unlawful manner.

I think this characteristic will make me
　　a good hero.

However, the society's need for a hero
　　has diminished.

Justice is not as important as power
　　and strength nowadays.

I guess this is why villains are more
　　popular than heroes now.

【中文翻譯】

這件事情不需要想。
我一定會成爲英雄。
英雄是邪惡的終結者，會捍衛正義。

我認爲自己是一個正直和勇敢的人。
我不能忍受其他人以不正當的方式取得他們想
要的東西。
我想這個特質能讓我成爲一個好英雄。

然而，社會對英雄的需要已經減少了。
現在正義已經不像權力和力量一樣重要。
我猜這就是爲什麼現在反派角色會比英雄還受
歡迎的原因。

**————————————————————

answer〔'ænsɚ〕 n. 答案；解決辦法
defend〔dɪ'fɛnd〕 v. 保衛
righteous〔'raɪtʃəs〕 adj. 正直的
brave〔brev〕 adj. 勇敢的
stand〔stænd〕 v. 忍受
unlawful〔ʌn'lɔfəl〕 adj. 非法的；不正當的
manner〔'mænɚ〕 n. 方式
characteristic〔͵kærɪktə'rɪstɪk〕 n. 特質
diminish〔də'mɪnɪʃ〕 v. 減少
nowadays〔'nauə͵dez〕 adv. 現今

7. **What are your views on plastic surgery? Would you undergo plastic surgery if you had the chance?**

你對整形手術有什麼看法？如果你有機會的話，你會整形嗎？

【回答範例 1 】

People want to be beautiful, and want to
　　be accepted.
It's a basic human instinct.
This is especially true nowadays, when
　　good looks often give you an advantage
　　over others.

So of course I can understand why people
　　want to have plastic surgery.
They just want to be attractive when their
　　original looks aren't.
If they have the money and courage,
　　why not?

If I had the chance to have plastic surgery,
　　I'd do it.
I would like to do my lips and make them
　　more "Angelina Jolie," as I like to put it.
I consider her lips to be extremely attractive.

【中文翻譯】

大家想變漂亮，而且想要被接受。

這是人類基本的本能。

現在尤其是如此，漂亮的外表常會讓你比別人佔
優勢。

所以我當然可以了解，爲什麼大家會想要整形。

當他們原本的外表沒有吸引力時，他們只是想變
得有吸引力。

如果他們有金錢和勇氣，有何不可？

如果我有機會整形，我會去做。

我想要整我的嘴唇，讓它們更「安潔莉娜‧裘
莉」一點，就像我喜歡說的。

我認爲她的嘴唇非常有吸引力。

＊＊───────────────

plastic surgery 整形手術

undergo〔ˌʌndɚˋgo〕*v.* 接受

instinct〔ˋɪnstɪŋkt〕*n.* 本能

advantage〔ədˋvæntɪdʒ〕*n.* 優勢

attractive〔əˋtræktɪv〕*adj.* 吸引人的

original〔əˋrɪdʒənḷ〕*adj.* 原本的

lips〔lɪps〕*n. pl.* 嘴唇　　put〔put〕*v.* 說

extremely〔ɪkˋstrimlɪ〕*adv.* 非常

【回答範例 2】

I totally disagree with plastic surgery.

Why mess with what your parents
　　gave you?

It's disrespectful and there's also a
　　chance it will fail, scarring you for life.

I think plastic surgery is a social disease.

People are made to think that they aren't
　　good-looking by a standard set by
　　"beautiful" people.

So they have to shell out money to
　　make themselves look like a beautiful
　　movie star.

Beauty is only skin deep, and even more
　　shallow when it's artificial.

I would never have plastic surgery.

I like how I look, and I care more about
　　what's beneath the appearance of others.

【中文翻譯】

我完全不同意整形手術。

為什麼要亂弄父母給你的東西呢？

這樣很不尊重父母，而且也有失敗的可能，讓你

終生留下傷痕。

我認為整形手術是一種社會疾病。

「漂亮」的人所設定的標準會使大家認為自己不

漂亮。

所以他們必須付錢去讓自己看起來像一個漂亮的

電影明星。

美麗是膚淺的，當它是人造的就更加膚淺了。

我絕不會去整形。

我喜歡我的外表，而且我更在乎別人外表下的東西。

** ────────────────────

mess〔mɛs〕v. 亂弄

disrespectful〔͵dɪsrɪ'spɛktfəl〕adj. 無禮的；不尊重的

scar〔skɑr〕v. 使留下傷痕　　***for life***　終生

good-looking〔'gʊd'lʊkɪŋ〕adj. 漂亮的

standard〔'stændəd〕n. 標準

set〔sɛt〕v. 設定　　***shell out***　付（錢）

Beauty is only skin deep.　【諺】美麗是膚淺的。

shallow〔'ʃælo〕adj. 膚淺的

artificial〔͵ɑrtə'fɪʃəl〕adj. 人造的

care about　關心；在乎　　beneath〔bɪ'niθ〕prep. 在…之下

appearance〔ə'pɪrəns〕n. 外表

8. **How long do you use the Internet every day and what do you mainly use it for?**

你每天花多少時間上網？你上網主要是為了什麼？

【回答範例】

I use the Internet for at least five hours per day.
The computer has become more powerful,
　　and so has the Internet.
I can use it to get just about everything I need.

I download my favorite songs and put them in
　　my iPod.
I google things I come in contact with.
I also chat with my friends using Skype.

I search for everything I am interested in.
From reports to discussion forums, I can choose
　　what I want to read.
Sometimes I will browse the online shopping sites
　　to see if there is any interesting merchandise.

The Internet is the quickest way to gain knowledge.
A life without the Internet is like a body without
　　hands.
I think as the Internet community grows, my time
　　spent on the Internet will become even longer.

【中文翻譯】

我每天至少會花五個小時上網。

電腦的性能已經變得更強，網路也是如此。

我可以用它來獲得幾乎我想要的所有東西。

我會下載我最喜愛的歌曲，然後把它們放進我的 iPod 裡。

我會用 Google 搜索我接觸到的事物。

我也會用 Skype 和我的朋友聊天。

我會搜尋所有我感興趣的事物。

從報導到討論區，我可以選擇我想看的內容。

有時我會瀏覽線上購物網站，看是否有任何有趣的商品。

網路是獲得知識最快的方法。

沒有網路的生活，就像是沒有手的身體。

我認為，隨著網路社群的成長，我花在網路上的時間將會
變得更長。

** ───────────────────

mainly〔'menlɪ〕adv. 主要地

powerful〔'pauɚfəl〕adj. 強有力的；有功效的

just about 幾乎　　download〔'daʊn,lod〕v. 下載

google〔'gugḷ〕v. 搜索（利用 Google 搜索引擎在網路上找資料）

come in contact with 與…接觸

Skype〔skaɪp〕n. 即時通訊軟體　　forum〔'forəm〕n. 論壇

discussion forum 討論區　　browse〔braʊz〕v. 瀏覽

site〔saɪt〕n. 網站　　merchandise〔'mɝtʃən,daɪz〕n. 商品

community〔kə'mjunətɪ〕n. 社區

PART 2　看圖敘述

1. **What is this place?** 這是什麼地方？

This is a lecture hall.　It is probably in a university
or a conference center because it is very modern
and high-tech.

這是一個演講廳。大概是在大學或會議中心裡面，因
為它非常現代化而且高科技。

**

lecture〔ˈlɛktʃɚ〕 *n.* 演講；講課　　hall〔hɔl〕 *n.* 大廳
conference〔ˈkɑnfərəns〕 *n.* 會議
high-tech〔ˈhaɪˈtɛk〕 *adj.* 高科技的

2. **What do you think this occasion is?**

你認為這是什麼場合？

I think this is a meeting of some kind. It could be a university lecture, but there are not many people in the audience. I don't think a small class of students would meet in such a large room.

我想是某種集會。它可能是大學演講，但是聽眾沒有很多。
我不認為一個學生人數不多的班級會在這麼大的地方集合。

3. **Who do you think these people are?**

你認為這些人是誰？

They could be students, but I think they are more likely to be professionals. Most of them are women, so I think they must be members of some female-dominated profession like teaching or nursing.

他們可能是學生，但我想他們比較可能是專業人士。大
部分的人是女士，所以我想他們一定是像教書或護理這
種女性為主的職業的成員。

** ————————————————

occasion〔ə'keʒən〕n. 場合
meeting〔'mitɪŋ〕n. 會議；集會　　some〔sʌm〕adj. 某一
audience〔'ɔdɪəns〕n. 聽眾　　meet〔mit〕v. 集合；聚會
professional〔prə'fɛʃənḷ〕n. 專家；專業人員
female〔'fimel〕n. 女性
dominate〔'dɑmə,net〕v. 支配；佔優勢
profession〔prə'fɛʃən〕n. 職業
nursing〔'nɝsɪŋ〕n. 護理；護士的工作

4. **Have you ever taken part in such an activity?**

你曾經參加過這樣的活動嗎？

I have attended lectures for my classes, but never in a
room as nice as this one. Our lectures are usually in a
regular classroom. 我參加過我課堂的講課，但不曾在像
這間一樣棒的地方。我們的講課通常是在普通的教室。

5. **If you still have time, please describe the picture in as
much detail as you can.**

如果你還有時間，請儘可能描述照片中的細節。

This is a meeting hall in which a man is speaking to a
small crowd. Most of the people in the audience are
women. They are spread throughout the lecture hall
and most of them appear to be paying attention to the
man. The seats look quite comfortable and there are
microphones placed around the room. There is a large
screen on the stage with some information projected
on it. The man is talking about this information.

這是一個會議廳，裡面有一位男士在和一小群人說話。聽眾
裡面的人大部分是女士。他們分散在會議廳的各個地方，而
且他們大部分的人好像都很注意聽那位男士講話。座椅看起
來相當舒服，這個地方的周圍有放置麥克風。講台上有一個
大銀幕，有一些資訊投射在上面。這位男士在談論這些資訊。

** ────────────────────

attend〔ə'tɛnd〕v. 參加　　regular〔'rɛgjələ〕adj. 普通的
crowd〔kraud〕n. 人群　　spread〔sprɛd〕v. 使散佈
throughout〔θru'aut〕prep. 遍及　　appear〔ə'pɪr〕v. 似乎；好像
microphone〔'maɪkrə,fon〕n. 麥克風
place〔ples〕v. 放置　　project〔prə'dʒɛkt〕v. 投射

PART 3 申述題

Some people don't think women can make good drivers and many people agree that women usually lack a sense of direction. Do you agree or disagree with these assumptions?

有些人不認為女人可以成為好駕駛，而且許多人同意女人通常都缺乏方向感。你同不同意這些假定？

【回答範例】

I think it is a myth that women make poor drivers. How well one drives depends on one's training and experience. It also depends a lot on patience, and I think women are often more patient than men. It is true that men tend to know more about cars than women do, but that doesn't necessarily make them better drivers. *Besides*, women can learn about cars too if they wish. Actually, I think that a person's driving ability is an individual thing and it doesn't depend on sex. There are bad women drivers, but there are also bad men drivers. Good driving takes skill and maturity. So I think those who are reckless and disregard traffic rules are the worst drivers, whether they are male or female.

【中文翻譯】

　　女人開車技術很差，我認為這是一種迷思。一個人的駕駛技術如何，取決於所受的訓練和經驗。這大多也取決於耐心，而我認為女人常常比男人有耐心。男人往往比女人更了解車子，這是事實，但那不一定會讓他們開車技術更好。此外，如果女人想學，她們也可以學會關於車子的知識。事實上，我認為一個人的駕駛能力是個別的事，而不是取決於性別。有差勁的女性駕駛，但也有差勁的男性駕駛。好的駕駛能力需要技術和成熟度。所以我認為那些魯莽和忽視交通規則的人，是最差的駕駛，無論他們是男性或女性。

**

myth〔mɪθ〕*n.* 迷思　　make〔mek〕*v.* 成為

depend on 視…而定；取決於

tend to V. 易於…；傾向於…

not necessarily 未必；不一定

wish〔wɪʃ〕*v.* 希望；想要

individual〔͵ɪndəˈvɪdʒʊəl〕*adj.* 個別的

maturity〔məˈtʃʊrətɪ〕*n.* 成熟

reckless〔ˈrɛklɪs〕*adj.* 魯莽的

disregard〔͵dɪsrɪˈgɑrd〕*v.* 忽視

中高級寫作口說測驗①

主　　　編 / 劉　毅

發 行 所 / 學習出版有限公司　　　☎ (02) 2704-5525

郵 撥 帳 號 / 0512727-2 學習出版社帳戶

登 記 證 / 局版台業 *2179* 號

印 刷 所 / 裕強彩色印刷有限公司

台 北 門 市 / 台北市許昌街 10 號 2 F　　　☎ (02) 2331-4060

台灣總經銷 / 紅螞蟻圖書有限公司　　　☎ (02) 2795-3656

美國總經銷 / Evergreen Book Store　　　☎ (818) 2813622

本公司網址　www.learnbook.com.tw

電 子 郵 件　learnbook@learnbook.com.tw

書 + MP3 一片售價：新台幣三百八十元正

2014 年 3 月 1 日新修訂

ISBN 978-986-231-031-1